Becoming

An Erica Murray Mystery

J E Nice

First published in Great Britain in 2020 by
Write Into The Woods Publishing.

ISBN 978-1-912903-16-0

Cover design by Jenny Lewis,
Write into the Woods.

www.jenice.co.uk
www.writeintothewoods.com

For the dog walkers
and our bravery of going through the woods not
knowing what we'll find.

Other Erica Murray Mysteries

Beginnings

Other Books By
J E Nice

The Last War Trilogy:
Matter of Time
Despite Our Enemies
In My Bones

No Masters Or Kings

Find them all at **www.jenice.co.uk/books**

Grab previews of the first book in each
series and get regular updates by signing up
at **www.jenice.co.uk/updates**

In The Woods

They were coming.

A silence fell over the woods, broken only by the odd chirp from a bird or rustle as a small animal moved through the undergrowth. The trees watched and waited. Dappled sunlight fell through the leaves, dancing across the ground as the branches bobbed and swayed in the summer breeze. The trees were a mixture of ages. Some had stood for centuries, when the landscape was made up of farmers' fields, their trunks often marking out boundaries, flanked by hedges. Others were younger, from when the woodland began to take shape and the rest were practically new, their trunks too thin to suffer yet.

The laughter sounded first, heralding their approach, then the stamping of feet, jumping down the steps, following the path that led between the trees. The trunks of the fallen had been arranged in a seating area in the immediate clearing and this is where they settled. Seating themselves, or crouching on the ground, collecting sticks and leaves, and preparing.

The pain didn't come straight away.

First, they created fire and the trees watched as the flames licked at their fallen brethren, devouring what had been piled up, scorching the earth.

Then the spray cans would come out. Some were

used to create more fire, sparks catching on the breeze and carrying them further into the woods. Others were used to create marks on the standing trunks surrounding the area.

Those marks had started off as curse words which, while bad, held no true power. Then came something much worse. Markings drawn over the tree trunks that burned into the bark. The trees watched, helpless to move away or stop them.

The marks continued to burn long after the humans had left. In the dark of night, as the canopy shielded the woodland floor from the moon and stars, something stirred.

It grew and grew, and soon it wasn't just the trees watching the dogs and children playing, the people walking and jogging, tennis balls being thrown and forts being made, foxes hunting, mice scuttling and badgers scavenging, birds singing, swooping between the trees.

Soon, there was something new that watched, and waited it for those humans to return.

1

Erica had chosen a table near the window. Not only was it a good spot for people-watching while basking in the morning sunlight, but it meant she would spot Jess arriving. In the meantime, she had a half-drunk latte and her laptop open on the table, finally connected to the coffee shop's free wi-fi. It was dodgy, going in and out of service despite nothing moving, but that was fine by Erica. She had two pages open and she was only staring at one of them.

A Facebook profile, not properly filled in and with full privacy settings enabled.

Erica didn't know what she'd been hoping for. She'd found the page within seconds of beginning her search two months ago and despite checking it at least once a day, nothing had changed.

The same profile picture stared back at her. A young man with dark hair and a full, sweet smile. It was a little blurry and the lighting was off, so perhaps he'd been in a pub drinking with friends when it was taken. Perhaps it was part of something bigger, zoomed in on his face to cut off the friends around him. Or to cut off a girlfriend.

She'd given this too much thought.

She hadn't recognised the smile at first but the eyes were almost the same. She could see past the youth and naivety to the man he would become. The moment she'd locked eyes with that photo, her stomach had danced and she'd slammed her laptop shut in shock, as if he would see her.

Not for the first time that week, Erica wondered what was hiding behind the privacy settings. A girlfriend? A child? She swallowed a mouthful of lukewarm coffee. A wife?

No. None of that rang true, it was her mind playing cruel tricks on her. Tricks that wouldn't stop until she sent him a message.

Her gaze moved from his eyes to his name.

Rick Cavanagh.

Leaning forward, she moved the cursor to the messaging option and clicked it. The box opened and Erica sat back, worried she might accidentally lean on the keyboard, type something and hit send all in one go.

She sipped at her coffee.

What did you say in this sort of situation?

Hi. You don't know me but in the future we're married.

No. He'd scoff and block her.

Hi. You don't know me yet but one day you will.

That would get her arrested.

Hi. Your future self sent me.

The Terminator theme sounded in Erica's mind. While that might be fun, she had to assume that would lead to him blocking her as well.

With a sigh, she leaned forward and carefully typed out a message.

Hi. How are you?

She leaned back and sucked on her lower lip. He would ignore it. It looked like the spam she got every now and then from strange male profiles.

Hi. How are you? A mutual friend suggested I get in touch. He thought we'd get on.

Erica smiled to herself. She could see how that conversation would go.

Oh? He would reply. Which mutual friend?

Erm, she would say after a lot of deliberation. You.

No. That wouldn't work either. She had to face the reality of the situation. The only way this was going to work would be to bump into him accidentally-on-purpose in the real world. Something that was difficult to do when he kept everything personal behind privacy settings.

Erica sighed, deleted the message and sat back again, hand wrapped around her latte. How did private investigators do this?

Of course, what would make this much easier would be if Rick, her Rick, from the future, would just come back to her. That was who she wanted. Looking at the fresh faced boy in the Facebook profile picture, she wasn't sure if that Rick could ever turn into her Rick.

Just how old was that photo?

Jess sat in the chair opposite and Erica jumped, glad that her coffee was almost gone. That would have left a nasty stain.

'Sorry I'm late.' Jess put down her coffee and

glanced at the back of Erica's laptop. 'What are you working on?'

Erica closed the laptop.

'Nothing.'

A smirk grew on Jess's lips but before she could say anything, Erica added, 'Just working on some marketing for our consultancy.'

'Oh.' Jess sat back, visibly deflating. 'You're still on about that, huh?'

'We need to make money somehow, Jess. The way I see it, our options are a marketing consultancy, stacking shelves at the supermarket or selling our bodies. A consultancy pays more than stacking shelves.'

'What I'm hearing is that we could be selling our bodies, which would be more interesting than running a marketing agency.'

'Consultancy, not agency, and you're not serious.' Erica opened her laptop again and closed Facebook but left their new website open. It was well-designed, if Erica did say so herself, and it ticked all of the boxes, but Jess was right. There was something clinical about the whole thing. Something stale and boring. 'Logic says that we should play to our strengths,' Erica murmured, as much to herself as to Jess. 'And we both have good backgrounds in marketing. This is the logical step.'

Jess leaned forward.

'Okay. Fine. I'll play the logic game. You have an excellent background in marketing, that's true. But you have a longer background with more experience in ghosts.'

A silence fell between the two as Erica looked up at her friend. 'I've found a job,' Jess added, pulling out her phone and flicking through it with purpose.

'Is this like the other jobs? Where we go into someone's house looking for a poltergeist to discover the cat's been moving things? Or someone just mislaid their keys?'

'No,' Jess muttered. 'Here.' She handed Erica her phone. 'Anyway, all businesses start off this way. We're finding our feet. Figuring out how to find the clients who actually do have something haunting them. Other than a bad memory.'

Erica looked down at the news article on Jess's phone as Jess sipped her coffee.

'It's a B and B,' Jess said while Erica was still reading. 'And it's haunted.'

'Looks more like a hotel,' Erica murmured. 'Aren't B and Bs small things? This one has forty rooms.'

'Whatever. They say it's haunted. Lots of people have had strange experiences there, and that got me thinking. You're always hearing about things like this, aren't you? Hotels being haunted. Maybe this is an untapped market.'

'I think the whole business could be classified as an untapped market by your definition,' Erica told her, going back to the beginning of the article.

'Do you remember in the film, Ghostbusters? Their business starts off in a hotel.'

Erica glanced up and caught the satisfied smile on Jess's face.

'Shame we're not in a film.'

'Oh, come on, Ric!' Jess leaned forward, trying to get her phone back but Erica held onto it. 'Aren't you curious?'

'They're not going to want to get rid of any spirits hanging around, I imagine they're good for business, and there are loads of paranormal invest-igation teams around that will go in for free. Why should we bother?'

Jess gave a small pout and Erica sighed. 'You already called them, didn't you?'

'It was either do that or let you talk me into a marketing consultancy that I really don't want to do.'

'Your mortgage provider will thank me.'

'Oh yes, that's what I'll be worried about on my deathbed. What my mortgage provider thinks.'

'I guess it depends on where your deathbed is. Is it in your own house or on the streets?'

'Probably a care home.'

'Paid for by the equity in your house.'

Jess stared at Erica and something sank in Erica's gut. She held up a hand. 'I know. I heard it. Sorry. Okay, change of tack. Let's do this your way. Have you mentioned payment with the hotel?'

'They know we're a business.'

'Do they want to get rid of the spirits?'

'They don't know yet. They don't even know if there really are spirits. I've offered them a full investigation and a report, to confirm or deny the existence of paranormal activity for a fixed fee.'

Erica blinked, marvelling at how close those words were to the ones she'd just written on their consultancy website.

'And they've agreed?'

'Not yet. I also offered a free thirty minute consultation at the premises. They can figure out if they trust us to hand over the money and you can work out if it's worth our time.'

Erica smiled and a grin grew on Jess's face.

'I really can't argue with that,' Erica told her.

'So, you'll come?'

Erica didn't want to admit the pleasure she took in closing the window showing their consultancy website and opening up a page to search for the hotel's history.

'Sure. When is it?'

'In fifteen minutes.'

Erica glared at Jess. 'Don't worry, it's only ten minutes away.'

'What if I'd said no?'

Jess beamed.

'Like you said, you can't argue with it.'

The history of the hotel wasn't glamorous, but as Jess said, they had to start somewhere. That somewhere was a terrace of Victorian houses that had been knocked through to create a forty-one bedroom hotel. Laptop safely stowed in the boot of Jess's car, Erica flicked through the about page on the hotel's website on her phone.

'I guess it depends on who lived there before,' she murmured. 'Looks like it was only made into a hotel over the last fifty years. Then again, someone could have died there last month for all we know. There's nothing coming up for something like that, though.'

'And there have been strange experiences there for at least thirty years, when the current owners took over,' Jess told her. 'We're dealing with the owner's daughter. She recently took over as hotel manager. I think she's probably looking for a marketing push. So, you know, technically, this probably counts as a consultancy job.' Jess glanced at Erica out of the corner of her eye but Erica pretended not to notice.

'There isn't much to go on,' she mumbled instead.

'Do you need much to go on?' Jess asked, keeping her eyes on the road. 'Surely you just walk in and see what you feel?'

'It's not that simple.'

'Well, you know what I mean.'

Erica sighed, locking her phone and gazing out of the window.

'I suppose the owner will know more of the history.'

'Exactly. You can ask her all about it when we get there.'

They drove in silence for a moment as Erica studied the houses.

'Do you know what you're doing for your birthday yet?' she asked quietly, her head still turned from Jess.

'You mean Marshall isn't planning me a surprise party?'

Erica blinked and looked at her friend, opening and closing her mouth. She should have put more thought into that question. Jess glanced at her and laughed. 'It's okay. I don't want a surprise party.'

'Oh. Good. Okay.'

'He's not planning me one, is he?'

'If he is, he hasn't told me.'

'Good. I think we're keeping it quiet. Maybe dinner with the people I love?'

'So...You, Ruby and Marshall?'

Jess frowned.

'No. Well, yes, but you too, and your parents and gran. And some others.'

'Gran would love that. Sounds like a party to me.'

'No, no, it's not a party, just a gathering of everyone I love and whoever they want to bring along. You know, you can bring a date.'

Erica glared at her.

'Who would I bring as a date?'

'I dunno. Have you looked for Rick yet?'

Erica stared back out of the window. 'Oh my God, Ric!' Jess cried. 'You've found him, haven't you? How did you find him? Have you contacted him?'

Erica shifted in her seat, desperately trying to think of a way out of this. There was none.

'I may have found him on Facebook and no, I haven't contacted him.'

'What does his profile say?'

Erica sighed.

'Nothing. He has all the privacy settings on.'

'Bugger.'

'Yeah.'

Jess gave a sigh and a shrug.

'Well, you're just going to have to contact him then.'

Erica rolled her eyes.

'Where's this hotel?'

'We're nearly there. Are you going to contact him?'

'I don't know, Jess. I don't know what to say. I'll do it in my own time. Okay?'

'Okay. Sorry. No pressure. Hey, if you don't want to contact Rick, you can bring Alfie to my birthday?'

Erica shot Jess a look and caught her friend smirking to herself.

'There's nothing going on between me and Alfie.'

'Hmm. Here we go,' Jess murmured, trying to hold back a smile as she slowed the car and indicated to turn.

There was nothing ominous about the hotel. A friendly sign hung outside and there were more signs at the front door. It looked like a regular, normal small hotel. Jess drove into the car park around the back and they climbed out of the car. Closing the door, Erica peered up at the windows of the back of the house. A part of her always expected to see a face, pale with wide eyes, staring down at her. Instead there were some clean looking net curtains and one window with a smear of bird droppings.

Erica followed Jess to the entrance where Jess rang the bell.

They both looked up at the building.

'Anything yet?' Jess whispered.

Erica took a deep breath. It would be too early to tell. She needed to be inside the building, and even then she wasn't sure if she would be able to sense anything.

What did a spirit feel like? She was sure she knew the sensation of a spirit nearby, she must have felt it often as a child. Her grandmother's house had had spirits coming and going, one or two had permanently resided there. They'd always been there but she'd purposefully invited them in after Erica's grandfather had passed on. Erica had asked her a couple of times why her grandfather's spirit hadn't come home. Her grandmother had only told her the once that her grandfather belonged elsewhere. It had made Erica sad at first, until her mother had pointed out that her gran needed her independence, she needed to move onto the next phase of her life, and her grandfather respected that. The concept made Erica happy, although she hadn't considered her grandmother falling into bed with someone else. Never mind a woman, especially not a woman who was also a fae. On the other hand, Erica hoped she was capable of such things when she reached her eighties. Erica's mother had brought her up to be wary of the fae. They were dangerous creatures, she'd said. But Erica's gran seemed happy with her fae lover. Erica had seen it for herself, just how protective Eolande was of her grandmother. She'd witnessed the love.

That was what the fae did, her grandmother had told her. They fell in love hard and fierce. Erica blinked and an image of Alfie, with his hands in his jean pockets and an easy smile on his charming face, filled her thoughts. She blinked again, trying to banish him. She wasn't sure she wanted to see him again, let alone invite him to Jess's birthday party.

Jess elbowed her gently.

'Hmm? Oh, no. Not yet,' Erica said, the hotel coming back into her vision with a distinct lack of ghostly feelings.

The hotel door opened and a woman appeared.

2

The short, blonde woman at the door looked them both up and down. Jess put on her best smile.

'Hello. Can I help?'

'Mrs Wilder? Jess Tidswell, we spoke on the phone?'

'Oh.' Relief hit the woman's eyes. 'Oh, yes. Welcome. Do come in.' She gave Erica a glance as she turned and led them into the reception area.

It was a narrow corridor, although decorated brightly with a large mirror on one wall. A door on the right led deeper into the hotel, there was a staircase leading to the next floor and in front of them was a reception desk. Given that the hotel was a number of houses knocked together, Jess was surprised that the reception area wasn't larger. Where were the seats for waiting around? Where was the bar?

Jess glanced at Erica. Was she wondering the same things? Or could she feel something? Erica's expression gave nothing away, although she gazed a little longer than normal at the mirror. Jess studied it for a moment before her brain gave her the image of a grey spectre standing behind them and she quickly looked away, checking once that it was just the three of them in the narrow space.

'So, how does this work?' Mrs Wilder asked, hesitating by the reception desk.

'It would be good if you could give us a quick tour while we talk through it all. We'll ask some questions, you can ask any questions you like, and then we can take it from there.'

Mrs Wilder nodded.

'Okay. Right. Where should we start?'

Erica, head craned back to look up at the ceiling, said, 'Where the last experience was.'

'Experience?'

Erica lowered her head to look at Mrs Wilder.

'Of your spirit.'

'Right.' Mrs Wilder led them up the stairs. 'This way. It all generally happens in one bedroom.'

There were paintings lining the white walls up the stairs and the carpet was a light cream that must have been hard to keep clean. Overall, it was bright and modern. Jess resisted the urge to look back to Erica as she followed Mrs Wilder. She was pretty sure if she did, she'd trip over the stairs or walk straight into the back of the hotel manager. It wasn't quite the professional appearance she was hoping for. Instead, she concentrated on Mrs Wilder's back and where she was putting her feet.

They stopped on the first floor and Mrs Wilder led them to the nearest door.

'This one,' she said, unlocking the room and letting them in. 'I haven't put anyone in here for a few days now. Not since the last...experience, as you called it. Incident, we've been calling it.'

'What happened to make it an incident?' Erica murmured, stepping inside and looking around. Jess stepped next to her.

It just looked like an ordinary bedroom to her. The room was square with soft grey walls and some interesting local artwork hanging above the double bed. There was a wardrobe and a door that likely led to an en-suite. It was clean and fresh and everything that Jess could ask for from a hotel room, if a little on the small side.

Not for the first time she wished she had some of Erica's gift. Just enough to know what it felt like. Just enough so that she could prepare for their next move the moment they walked in the room. She watched Erica, trying to read her but her friend was expressionless, as she always was when Jess presented her with a potential haunting.

It didn't help that they hadn't actually found a haunting yet. Jess was close to deciding that spirits didn't exist. If it wasn't for Erica and her family being so adamant about their existence, Jess would have already come to terms with the fact that ghosts weren't real.

She wondered what she'd be doing now, if that were the case. The idea of working in marketing still made her feel a little sick. After just over a decade of working for agencies, dealing with problematic clients and bosses not quite liking her ideas enough to give her credit for them, she was ready for something new. Something fun that would also pay the mortgage. That had to exist, didn't it?

If it did exist, Jess was pretty sure this was it. Finding ghosts, explaining hauntings and getting paid for it. The idea itself was exciting, the idea of running her own business and not dealing with marketing clients was thrilling. She hadn't given much thought to what she'd do if they actually found a ghost. She'd deal with that when it happened, which she hoped would be soon, seeing as how they needed to get paid.

Erica had always been sceptical of people talking

of strange happenings. She seemed to know what was real and what wasn't so quickly, sometimes without even being there. The fact that she had proven each and every job they'd had so far was not paranormal in any way didn't bode well for their bank balance.

Maybe the free consultations were the wrong way to be going about it, Jess pondered. Perhaps she should be charging a fee for this. She snuck a glance at Mrs Wilder who was watching Erica intently.

'The latest incident was with one of my staff. One of my housekeepers. She was making the bed when she said she felt a rush of cold air and then she heard a voice. She thought it was the other housekeeper down the corridor, or another member of staff, so she ignored it. Then she heard it again, so she called to the other housekeeper, but of course it hadn't been her. There was no one else around and she said the voice was incredibly clear. They both checked out the room but couldn't find an answer and then she refused to step foot in here again. I had to come up and finish the room myself.'

Erica had walked around the room while Mrs Wilder spoke, running her fingers over the walls. She peered out of the window, giving the view a thorough inspection, before opening the door and glancing around the en-suite.

'What did the voice say?' she asked, studying the bed before ducking to look underneath it.

Mrs Wilder took a deep breath.

'It's here.'

Jess frowned.

'What's here?'

'I don't know. That's all it said. And it repeated

it three times. It's here. Do you think she could have heard someone talking outside? Only, the girls are adamant there was no one there.'

Erica stood up and blew out her cheeks, gazing around the room again.

'Is there any history to this room?' she asked. 'Any known deaths, in here or in the hotel in general? While you've owned it or before?'

'Well, of course. So many people have stayed here over the years, there's always going to be at least one case of someone going to sleep and not waking up. We have quite a few elderly people coming through, coach parties and things.'

Erica nodded.

'But no murders? No suspicious deaths? No violence at all?'

'Not since my family have owned it.'

Erica sighed thoughtfully and Jess pricked her ears up. That was a good sign. In all of the other jobs, Erica's shoulders had sagged a little. She'd asked her questions with minute shrugs as if she already knew the answers but this was different. She was genuinely interested.

Jess's chest tightened with the anxiety of it. She'd been keeping it as quiet as possible, just how much she needed this business to work, and now there was a glimpse of hope, no matter how small.

She pressed her lips together, so that her hopes and begging pleas to the universe wouldn't slip out.

'Okay. Do you mind if I run a couple of little tests?' Erica asked. Mrs Wilder nodded.

'Of course not. What sort of tests?'

Jess shot to attention as Erica turned to her.

'Can you take Jess here to the room directly above. Move around the room talking.'

Jess nodded and, holding back the grin, let Mrs Wilder escort her to the stairs.

'This is all part of the free consultation you mentioned?'

'Oh, yes. We're not scam artists, Mrs Wilder. We only charge if there's something actually here.'

'And your friend can tell if there's something here?'

'She can.'

They took the stairs in silence for a moment.

'How?'

'Erica grew up in a house full of spirits.' It wasn't strictly true but it was close enough. 'She has a gift.'

'Hmm.'

'She's also one of the biggest sceptics I know,' Jess told her. 'Trust me, if there's nothing here, she'll say so. You wouldn't believe the amount of lectures I've had from her about most hauntings being a load of rubbish.'

Mrs Wilder glanced back to Jess over her shoulder as they reached the landing.

'And then you wouldn't charge?'

'Absolutely not. It's the main reason we're going to go out of business.'

Mrs Wilder gave her a curious look and then led her to the room, unlocking the door and allowing Jess inside.

'Lucky there's no guests in here, I guess,' Jess murmured, stepping into the clean and tidy bedroom. It was the exact image of the room downstairs.

'We're quiet this week.'

Jess stepped over to the window and glanced down at the road below.

'So, now we talk and see what Erica can hear.' She turned back to Mrs Wilder. 'Have there been any other experiences in this place? From your staff or your guests?' Jess gestured for Mrs Wilder to walk around the room, which she did, slowly and awkwardly.

'Some. Footsteps have been heard, but it's an old building. It creaks.'

'And then there's that chill your housekeeper mentioned.'

'Well, that could have come from an open window.'

'Was the window open?'

'No.'

'Have you ever experienced anything?'

Mrs Wilder went quiet, stopping by the window and looking out. Eventually she turned back to the door, avoiding Jess's gaze.

'Should we do this in the car park too? Maybe the voice came from out there.'

Jess's pocket vibrated. Pulling out her phone, she answered as soon as she saw the name flashing up.

'Everything okay?'

'I can hear you walking and very muffled voices but I can't make out the words,' said Erica. 'There's definitely something here but I'm not quite sure what. Come back down and we'll try something else.'

Jess stopped herself from jumping up and punching the air as she hung up the phone.

'She can't hear us clearly. She wants us back downstairs to try something else.' This time Jess didn't hide the grin and trotted down the stairs, Mrs Wilder jogging to keep up.

They found Erica still in the bedroom, peering

into the wardrobe, her brow furrowed.

'Have you got battery on your phone?' she asked as Jess entered. Jess nodded. 'Can you film me and the room?'

'Sure. What are we doing?'

'Making contact.' Erica glanced behind Jess to Mrs Wilder and then took out an old Dictaphone. She pressed the buttons to make the Dictaphone record and held it up. Jess began filming her.

'Hello. My name is Erica Murray. If you can hear me, please try to talk to me. I might not be able to hear you but this machine will.' She paused. 'Did you tell a woman in here that it's here? What's here?' She paused again, moving around the room.

Jess realised she was holding her breath and forced herself to exhale. A shiver ran up her right arm, goosebumps shooting up on her skin.

'Ric,' she murmured, holding out her arm for inspection. 'Did you feel that?'

'I did,' Mrs Wilder whispered, hugging herself.

'You're here, aren't you?' Erica continued, watching the women. 'What's your name?'

There was a silence which Erica allowed to drag on before she stopped the Dictaphone and rewound the tape.

'I thought there would be more sophisticated technology by now,' Mrs Wilder murmured. The words were condescending but the quiver in her voice gave her away.

'Sometimes the old ways are the best ways.' Erica shrugged.

'You'll be bringing out a Ouija board in next, I imagine.'

'Oh, no.' Erica stopped the Dictaphone and beckoned Jess to join her, holding the machine up between their ears. 'We don't need one of those.'

She pressed play.

Erica's voice rang out, talking to the room, and between the questions there was the buzz of dead air.

'What's your name?' asked Erica's voice.

Jess jumped back as a low noise sounded, garbled and hissing with the unmistakable sound of the word "here".

Erica rewound the tape and they listened again. This time Jess didn't flinch, she leaned into Erica trying to get as close to the noise as possible.

'Here,' she murmured, catching Erica's eye. 'It's here.'

The women looked around the room.

'What's here?' Jess asked.

'Here in this room?' asked Mrs Wilder. 'Look. I'm not sure I like this.' She took a step back.

'Just because there's a presence in the hotel doesn't mean anything bad,' Erica told her. 'And yes, there is something here. A spirit isn't necessarily always a big presence. Some come and go while others stay put. Some like to make their presence known while others will stay quiet until something happens. Maybe something's happened to make this one start to speak up. But it doesn't mean it's bad and it doesn't mean that this spirit means anyone harm. A spirit isn't always a conscious being. Often they're memories, attached to the brick and mortar of a building.' Erica looked to Jess. 'I guess, where we go from here depends on what you want to happen next.'

Jess, putting on her most professional smile, turned to Mrs Wilder.

'Yes. You have some options now. We can find

out the spirit's motives, work out who they are and why they're making contact—'

'Can you get rid of it?'

Erica stiffened beside Jess and Jess cleared her throat.

'There are consequences to that and it's often not necessary.'

Mrs Wilder, her eyes watery, shook her head and took a shaky breath.

'I think you need all of the details and some time before you make any decisions,' Jess told her. 'Is there somewhere we can go talk? An office or a bar or something?'

Erica was glancing around the room again, closing her eyes for a moment as if listening.

Another shiver ran over Jess.

'The bar,' agreed Mrs Wilder, leaving the room without looking back. Erica followed. Jess was the only one who glanced back to the room over her shoulder, just before she closed the door. She wasn't sure what she'd expected to see, if anything. A girl weeping on the bed, a figure looking out of the window.

There was nothing.

It was an empty hotel room.

Jess closed the door with a click and followed Erica and Mrs Wilder down the stairs, along a corridor and into a large bar area.

'Can I get you a drink? Tea? Coffee?'

'Coffee would be good. Thank you. A flat white, please,' said Jess, taking a seat at the table Mrs Wilder gestured to.

'Same for me, thanks,' said Erica, sitting next to Jess.

While Mrs Wilder turned her back on them to

tend to the large coffee machine, Jess caught Erica's eye.

'So?' she hissed.

'There are a few spirits in this place,' Erica murmured. 'They're not strong enough, I guess, to come and talk to me. Or they don't want to. They don't feel malicious. I'm not happy about moving them on. It's strange though. *It's here.*' Erica sighed, her eyes glazing over in thought.

'A new spirit is here?'

'It, though. Not he or she or even they. It.'

'So, not a spirit? It's here. The end of times?' Jess chuckled and then caught herself. 'It's not that, is it?'

Erica watched Mrs Wilder.

'I don't know. Recommend some further investigation. If we can figure out what the spirit means, maybe they'll go back to being quiet and then problem solved.'

'Okay. I'll do the talking, but chirp up if I get anything wrong.'

Erica nodded and they watched as Mrs Wilder approached with a tray of three coffees.

'Thank you,' said Jess, taking her drink. 'Okay, so, there are a few options, as we mentioned. The first, of course, is to do nothing. But we're curious as to what "it's here" means. So, option two involves some further investigations, which we would highly recommend, to see if we can get to the bottom of this. The theory being that once we've understood this message, the spirit will go back to being quiet and you'll get your hotel back.'

'And option three?' asked Mrs Wilder.

'Exorcising a spirit is incredibly dangerous,' Erica told her. 'Not just because it can anger something that is stronger than you think, but because it opens a door and doors work both ways. Things can leave but things can also enter. Helping spirits to pass is a last resort, and I would say only if you can't afford to sell the hotel and move on.'

Jess held her breath. Those weren't the words she'd have used.

Mrs Wilder stared at Erica.

'Then I suppose I need to hear more about option two.'

In The Woods

Laughter rang through the trees and somewhere a dog was barking, running full speed down the path after a squirrel. A group of five teenagers were gathered around a tree trunk, collecting sticks and leaves.

It felt the fire before it saw it. Felt the fear in the trees around it. That ancient scent passed down from oak to ash at the quiver of a spark. Metal cans were used. That was new. Gas sprayed that made the spark burst into full flame.

The laughter sounded again, with yells and screams.

It was delightful.

The warmth, the chaos.

The fire was soon brought under control, turning to small flames as the twigs and leaves caught. Someone stamped on the wandering sparks that sputtered out.

Nothing was to come of this. Not yet.

On the other side of the woods, the dog had gone quiet, following its owner home. The birds were singing. A murder of crows perched at the top of one tree filled with nests, argued and called to one another.

They had a problem. There was something there that shouldn't be.

It listened intently to them, its eyes still fixed on

the fire and the teenagers.

There was a new danger in the woods, something bigger than the fire, something worse than the teenagers with their cans of gas.

Nearby the sparrows sang angrily, protecting their branches. The starlings echoed and called. A robin watched curiously, flitting away as soon as it was seen.

Those crows kept chattering to one another.

Soon the sounds of the other birds dimmed until only the conversation of the crows could be heard.

They should tell someone.

But who?

There was no one to tell. No one to go to.

These woods were small and young and, it transpired, so far undiscovered.

These woods were unprotected and there was so much blood to be had.

3

'Could you really feel a ghost in there?' Jess asked as they climbed into Jess's car. Mrs Wilder had closed the door as soon as they'd left, as if happy to see the back of them. Erica couldn't blame her. This was going to cost her, but Jess had ended up waxing lyrical about the marketing opportunities of having a haunted hotel.

It seemed like that would become an extra to the investigation. Mrs Wilder would likely be left with a marketing plan for her next moves once they were done.

It's here.

The words echoed around Erica's head.

It was too open. There were too many possibilities.

It could be a warning that something was coming, perhaps a stronger spirit had found a way into the hotel and the resident spirits were threatened by it. Or it could just be a memory, caught in the fear of death and repeating itself over and over.

Perhaps "it" was death.

Erica sighed.

It was a puzzle but she had to admit, the potential was more exciting than the idea of going back to work on their networking skills for their own marketing consultancy.

'There's definitely a spirit,' Erica told Jess as her friend pulled the car back out onto the main road. 'But I can't tell the strength of it. Either it's very weak, maybe only a memory, or it's strong but it's hiding.'

'And we'll be able to figure that out?'

'Yes. I think that went well. We did everything we could. What do you think?'

Jess beamed.

'I think this is a sign that everything's going to be okay.'

'You think a spirit saying "it's here" is a sign that everything's going to be okay?'

'Well, yeah. It's here. The business is here. Our financial worries are over.'

Erica laughed.

'If only it was about that.'

'What do you think it's about?' Jess glanced sideways at Erica.

'I don't know. That's what we need to find out. Along with who this spirit is. And I imagine the two are connected, so we won't be able to find out one without finding out the other.'

'Right. So, what's our action plan, then? What do we need to do before we go back tomorrow?'

'Is tomorrow a good idea? You haven't even ordered the cameras yet.'

'One day delivery. I'll order them when we get back to the coffee shop and then we'll head to the hotel as soon as they arrive. You're not busy tomorrow, are you?'

Only working on the consultancy, Erica thought.

'No,' she said.

'Perfect. We probably need other equipment too,' Jess mused, waiting at a roundabout.

'Like what?'

'Well, you're the ghost expert, I thought you'd know.'

Erica stared at Jess.

'Oh, come on. You're dying to tell me.'

Again, Jess grinned.

'Yeah, all right. I might have done a spot of research. So, there's this thing you can get. An app on your phone and apparently the spirits use it to give you words. They use energy, or something, to make words turn up on the screen and they can communicate with you.'

A smile touched Erica's lips.

'Okay. There's an app for that. Is it expensive?'

Jess shrugged.

'Business expense. My question is, is it worth trying? If you can talk to ghosts, then do we really need something like that? But if this one isn't strong enough or is being cagey...well, if it's weak, could it use something like that?'

Erica chewed on her lower lip.

'I have no idea. Get it if you want to try it. If we're going to take this business seriously, we should try things like that. You never know. It might help.'

Jess nodded.

'I'll download it when I'm home. I can try it when we go back tomorrow.'

'We really should have bought the equipment before. What if the cameras don't arrive in time?'

'They will. Don't worry. And if they don't, there's a shop in town that sells things like that. It's just I found these particular ones I thought would be good. It'll be fine. Don't worry. That's all my part of the job.'

'Is it? Along with talking to clients and dealing with the admin and contracts? What exactly is my job?'

Jess pulled a face at Erica.

'Dealing with the ghosts. What else?'

'Right.' Erica stared out of the window. She was the freak in this show, she'd almost forgotten. She was the freak and Jess was her manager. 'I'd quite like to do some of the business stuff though.'

'Okay. Why don't you do the marketing? I feel like I've had enough of that these days. I'd quite like to deal with the money, to be honest. You can do the admin too, if you like.'

'Nah, that's okay, you can do the admin.'

The women glanced at one another.

'Maybe we need to work towards hiring an assistant,' Jess suggested.

Erica nodded.

'Perfect. And this marketing consultancy. Are we still doing that? Given that you're sick of marketing?'

'Oh God, Ric, I don't know. How many clients do we have for that?'

'Well...none.'

'And how many clients do we have for the paranormal investigation agency?'

'One.'

'Which is more than none.'

'You haven't answered my question.'

'You know, we need a name for this investigation business. Tidswell and Murray Investigates? Probably too long. T and M Investigates. TM Investigations. A bit boring. Maybe a play on words?'

'So, you're just not going to answer the question?'

'I don't know. I get the logic, I do. We need to earn money and a marketing consultancy is a logical way to do that. It's just...'

'What?'

'The idea makes me feel sick.'

Erica shuffled in her seat.

'Yeah. I get that.'

'I've been working in marketing for so long, been treated badly over and over again, and I'm sick of it. And I know we're the bosses now, but do you remember how our clients used to treat us? We'll still get that. Whether we're the bosses or not. We'll still get treated like crap.'

'Okay. But what's the difference between those clients and these investigation ones? You saw the look on that woman's face. Not only is she not keen on paying, she's not keen on us being there full stop.'

'She will be. When we give her results. And at least she's not patronising us.'

'Yeah, well, she hasn't had the bill yet.'

'I just feel like there has to be something more to life than a marketing agency,' Jess murmured.

Something in Erica gave way. Jess needed a way out and Erica could give her that.

'Okay. How about this.' She took a deep breath as she thought through what she was about to say. 'Our marketing consultancy just got its first client, and I'll deal with all of it.'

Jess frowned and glanced at her.

'What are you talking about?'

'Us. We're our first clients. Erica and Jess Investigate, or whatever. And I'll deal with it. You don't have to do anything. I'll run the consultancy. You could even be a silent founder or whatever they're called, if you want.'

There was a silence as Jess waited until they stopped at a red light, then she turned in her seat to Erica.

'I can't let you do all of the work. That's insane.'

'Think about it. You're doing most of the work for the investigation stuff. I just walk into a building and tell if you there's something there. Plus, you have a little girl and big dog that need you. I just have me. Your hands are full without worrying about the consultancy. So, I'll do that. At least, to begin with, and let's see what happens. Let's see where each business goes.'

Jess fretted, tapping her fingers on the steering wheel. 'There's no other way of us both being happy and building both businesses without us going mad,' Erica added. 'And it's worth a try. You build up the investigation side of things and we'll ditch the consultancy.'

'Really?'

'Really.'

'Because, you know, I've been thinking. We could run workshops or do tours and all sorts.'

'Let's not get ahead of ourselves,' said Erica with a smile. That smile faded as a fire engine came roaring towards them. Jess pulled the car out of the way and both women screwed up their faces at the sound of the sirens, as if that would protect their ears.

'I hope everyone's all right,' Jess murmured, pulling the car back out and heading towards the coffee shop car park.

Erica had turned in her seat, watching the fire engine go.

'Maybe a cat's stuck up a tree,' she said. 'It's

headed towards the woods.'

4

Their table was occupied when they made it back to the coffee shop, so they set up their laptops in a booth towards the back. The lighting wasn't as good but at least they were out of the way. The noise level had risen as the local schools had emptied and parents gulped at drinks while their children talked about their days. The sound of the machines hard at work broke through, hissing and banging, and the strong scent of coffee beans filled the air.

Erica cradled her coffee and watched Jess get settled.

'So, you're ordering cameras for tomorrow.'

'And writing up the brief, contract and sorting the first invoice.' Jess bounced a little on the soft seat. 'This is the exciting bit. We should have something better than coffee to celebrate.'

'Let's do that once she's paid. Do I need to do anything?'

'Find our next client?'

'Right.' Erica smiled. 'On it.' Except that she wasn't. She'd helped to promote clients from various industries but never a paranormal investigation company.

She took out a notebook and began by making a list of everything she could think of that other investigation groups did. She tried to ignore the fact that they did this for free.

A police car, sirens blaring, whizzed past the large windows at the front.

It niggled at Erica.

They were near the motorway, sirens and emergency vehicles were common place around here. It wasn't a strange occurrence, so why was it bothering her? Maybe because they'd been going in the opposite direction of the motorway, the same as that fire engine.

'Do you think we need to be on YouTube?' Jess asked, pulling Erica out of her thoughts.

'Err, I'm marketing, you're doing the contract and invoice.' After a moment's hesitation, Erica wrote *YouTube* on her list. Then she crossed it out and wrote *Social media – Videos*. That was better.

Jess had mumbled something under her breath and gone back to typing away at what Erica assumed was the client's brief.

While Jess was preoccupied, Erica opened a browser window on her laptop. She stopped her fingers from going to Facebook and instead searched for news in the local area. What was going on that might need a fire engine and a police car.

A traffic incident was the likeliest. Erica hoped no one was hurt.

The search brought up the usual suspects. Accidents, crashes and then something caught her eye. She brought up the story. It was a small article from the local magazine, written and edited by a resident.

Teenagers Set Fire In Woods

There weren't many details. A group of teenagers had been caught lighting fires in the woods using aerosol cans. It was dangerous, and it potentially explained the emergency vehicles.

'Are these the woods you walk Bubbles in?' Erica pushed her laptop over to Jess who gave the screen a cursory glance and then did a double take.

'Yeah. Why? What's going on.'

'Teenagers setting fires.'

'Hmm, I've seen the mess they leave behind.' Erica nodded.

'I wonder if that's where the fire engine was headed.'

Jess glanced up at the window and shrugged.

'Maybe. Wouldn't surprise me. Oh, shit.'

'What?'

'I just remembered. I have to go to this thing at the school this evening.'

Erica checked the time. It was just turning half two.

'Okay.'

'And Marshall's got this job he can only do in the evening.'

'Right.'

'And, I don't suppose you could check in on Bubbles and maybe give her a walk, could you? It's just, I have to go get Ruby from school and give her something to eat, and feed Bubbles, and then we go back to school, and by the time we're home again I'll have to cook something and then it'll be nearly bedtime, and—'

'It's okay. I don't mind.' Erica really didn't. She had two dogs at home and her family would often argue over who got to walk them. Her father always won. The youngest was technically her mother's dog, but both followed her father around, awaiting whatever spool of wisdom would fall next from his lips. Wisdom such as *dinner*, *ball* and *walk*.

Bubbles, on the other hand, listened to Erica. Walking Bubbles was less about frantically playing ball and more about sniffing and exploring and a little bit of togetherness.

'Actually, I'd love to.' Erica didn't expand. Jess had been on her own with Ruby for nearly five years now. Whether she remembered living with her parents or not, she didn't know what living with your parents in your thirties was.

'Oh, thank you. You're a lifesaver.'

'No problem.'

A silence fell between them again. After a moment of trying to remember what she was supposed to be doing, Erica opened up a new window, found Facebook and began typing "Rick Cavanagh" into the search bar.

In The Woods

It had watched dog walkers come and go since it
had arrived but this one was special.

Witch.

The trees whispered the word.

Witch.

A human woman with a large brown, black and
white dog who she promptly let off the lead before
starting down a winding, narrow pathway between
overgrown ferns and clumps of grasses. She gazed
up at the canopy, closing her eyes against the gentle
breeze, while the dog bounded off ahead.

It pressed itself against the branch it crouched
on. Would she notice it? Would she see it?

The leaves above their heads rattled and it gave a
low hiss. The trees were trying to warn her.

Witch, witch, they cried. *Help us.*

The witch didn't flinch, she didn't stop. She
opened her eyes and continued down the path after
the dog.

If it had a face, what grew on it could be loosely
described as a grin, although it wasn't a happy
sight. It moved from branch to branch, the trees
beneath it trembling and moaning. It ignored them,
and it appeared the witch didn't hear their
complaints or their calls for help.

A young witch. Naïve, untrained. She wasn't a

threat.

No, there were no threats in this place.

It hopped to the next tree, keeping the woman where it could see her. The dog had found something up ahead. The witch called to it.

'Bubbles! Don't get lost, I'll never be forgiven,' she mumbled. 'Where are you? Bubbles? There you are. Leave that. Now.'

The dog was snuffling at something on the ground.

It stiffened as the witch pulled the dog away and stared down at the limp corpse lying curled on the dirt. A mouse. A simple creature that had screamed until it had cut off the mouse's breath. A small meal but it had been enough.

The witch studied the animal and whispered under her breath, 'Poor thing.'

They continued their walk, without even a glance up into the trees, and it relaxed, hopping to the next branch to follow.

The murder of crows, high in their canopy, began calling and crying out to the witch. It cocked its head, watching, waiting. Would she hear them? Would she notice?

The witch did look up then, at the crows, stopping to study and listen. Then she continued. She heard them but she didn't understand them.

Poor, naïve young witch.

It followed the woman and her dog, only stopping, hanging from a branch, when the woman shouted, 'Bubbles! Leave it!'

The dog sniffed at the large white mound on the path leading out of the woods.

In hindsight, it should have been more careful. But it had been so hungry. So ravenous. It hadn't given any thought to leaving the body in the middle of the path.

Again, the witch stopped, hovering over the dead seagull, her brow creased.

Then she turned and looked up into the trees and it held its breath. The witch's eyes didn't see it and she quickly looked down, searching for signs of a ground predator.

Yes, little witch, it thought. That's what did this. A ground dweller. Not something that swooped from the trees.

The witch, frowning and studying the trees around her, stepped over the seagull and led the dog away, out of the woods and out of sight.

It leaned back against the tree trunk and began to shake, silencing the birds as its laughter rippled through the woods.

5

Erica closed the driver's door of her Mini Cooper and stretched her hands up to the sky. The air in the cemetery was crisp. The afternoon was turning late, the clouds in the sky shifting to show off the blue behind. It was a beautiful day. It was a shame about the roar of road noise filtering through the trees but that would disappear soon enough.

The cemetery had been built by the Victorians as a proud garden to bury the wealthy and prominent in the city. Then it had been forgotten. A team of volunteers now tended to the graves and tall trees that grew across what had once been lawn. Nature had taken the cemetery back. It was something Erica's grandfather could talk about for hours, which was the main reason her grandmother and his wife, Minerva, had suggested he join the volunteer team. For over a decade he had fought to protect the trees, learned the histories of each grave and chatted with the dead and squirrels alike. Which was why the organisation now in charge had allowed him to be buried in a plot designated for those who had made a contribution to the cemetery.

Erica first went into the small café that joined onto the Victorian chapel. With a steaming cup of coffee and a brownie, she made her way to her grandfather's grave.

He was waiting for her, pulling at the weeds

growing over his grave, although his hand went straight through the plants. He sat back on his haunches and grumbled at her as she approached.

'Can you get these?'

'Nice to see you too, Granddad.' Erica smiled, placing her coffee and brownie on the grass and carefully pulling up the three weeds.

'Stick them over there, under that bush.'

Erica did as she was told and then patted the grass. Finding it dry, she sat down and broke a piece off the brownie. Her grandfather watched and then sat beside her.

'You know, there's a lot to like about being dead. One of my favourites is that my knees don't hurt when I do this.'

'That's good. Mine hurt and I'm only in my thirties. I'd offer you this if I could.' Erica popped the brownie piece into her mouth.

'Hmm.' Her grandfather watched. 'That's one of the downsides. I do miss chocolate more than I thought. And weeding.'

'Never thought I'd hear you say you miss weeding.'

Her grandfather laughed.

'Me neither.'

'Has Gran been to visit today?'

Her grandfather nodded, running his fingers through the blades of grass at his hips.

'How's your day been?'

'Good, actually. We got a client. An actual client, this time. A hotel manager with definitely more than one spirit, although I don't think she knows there's more than one.' Erica stopped and cleared her throat. It had only been a couple of months since she started being able to see her grandfather and it was still strange. Their conversations were always normal despite the questions about death knocking at the back of Erica's mind. She'd asked him if he was in pain, if he was stuck. He'd told her no.

Did he have unfinished business? she'd asked.

No, he'd told her gently. He was at peace, everything was calm and he was ninety-nine per cent sure this was his heaven. In his Victorian cemetery, among the trees, with other spirits to talk to and where his wife, daughter and granddaughter visited regularly.

'What more could I want?' he'd told her.

'And the fae?' she'd asked, worried about upsetting him. He'd laughed and shrugged and told Erica that he didn't blame Minerva one bit. Given half the chance, he'd be doing the same.

That had made things easier and allowed Erica to relax. Still, there were questions that she was burning to ask, which was difficult when her grandfather kept the conversations so *normal*.

'Did you talk to the spirit?'

'No. Not really. It's only said two words, first to one of the housekeepers and then to us.'

'What two words?'

'It's here.'

Her grandfather frowned.

'What's here?'

'I don't know. I don't even know if it's a who or a what.'

'It sounds ominous.'

Erica studied him. He looked exactly how she remembered him, although with fewer lines on his face. He'd always called them his worry lines. He looked younger with them gone. He was also slightly translucent at times, when the light hit in a certain way, and through him she could just make out the trees and gravestones beyond. They were always careful to have these conversations by his own grave. It was where he felt most comfortable, but it also meant that any passers-by would mistake Erica for someone sat, talking to her grandfather's gravestone. She'd received a number of sympathetic looks and smiles while her grandfather waved at them and said hello.

'Really? I wondered if it might just be a memory repeating itself.'

'Perhaps. But there's been some talk of something around here. Of something dark coming. It might not be connected.' He shrugged and pointed to an overgrown patch of shrubs with an ash tree growing between a huddle of Victorian gravestones. 'They talk about it. They've been here long enough to feel these things. Me? I can't feel anything different. They said it's because whatever it is isn't close enough.'

This time Erica frowned.

'So, the spirit might be warning us?'

Her grandfather looked her in the eye.

'Since when has a spirit ever guided you wrong?'

Erica looked down at her brownie. He was right.

'Shit — sorry— wow. There was me celebrating our first paying client, but it sounds like I need to get on with figuring out how to talk to this spirit.'

Her grandfather smiled.

'Well, that is exciting. That the client is paying. Not enough to pay the bills I guess? But a start.' Erica nodded. 'And what about Rick?'

The sound of his name made Erica's stomach

clench.

'What about him?'

'Have you found him yet?'

Erica sighed.

'I might have done.'

'Have you talked to him?'

'Nope.'

'Why not?'

Erica looked up at her grandfather.

'I don't know what to say. Oh, hello, you from the future told me to find you. I'm your future wife. How do you do.'

Her grandfather laughed.

'I see your point. But don't worry.' He reached out a hand and attempted to hold hers. His fingers went straight through her palm, sending a chill up her arm and goosebumps in its wake. 'You'll figure it out. You always were determined. Which is why this ghost hunting business of yours is going to work too.'

'And my marketing consultancy.'

'What? What's that? I thought it was a ghost hunting agency?'

'Paranormal investigation agency. And yes, we're doing that but as you said, it's not paying the bills and if the last month has taught us anything, it's that it probably won't be able to steadily pay the bills. So we're sticking with the marketing consultancy as well. It's fine. We can do both.' Erica glanced at her grandfather out of the corner of her eye. 'Plus, I promised mum.'

Her grandfather grinned.

'Ah. Yes. Darling Esther still doesn't want you to tow the family line.' He shook his head. 'If she really wanted that, she shouldn't have let Min get her claws into you when you were little.'

'Claws? You can't talk about Gran like that.'

'I can talk about her however I like. We were married over sixty years and I'm dead.' He flashed her a mischievous smile.

Erica shook her head.

'Mum doesn't mind me doing some of the stuff. I've been working with her herbs since I was little. It's just some of the spirit stuff she wants me to stay away from, not all. And definitely all of the fae stuff.'

There was a pause at the mention of the fae. Her grandfather looked past her, in the direction of the almost hidden gate and the walled garden that the volunteers had nicknamed the secret garden, purely because the general public assumed they weren't allowed in there. Knowing what she knew now, Erica wondered if the fae had something to do with that. What magic lurked on that gate?

She followed her grandfather's gaze.

'Have you ever considered,' he said slowly and with purpose. 'That the reason you haven't contacted Rick is because of Alfie?'

Again, Erica's stomach lurched. She looked back to him. Her cheeks warming, she attempted to nonchalantly brush them as if the mere touch of her own cold fingers would get rid of the redness.

Her grandfather didn't care though, he was searching her eyes.

'You think I want to be with Alfie?'

Her grandfather blew out his cheeks and turned away, gazing across the cemetery. He looked back at her.

'Do you?'

Erica struggled, staring down at her coffee while

she tried to sort through her feelings.

'No. But then a little bit yes. But then a massive no. But then yes. But if I'm feeling like that, then the answer is probably no.'

'Except when it's yes?' Her grandfather smiled gently. 'What's behind the no? What makes you think no? Is it just because he's a fae?'

'You can't say that lightly, Granddad. Being a fae is big. They're powerful and dangerous, and if I let him get that close...'

Her grandfather nodded.

'I used to worry about Min, too, when she would go and talk to them. The thing is, from what I could gather, fae are powerful and they are dangerous, to the likes of me and your father, and Jess. But to you and Esther and Min...Ric, they're allies. They're your allies.'

'I don't know. They didn't really help that much when it came to getting Steve's baby back.'

'Okay, no, but they did warn you about his wife being from another time. And just because they're selfish, doesn't mean they're not helpful some-times.'

Erica sat back and raised an eyebrow at her grandfather.

'Why are you doing this? It's like you want me and Alfie together. Has he been saying things?'

'Of course he has. You forget, he translated for us, before you could see me.'

Erica hadn't forgotten. She had strangely fond memories of that moment.

'What's he been saying to you?'

Her grandfather smiled.

'He asked me to build him up to you. He really likes you, you know, and he has a point.'

'Oh?'

'If this Rick is the man you're going to marry and potentially be with for a long, long time, then why not have some fun with Alfie now? Better to have fun now than wait until you're Min's age.'

'Gran would say it's better to do both. To have fun before and after.'

Her grandfather shrugged.

'She almost makes marriage sound horrible.'

Erica smiled.

'She loves you, Granddad.'

'I know. So, why not take her advice? And mine? Go have some fun. Just until you've found the right words for this Rick fella.'

'You know, I didn't come here to talk about my love life,' said Erica, finishing off her brownie. 'I came to ask you about this spirit.'

'What about it?'

Erica drank the last of her coffee and considered her wording.

'How can I make contact? Is there a way to know if it's being cautious or if it's just too weak?'

'What have you tried so far?'

'EVP.'

'What's that?'

'Electronic voice phenomena. It's when we record a conversation and when you play it back, sometimes you can hear a voice where there wasn't one before. That's how we heard it telling us "it's here". I asked it to talk to me when I was alone in the room but nothing happened, even though I could feel it there. We're getting some cameras to see if we can record anything and Jess has some other techniques she wants to try. But I find it strange that I can talk to you but not to this spirit.'

'You couldn't always talk to me. It's only recently you could see me, but I was here all along, talking to you.'

Erica sighed. She still felt guilty about that. 'Maybe it's not just a question of whether this spirit is strong enough,' her grandfather continued. 'It obviously wants to communicate if you heard its voice. Maybe it's also about what you believe and what you want to happen.'

Erica blew out her cheeks.

'Wonderful.'

'Maybe you should ask Alfie.' Erica shot her grandfather a look. 'If you like, I'll keep an ear out on the Victorians over there. See if they know anything more about whatever it is that's here.'

Erica relaxed a little.

'Thanks. That would be good.' She snuck a glance to the gate leading to the secret garden.

'Well, now that's sorted, why don't you go see Alfie?'

Erica groaned.

'Aren't you worried he'll hurt me?'

'Are you kidding? You've met your grandmother, yes? Can you imagine what she would do if he hurt you?'

'Fae are more powerful.'

'You've met Eolande, too? Your grandmother's lover?'

Erica turned back to her grandfather.

'You know about that?'

'Oh, yes.' There was an unmistakeable twinkle in her grandfather's eyes. 'You know, she never let on that she might be interested in sex with another woman.'

'Oh, and you would have been okay with that?'

He shrugged.

'I'm okay with it now. But then, these things matter less when you're dead.'

Erica put the napkin her brownie had come with inside her empty coffee cup.

'Could Alfie hurt you?' she asked.

Her grandfather thought about this.

'Probably. Maybe. Probably not. Who knows. Can ghosts feel pain?'

'I don't know. Can they?'

'My joints don't hurt anymore. You probably don't remember the amount of painkillers I had to be on for them.'

'But that's because death cured your arthritis.'

Her grandfather laughed.

'That's one way of looking at it. Okay, well, I walk into things and it doesn't hurt.'

'Because you go straight through them.'

'So, how is Alfie supposed to hurt me?'

Erica shrugged.

'Magic. Twisting your ectoplasm or something?' She looked up into her grandfather's wide eyes.

'That does sound painful and I don't even know where my ectoplasm is.'

'You'd tell me, if any of them tried to hurt you, right?'

'Of course.'

'And if he's saying anything...I don't know, if he's putting pressure on you?'

'Of course. And you're not to have anything to do with him if you feel he's pressurising you either,' he told her.

'Except that he is, isn't he?'

'He's persistent.'

'When does persistence turn into pressurising?'

'Do you feel pressured into being with him? I would hate for you to feel that. I just want you to be happy. Don't say no to him just because you think you'll upset Esther. Boy, the things Esther used to do that upset your gran and me.' Her grandfather whistled through his teeth.

'Yeah? Like what?'

'Never you mind. Just remember, when it comes to Alfie, you need to put yourself first. What do you want?'

'Everyone keeps asking me that,' Erica murmured.

'You're at that time of life, Ric. It happens to us all, one way or another.'

'When did it happen to you?'

'Well, it didn't happen in quite the same way for me, did it. Back in those days, no one asked what you wanted in life. No one asked me what I wanted.'

'What did you want?'

'I wanted to join the police.'

Erica stared at her grandfather.

'Really? Why didn't you?'

'Because I joined the army instead. I didn't have much of a choice, remember?'

'You could have joined the police when you came back.'

'I'd had enough of men being bad to each other by then.' Her grandfather sniffed, staring off into the distance. 'But when I was young enough, I wanted to make the city a better place. I wanted to defend the vulnerable. Be a protector.'

Erica grinned, leaning into her grandfather but not enough to lean through him.

'You became a protector of your family. And of

this place. You protected these trees until your last day, and even death couldn't stop you. You're still here, watching over them.'

Her grandfather smiled knowingly.

'Like I said. It's heaven.'

'When do the Victorian spirits come out?' she asked, staring over at the clump of trees he'd pointed at.

'Whenever they like.'

'So, you could go ask them now? About this ominous thing?'

'All right.' Her grandfather stood and moved over to his gravestone. 'I get the message. No more talking about what you want, or Alfie or this Rick fella. Are you going straight home or will you go to the garden first?' He gestured to the secret garden gate.

'Home. Mum's making a big casserole.'

'Oh, I loved those.'

'Sorry. I'd bring you some if I could.'

'I know, love.'

'You'll talk to the Victorian spirits?'

'Of course.'

'I'll come back tomorrow, if you like?'

'Sure. Get home and stay safe.' Her grandfather blew her a kiss and she blew one back. It was the best they could do given the circumstances.

Erica made her way back to her Mini, trying to ignore the heavy sensation of being watched.

6

Jess ran up the stairs with a piece of toast in her mouth. Bubbles followed her up. She reappeared moments later clutching her laptop she'd scooped from her bed, pausing half way down to let the puppy bound down in front of her.

She sat at the kitchen table and opened her laptop. If she had to choose, the kitchen was her favourite room in the house. The cabinets and work units ran along one wall with the fridge at one end and the door to the hallway at the other. Opposite the cabinets was a floor to ceiling window over-looking the garden. In the small space between, near the fridge covered in Ruby's drawings, was the tiny table with four chairs. It was just large enough for the three of them to sit down to eat together and just the right size to act as Jess's desk.

She tapped in her password and ate her toast as the desktop loaded.

The first thing she did was check her emails. There was nothing about the cameras she'd ordered being delivered but then it had only just gone half nine in the morning. There was still time before she'd have to make the decision to go into the city and buy the cameras there and then at full price.

What there was, however, was an enquiry. Frowning, a lead ball dropping into her stomach, Jess opened the email and checked the name. It was a client from her and Erica's old marketing agency. They'd been careful not to poach anyone but Erica had mentioned that her and Jess were setting something up. This client must have discovered them somehow. How much marketing had Erica done? How had this woman found them?

It didn't matter. Jess should have been happy. As far as she knew, this was their first enquiry, but instead she closed the email and then her laptop and stared down at Bubbles, sitting patiently by the table waiting to catch Jess's eye.

'I should probably read that, shouldn't I,' she murmured.

No. You should take me for a walk, said Bubbles' big brown eyes.

'Oh come on, it's not like you're desperate. You've been in the garden,' she told the puppy.

That's not the same, Bubbles stared.

'I know, I know. Hang on.' Jess opened her laptop and reopened the email, scanning it quickly. 'Blah blah blah, wonderful you're setting up together, blah blah blah, social media management, blah blah blah, content marketing. Bleugh.' Jess put a hand on her stomach in an attempt to settle it. Pulling her phone from her pocket, she messaged Erica.

Morning! Have you checked the consultancy emails? What do you think?

She knew what Erica would think. Erica would jump at the chance. This client was easy albeit boring money. With a sigh, Jess looked around her kitchen. It would be nice to be able to pay the mortgage this month.

'Ric said she'd deal with all this, so I'm going to let her,' Jess told the puppy who jumped up, wagging her tail. 'Yes, yes. Your turn.'

Leaving her laptop behind but taking her phone, Jess grabbed Bubbles' lead and her keys. 'Where do you want to go? How about a peaceful walk in the woods? A bit of bird song and some trees, see if it'll stop me feeling sick, yeah?'

Bubbles didn't reply, she was already waiting by the front door.

It was a short drive or a long walk to the woods. They walked, Bubbles getting stronger and stronger as they neared the path that would take them between the trees. Jess stopped every now and then, making Bubbles sit for a moment in an attempt to teach her patience. The puppy would stay calm for a few steps when they started walking again only to get overcome by excitement and go back to pulling.

Jess took a deep breath when they reached the tree line and told Bubbles to sit. The puppy obeyed, looking up at her with those large eyes that got her whatever she wanted. Jess unclipped the lead.

'Don't wander too far,' she told the dog. Bubbles sprang forward and immediately buried her nose into a clump of grass. 'And don't eat anything!' Jess called to her as she walked past the dog, letting Bubbles' bushy tail brush against her fingertips.

Jess walked into the dappled shadows and took another deep breath, waiting for the relaxation that always came over her on these walks.

Nothing happened.

Jess tried again. This time with her eyes closed.

There was no relaxing, her muscles stayed tight, her stomach cramped.

She opened her eyes and looked up into the trees.

There was silence and not a peaceful one.

'Where are the birds?' she murmured as Bubbles trotted past her, oblivious. There was no bird song, no rustling noises, no magpies screaming at each other or pigeons whistling from branch to branch. Frowning, Jess followed Bubbles as the puppy ambled along the path, sniffing.

If the dog wasn't concerned, then Jess wasn't either. She led Bubbles further into the woods, smiling as the puppy rushed past her in a fit of joy.

For a moment, the silence was forgotten and Jess's mind wandered back to Mrs Wilder at the hotel. Were the cameras being delivered now, while she wasn't home? She checked her phone. There were no new notifications. She'd finished filling in a contract of work and sent it along with an initial invoice to Mrs Wilder late last night. She hadn't responded yet. Maybe there was something wrong with her internet connection, or with her data, or with technology in general. Jess bit her lip. No, there was something wrong with her patience. There she was, telling Bubbles to be patient about going into the woods and she couldn't even wait less than twenty-four hours for a client to respond.

A twig snapped above her head.

Jess stopped and looked up.

That was odd. She'd expect the sound of a twig snapping behind her, or in front, or anywhere around her. There were foxes in these woods, and birds sifting through the detritus on the floor and a large puppy up ahead, tripping over her own feet. But from above?

Narrowing her eyes against the sunlight, Jess couldn't see anything other than the green leaves of the canopy. What had she been expecting? A bear?

She laughed at the thought and walked away from the spot a little faster than usual.

They continued on through the woods and Jess began to get lost in her thoughts again. It was all well and good that they'd found one paying client —if she paid—but they needed more. The hotel market seemed a good one to tap into. Maybe she would do a quick search for supposedly haunted hotels in the local area when she got home. No, Erica said she'd deal with the marketing. Jess had to focus on the client they did have rather than ones that didn't exist yet.

Jess blinked out of her thoughts as she fell over Bubbles. The puppy had stopped in the middle of the path, the fur on the back of her neck rising as she growled.

Jess had only heard Bubbles growl once before. Inside the secret garden at the cemetery, when she had been foolish enough to go searching for the fae to ask for help.

Wide-eyed, Jess looked around them, feeling the comforting warmth of Bubbles against her leg.

'What is it, Bubs?' she whispered.

Should she call out? That would draw attention to them. What if there were fae living in these woods? They'd only been walking here for a couple of months, since Jess and Ruby had moved into their house and Ruby's father had pretty much thrown Bubbles at Jess claiming that she was a gift for Ruby. The woods were small, so Jess already knew them well, but she didn't know them well enough to know how the woods changed between the seasons. Or what might be lurking between the trees that the average human didn't know about.

She looked down at Bubbles. The dog had

relaxed and returned to sniffing a nearby fern.

Jess exhaled.

'What was that about?' she asked. 'Maybe we should go a different way. Or, you know, go home.' She was about to clip Bubbles' lead on when the dog spurted forward, head nestled in the under-growth. Her tail started wagging furiously.

'Oh, no. What have you found? Bubbles, this isn't the right time. It really isn't,' Jess hissed at her dog, grabbing her by the collar and pulling her away.

There, between the clumps of grass, ferns and brambles, were the glassy eyes of a dead fox.

Jess gave a small squeal, her heart pounding and she pulled Bubbles closer to her.

As her heart rate slowed, she took another look.

'Poor thing,' she murmured. She'd expected the fox to be curled up. How else did a fox die in the woods like these but from an illness or old age? But no, it almost looked as if the body had been thrown there, except that...yes, Jess counted, there were only three legs.

Instinctively, Jess scanned the area surrounding the fox and found the fourth leg nearby.

'How weird,' she murmured. 'Who did this to you?'

The fox didn't reply.

Letting go of Bubbles but attempting to keep the dog away with her leg, Jess took out her phone and snapped some photos of the fox and its leg. She'd send them to the police, or the RSPCA, or the local press. Someone would show an interest, and if someone was going around killing foxes, they had to be stopped. She wondered if a dog did this.

Jess glanced at Bubbles who was staring intently

at the fox.

There were no signs of ripped skin that she would have expected from being torn apart by dogs. Jess pulled a face at the thought.

'Strange,' she said, straightening and clipping Bubbles' lead on. 'We're definitely going home now. Come on. Fastest way out is back the way we came.'

The birds were still silent and as Bubbles could no longer stop to sniff, the world became eerily quiet as they rushed back through the woods.

As they reached the path that would take them out and home, Jess stopped. She turned and studied the trees.

'Is someone there?' she asked, not quite loud enough for anyone to hear. Her gut twisting, she dragged Bubbles out and away from the woods.

She could have sworn she'd heard a voice, something deep and guttural, although even as the noise repeated in her head, she couldn't make out the words.

Once home, Jess locked the doors and stopped. Her eyes filled with tears and she wiped them away as soon as they fell.

'Don't be ridiculous,' she told herself, sitting at the kitchen table and heaving a trembling sigh. Bubbles put her chin on Jess's lap and wagged her tail. Jess cuddled the dog, digging her fingers into the puppy's fur and breathing her in.

After a while, her body relaxed and her stomach grumbled for food. Jess sat up and Bubbles lay down at her feet. Taking out her phone, Jess messaged Erica.

Just took Bubbles for a walk in the woods and had a strange experience. Are there fae in those woods?

She put the phone down and moved to make herself a cup of tea. Bubbles watched her. Feeling the dog's stare on her back, Jess found a carrot and gave it to Bubbles in return for the dog placing her paw in Jess's hand.

Her phone beeped.

Sorry, only just saw these. I saw the email. I'm replying now. Don't worry, I'll deal with it all. Any sign of the cameras?
Funny you should say that about the woods. We found a dead seagull there last night. I've never seen a dead seagull before. I've never seen a live seagull in woods before.
I don't think there are fae there. I can find out? What happened?

Jess reread the message a couple of times. A dead seagull was strange, she wasn't sure she'd seen one before either.

Too much to tell like this. I'll tell you later.
No sign of the cameras yet. I'll keep you posted.

She sat back, sucking on her lips. Then added to the message.

Ask about the fae.
I found a mutilated fox. Very strange. I took photos. Should I send them to the police or the RSPCA?

She sipped at her tea.

Horrible! Poor thing. Send them to both? I'll ask about the fae. They wouldn't kill a fox but they'll want to know about it. I think.
See you later x

Jess responded with an acknowledgement and a kiss, and then opened her laptop. She'd deal with the fox photos before she started worrying about the cameras arriving.

In The Woods

The woods pulsed. Fear, the tingling of pain, touched every branch, every leaf and the eyes of every animal. The birds had stopped singing. Those that hadn't flown away, leaving the woods behind, huddled together in the branches. Through the silence, it waited and watched, as dog walkers came and went, as joggers hurried between the trees.

It waited, until it heard the sound of young voices approaching.

Licking at what could have been considered lips, it moved closer, eager and hungry.

Four teenagers strolled into the woods with carrier bags and cigarettes. The smoke and red of the flame touched at it, making its stomach growl with anticipation. The teenagers didn't hear. They were too busy making noise, trying to be heard over one another, laughing loud.

They stopped at the ring of carefully placed tree trunks and began to unpack their bags. Two males and two females. One of the females was frightened. It darted out a long tongue to taste her fear.

The other three were heavy with musk and lust. The frightened girl sat down, staring at the ground while a boy wrapped his arms around the other female. The couple kissed.

While the remaining boy pulled out an aerosol can and began spraying a large, charred branch left behind by others, the couple left and followed a path deeper into the woods.

'Where are you going?' the frightened girl called.

'We'll be back soon,' her friend giggled.

The frightened girl sat huddled, avoiding the remaining boy. It watched and then decided against her. It wasn't strong enough for her yet, and through the fear she would put up a fight.

No, it turned its attention to the leaving couple, following them, hopping from branch to branch. If they felt what that dog walker earlier in the day had sensed, they didn't show it. Their attention was only for each other. Hands grasping and groping as they walked, until the boy found a small clearing, with a fallen tree trunk and the remains of a fire left by others. He pulled the girl in close, kissing her hard, pressing their bodies together.

It felt their blood pulsing, their breathing coming hard. It could almost feel the heat of their skin touching, the fire of his hands on her as he clumsily pulled at her clothes.

It slithered down a tree trunk, the tree gasping and crying out but there was no one around to hear. In fact, there was no one around to hear any of the trees screaming warnings at the couple.

It had a decision to make. The boy or the girl. The boy was full of strength but the girl had something more about her. An innocence and a softness and no sign of the weakness that hid behind the boy's strength. No, the boy would give it a small hit of vitality but the girl was just what it needed.

It waited until they were fully engrossed in one another, the boy's head at the girl's chest. The girl moaned and giggled and that was when it slid down to her arms, stroking at her long hair that fell down her back.

The girl flinched.

It wrapped itself around her legs, feeling the softness of her thighs beneath her thin skirt and the girl gasped. Running its tongue up her neck, it pulled sharply.

The girl fell forward, collapsing onto the boy, before it yanked the girl away.

She yelled at first, unsure of what had happened, and then feeling the tightening around her legs, she screamed and kicked. It was too late. The kicks didn't land. It held her legs together fast and pulled her closer. The fight was strong in her and now the fear had arrived. The wonderful taste of the fear and lust mixing together gave it a head rush and with renewed energy, it pulled her up the tree in one swift movement.

7

Erica drove into the hotel car park to find Jess already there with the boot of her car open. Erica parked her Mini next to Jess's old car and climbed out, closing the door and wandering around to Jess.

'Good afternoon.' Jess flashed her a smile that was a little too wide and waved a box at her.

'The cameras arrived then?'

'Yup. Thank God. I was just about to jump in the car and drive all the way into town in a panic when they arrived. Talk about nick of time. No idea how to set them up though.' Jess handed Erica one of the boxes. She read the writing on the side and squinted.

'I'm sure we'll figure it out.'

'Yeah. How hard can it be?' Jess didn't sound convinced but still that smile stayed on her lips. Erica watched her.

'Are you okay?'

'Hmm? Yeah. Of course. I've told Marshall we might need his help. He's on standby.'

Erica grinned and tutted.

'Remember the days when you were a strong, independent single mum who didn't need a man helping her with stuff like this? You built your kitchen table all by yourself.'

'Yes, and I remember all the swearing involved. It took me hours. That's all well and good but when you have a handyman boyfriend, you use him. I like to think the universe sent him to me for a reason.'

Erica laughed. 'Hold out your hands.'

'Why?' Erica did as she was told and Jess started piling the boxes between her outstretched arms. 'Oh. Okay.'

'Come on. Sooner we start, the longer we can stare at the instructions and wonder what the hell we're doing.'

Erica followed Jess to the front door and waited while she rang the bell. The boxes were starting to get heavy. She shifted her weight to see if that would help. It didn't.

Finally, the door opened and Mrs Wilder appeared, or so Erica assumed. She could see a pair of feet and hear Mrs Wilder's voice but the boxes prevented her from making a clear iden-tification.

'Come in, ladies.' Mrs Wilder led the way into the reception area where Jess unburdened Erica of some boxes. 'What's all this?'

'The cameras we discussed setting up. I hope that's still okay? We may be a few hours, we'd like to take another look around. We don't want to be a bother though,' Jess explained.

'I'll give you the key to the room. Do you need anything else?'

Jess looked at Erica who shook her head.

'No, that's all great. Thanks.'

Mrs Wilder fetched the key and led them up the stairs to the haunted room, unlocking it for them and handing the key to Jess.

'Let me know if you need anything.'

'Thank you,' Jess called after her as Mrs Wilder walked away. She turned, beaming, to Erica. 'I've got a really good feeling about this. She paid so fast.

Makes me wonder if we're charging enough,' she whispered.

'Don't push our luck,' Erica murmured back, dumping the boxes on the bed.

There was a moment's pause as Erica looked around the room. Nothing had changed from the day before.

'Can you feel anything?' Jess asked.

'No. Can you?'

Jess pulled a face.

'Of course not. I don't even know what I'd be looking for in a feeling, if you know what I mean.'

'Well, I don't usually either. It's just a...feeling. It's hard to describe, and it tends to be a little different each time.' Erica waited to see if there was a chill in the air or a whisper at her ear, but the room was quiet and suitably warm. 'Let's get these cameras sorted first.'

Erica turned one box over and read the small print.

'A heat camera.' She looked up at Jess. 'Are these all different?'

'Yup. We've got a normal camera, one that registers heat and a night vision one.'

Erica looked down at the boxes on the bed. There were definitely more than three.

'And the other boxes are...?'

'Other equipment.'

Erica stared at Jess.

'What did you buy, Jess?'

'Well, cameras need other things, apparently. Plus there's an EMF reader, a portable heat camera I thought might come in handy, a couple of power packs and something called a ghost cam I thought we could try.'

Erica blinked and stared at her.

'You didn't think that maybe we should start off slowly? Maybe one or two cameras and go from there?'

Jess shrugged.

'I found a website that basically sells everything you need to hunt ghosts. I admit.' Jess held up her hands in defeat. 'I may have gotten carried away.'

Erica looked back down at the boxes on the bed.

'How much did all of this cost?'

'Oh don't worry, this job covers it.'

A silence followed and Erica glanced at Jess suspiciously.

'So, how much profit are we making from this job, if you take all of this gear into consideration?'

Jess pursed her lips and ripped open a box. 'That much, huh?' Erica mumbled. 'Jess, our main aim here is to make a profit.'

'Ethically and with happy customers,' Jess added.

'Yes, and with a profit.'

'All start-ups require investment, Ric. This is our investment. It means that the next job will be all profit.'

Erica sighed and looked back down at the boxes.

'What the hell is a ghost cam?'

'Oh, that does everything. Covers the whole room, has night vision and normal vision, and connects to our phones so we can be watching from the car park or something.'

'So...what do we need these other cameras for?'

Jess hesitated.

'Well, I didn't know if it would work.'

Erica suppressed a low groan.

'Okay, well which was the most expensive?'

'The ghost cam, why? Oh, Ric.'

'Don't open it, okay? Maybe we can return it.'

'But we might need it.'

Erica shot Jess a look and her friend closed her mouth and started reading the instructions for the camera she'd opened. Erica picked up the night vision one and started unpacking it.

'We might be here for a while,' she murmured, staring at the small device. At least things were wireless now, so there weren't endless cables to sort through. 'Who's got Ruby?'

'She's at her dad's tonight and tomorrow.'

'And what about Bubbles?'

'She's home alone for now. She'll be fine. Marshall's going to check in if I'm going to be late.'

'You should have said. My parents would have had her.'

'Oh, no. I know what your parents are up to. Oh, Jess, we'll look after the puppy, it's no problem. Until one day, when my guard is down, boom! She chooses them over me and suddenly she's their dog. Nope. That's not happening.'

Erica grinned. Jess wasn't wrong.

'You picked up on that, huh?'

'I see the way they look at her. And I see how excited Bubbles gets when she sees them.'

Erica laughed.

'All right. Best get this done then, so you can go home to her. Where are we putting these cameras?'

'Erm, well, we need to try and cover the whole room, so above the window?'

Erica bit her lower lip as she looked up at the ceiling, considering the options.

'Okay. Might need a ladder.'

'Yeah.' Jess looked around the bedroom. 'Take your shoes off and stand on the chair.'

'Very professional.' Erica did as she was told and checked the positioning of the camera.

It's here.

Erica wobbled on the chair and held her breath. The hair on the back of her neck stood on end and a chill ran up her spine making her shiver. Slowly, she turned to face the room but there was nothing there, other than Jess frowning at some instructions and then tapping at her phone. Erica waited a moment. There were no strange shadows, no movement and no odd feelings of being watched.

'You okay?' Jess asked.

'Hmm? Yeah. I just...I heard it again.'

Jess lowered her phone and faced Erica.

'Heard what? The voice? It's here?'

'She,' said Erica. 'It's a woman's voice. She said "it's here" again.'

'What's here?' Jess glanced around the room. 'What's here?' she shouted.

Erica grimaced.

Nothing happened.

'We really need to get these cameras set up.'

'You think they'll work on this?'

'You don't?'

Erica sighed and stepped down off the chair.

'Worth a try. I can't see her and right now I can't feel her. I don't know. Did I tell you about Granddad? He said the Victorian ghosts think something's up. I asked him to talk to them.'

'What do you mean by something's up? Like what?'

'I have no idea.'

Erica turned on her camera and stuck it to the

wall above the window using a sticky wall hanger, the type that didn't leave a mark. She checked on her phone that it was connected and working. 'This one's done I think.'

'Good. Do this one, will you?' Jess handed her the other camera.

'You can't figure it out? It's easy.'

'I'm this close to chucking it and my phone out the window. You do it.' Jess picked up the EMF reader box.

'Ah! If you can't handle a camera, I doubt you can handle that.'

Jess glared at Erica and then her eyes lightened in a worrying way.

'Oh, I saw this thing on TV the other night.'

'Oh?'

'These ghost hunters investigating someplace in the U.S. and something spoke to them using their phone. Siri or whatever.' Jess opened up the AI on her phone and placed it on the bed. 'Hello? Can you use this to communicate with us? We don't want to hurt you. We just want to help. We want to know what's here? Is it here in the building?'

'That's a lot of questions,' Erica mumbled, fiddling with the night vision camera.

There was no response. Jess's phone went dark due to lack of activity.

'Try the EVP again,' Erica suggested. 'That worked last time.'

Jess nodded, finding the Dictaphone and hitting record.

'Hello? We don't want to hurt you, we just want to help. What's your name? What's here? Is it in the building?' She paused to give the spirit time to reply and then hit stop and played it back.

Erica caught herself holding her breath from the effort of trying to hear something. There was static after Jess's voice and then a whisper, or perhaps a groan. Jess rewound and played it again, holding it closer to her ear. She shook her head.

'There's something, but I can't figure it out.' She handed it to Erica who did the same, playing it again close to her ear. There was a gap between Jess's voice and then the strange noise began. There were words there but garbled and slurred. Erica played it again, this time closing her eyes and focusing on the sounds.

'It's here,' she murmured, rewinding and playing it again. 'It's here. Help. Them? Help them?' she asked the room.

From the bed, Jess's phone beeped and both Jess and Erica jumped, spinning around to face it. Jess sidled over and peered at the screen before visibly relaxing.

'It's Marshall.' She picked up the phone and read the message in full. 'He's finished early and is checking if we need help. Do we need help?'

That was a loaded question. Erica shrugged.

'I think we're okay.'

She finished setting up the camera and positioned it on the wall next to the other one. 'There. Good to go. Now what?'

Jess was staring at the Dictaphone.

'What else can we do? How else can we contact her? A séance?'

'Absolutely not. That's too dangerous. We'll figure this out, don't worry. Now,' said Erica, addressing the room. 'We've set up cameras here and here.' She pointed. 'One will catch anything you move, or if you're strong enough to materialise.

The other picks up heat, so if you're able to make something very hot or very cold. Please, try to do something tonight so we can see it. And, erm,' Erica paused, her heart racing. 'Who do we need to help?'

T-t-t

Erica spun round to face the voice but there was nothing there. Had it even been a voice? It had sounded like a tutting in her ear. Did the spirit not approve?

'What is it?' Jess whispered.

'She's here. She's in my ear,' Erica murmured. 'I hear you,' she told the spirit. 'But I don't understand. Please, keep trying.'

A silence followed. No more whispers sounded and eventually Erica admitted that the spirit had gone quiet.

They left the room, locking the door, and went back to their cars. There wasn't much else they could do until that night.

Jess hesitated by her car, staring down at the keys in her hand.

'You okay?' Erica stopped, her keys out, fighting the urge to glance up at the hotel windows.

'Did you hear the news on the way over here?'

'No. Why?'

'Apparently a girl went missing earlier today from the woods.'

'Your woods?'

'Yeah. It'll be crawling with police. I'll need to find somewhere else to walk Bubbles.'

Erica studied Jess a moment.

'I'm sure she's okay,' she said, walking over and touching Jess's arm. 'She'll have run off with her boyfriend or something.'

'Yeah. I guess. Only...' Erica waited for Jess to

find the words. 'That fox. Did you, I don't know, feel anything when you found that seagull?'

'No. I don't think so. Maybe.' Erica struggled to recall the memory.

'Last time I went into the woods the birds weren't singing,' Jess murmured.

'Maybe they were but you just couldn't hear them. They don't sing all the time.'

'I guess. It's weird though. It freaked me out.'

'There'll be a logical explanation, Jess. It'll all be okay. Go home. Drive safe, let me know when you're home and don't worry. If you want, you can always bring Bubbles to us and we'll walk her over the fields. I promise you my parents won't feed her treats and make her love them.'

That did the trick. Jess smiled and shook her head.

'I've got a gorgeous handyman waiting for me at home with no child and a dog that I can walk around the houses. I'll see you tonight.'

Erica laughed and unlocked her Mini, allowing herself one last fleeting glance up at the hotel windows before she got into her car. The windows were empty, but just as she looked away she swore a shadow passed over one of them.

8

The confidence that Jess had feigned for Erica lasted all of two minutes, until Jess was on the road and Erica was lost in the traffic behind her. She wouldn't walk Bubbles in the woods, that was obvious, but it didn't change the fact that a girl had gone missing or that it had been her boyfriend and friends who had reported it.

That was enough to give Jess a queasy feeling without the memory of the mutilated fox and its dead eyes staring past her.

It was a coincidence that there had been two strange animal corpses right before a girl had vanished. What else could it be? But the thought wouldn't leave Jess alone.

She made a turn she shouldn't have, taking a longer route that would pass by the main entrance to the woods. The skate park next to it was open, although there was no one skating, but the road had been cordoned off. There was a gathering of vehicles in the car park, some of them marked police cars. Jess assumed the others were unmarked ones.

Police tape fluttered by the woods and there were uniformed officers standing by the car park entrance.

Jess went around the roundabout, slowly down the road past the turning and parked her car, pretending with all of her might that she lived in the flats she'd parked next to. From there, she studied the scene. She couldn't see the whole car park from there, but she could see enough. Men and women walking in and out of the woods, talking to one another, discussing things in groups. She wished she could hear what they were saying.

Had they found something? Had they found her?

If this were a TV show, Jess thought, she'd walk over and start a conversation with the officer standing at the car park entrance. Or she'd sneak in through the skate park to hear what was being said.

But this wasn't a TV show, Jess had no reason to get involved other than her own nauseating curiosity and, most importantly, Jess didn't really want to know.

Still, she didn't restart the ignition. She stayed there, watching.

She watched as an old Mini, an ancestor of Erica's car, pulled up and the uniformed officer leaned to speak to the driver before waving them through. The car drove in, parked and a woman stepped out. She looked around Jess's age with long black hair tied neatly back and she was wearing a suit, jacket and trousers, that looked like it belonged in an office.

As police approached her, she flashed a badge of some sort at them and began talking.

Jess frowned, wishing she could hear what was being said. Was this the detective inspector arriving?

Jess's stomach dropped. That meant this was serious. A murder? A kidnapping? Jess unstuck her tongue from the roof of her mouth and gripped the steering wheel.

This was stupid. This wasn't work related and she couldn't hear anything. All she was doing was winding herself up.

Jess took a deep breath and started the ignition. Slowly pulling the car away, she drove past the woods and towards home.

The scene niggled at her all of the way, as she pulled her car into her driveway, blocking in Marshall's van. Her eyes remained glazed in thought as she walked to the front door and found her keys.

'Jess?'

Marshall's voice broke through the panic that was rising from her gut and Jess smiled as he appeared from the kitchen. She opened her arms and he mirrored her, wrapping her up as she snuggled into his broad chest.

To many, Marshall would be intimidating. He wasn't just tall, he was wide, and only some of it was fat. But, like most giants, he was gentle and never more so than with Ruby and Bubbles. That alone had made Jess fall in love with him. The fact that he could seemingly fix anything around the house helped too. As did the feeling of those arms wrapping around her, whether they were lifting her up, pulling at her clothes or giving her warmth and comfort.

She breathed in his scent of musk, testosterone and that distinct smell that all tradesmen have, which lingered for a while whenever he came through the door.

'Hello,' she murmured into his shirt.

'Everything okay? What happened?'

'Nothing. I'm fine.' Jess flashed him a smile before leading him back into the kitchen where he'd been cooking. The worktops were a mess of chopping boards and discarded pieces of vegetables. A meat tray sat sadly at one end, waiting to go in the bin. On the hob, a pot was bubbling and the smell coming from it made Jess's stomach grumble.

'Spag bol?' he asked, moving to stir the pot. Jess nodded.

'Lovely. Wine?'

'I'll have a beer.'

'Good. Beer sounds good.'

Jess went to the fridge and pulled out a couple of cans. She opened them both, leaving one on the counter for Marshall and taking a good glug of her own before pouring the rest into a glass. She closed her eyes as the taste danced on her tongue and the cold alcohol trickled down through her body. That was better.

Marshall watched her.

'So, everything went all right with the cameras?'

Jess nodded.

'It was fine. Actually, Erica made contact again but we didn't learn anything new. It's frustrating. It's like the ghost can't quite talk to us properly. Erica says she's probably too weak.'

'She?'

Jess shrugged.

'So Erica says.'

'Is there a way of giving a ghost strength?'

Jess paused with the glass to her lips.

'I'm not sure if that would be a good idea. It's probably nothing anyway. It's here. That could mean anything. The delivery is here. Summer is here. The baby is here. It's probably a memory from the ghost's past. That's what Erica always says about these things.'

'Is that what she's saying now?'

'She mentioned it.'

Marshall studied Jess.

'Something happened, though?'

Jess searched his eyes before relenting. From the moment they'd met, he'd been able to read her.

'There was something online, in the local news, about a girl going missing in the woods. I just drove past and the place is crawling with police.'

Marshall put down his stirring spoon and gathered Jess back up in his arms.

'I hadn't heard. When did it happen?'

'Earlier today.'

Marshall squeezed her.

'I'm sure everything's okay. She's probably gone off with a boyfriend or girlfriend or something.'

'That's what Erica said, but the friends and boyfriend are the ones who reported her missing. It just seems weird, that's all.'

'How so? This happens. You don't know who she was, do you? Right. So she could have had a troubled past. Maybe she's run away. This doesn't have anything to do with you or Ruby, you know.'

The tears came suddenly, tumbling down Jess's cheeks.

'Oh, baby. I'm sorry. I didn't mean...' Marshall hugged her tight, until she had trouble breathing. She laughed through the tears, pushing him away.

'No. You're right. I'm okay. Sorry. Guess you hit on something there.' She turned her back on him to wipe her eyes and blow her nose. 'I'll go get ready for dinner. It smells amazing.'

'Why don't you go give Paul and Ruby a call? Might make you feel better?'

Jess stared at Marshall, her chest aching with how much she loved him in that moment. She stopped to kiss him hard on the lips as she passed.

'Thank you,' she murmured. 'I won't be long. Promise.'

When Jess came back downstairs, it was with a strange mixture of feeling buoyant and grief-stricken at having spoken to Ruby and then having to face the house without her, Marshall had put dinner on the table. Bubbles, following Marshall closely, pondering if any of it was for her, wagged her tail and trotted over to greet Jess.

'This looks good,' Jess said, giving Bubbles a quick cuddle. 'Ruby sends her love. To both of you.'

Marshall gave Bubbles a chew to work on and then sat down to eat. Jess watched them for a moment before picking up her fork.

'How are you feeling?' Marshall asked.

'I'm okay. Sorry about that.'

'Nothing to be sorry for. A kid's gone missing in the woods. I get it. But Ruby's okay. We're all okay.' Marshall took Jess's hand and kissed it as she chewed her first mouthful. 'Ruby is safe at her dad's. How was she?'

Jess nodded and swallowed her food.

'She's good. Actually, I think she's enjoying herself. Paul ordered pizza and they're watching a film.'

'There you go.' Marshall smiled around his food. 'So, we're back to just the two of us. A whole evening together. Shame you have to work tonight but we still have time. What do you wanna do?'

In a moment, the missing girl in the woods was

forgotten as Jess's stomach tingled.

'I want to enjoy having this house all to ourselves,' she told him.

Marshall winked at her and went back to his dinner.

'You know,' he said after a moment. 'I seem to be spending a lot of time here. We never spend the night at mine when Ruby's at Paul's.'

The tingling sensation evaporated and Jess shoved a forkful of food into her mouth to buy time. Then she gestured at the dog, licking the remainders of the chew from her paws. 'No, I know,' said Marshall, looking down at Bubbles. 'We can't leave the dog and it's silly to take her all the way to mine or to ask someone to look after her. I get it. I do. And it's fine.'

Here we go, thought Jess.

'I just wonder how much money I—we—could save if I...I don't know, got rid of my flat.'

The words hung in the air between them as Marshall watched Jess and Jess stared at her plate, trying to find the right words.

'We've been together two months,' she started.

'I know. It isn't long. But isn't that for teenagers and people in their twenties? When you're that young, two months isn't long enough to move in together. But for us? You've got a mortgage and a child and a dog and a growing business. I've got a fully-fledged business and I'm paying out rent each month because I never felt I could settle and buy. Except that now I feel like I could, with you.'

Jess looked up at him.

'You want to buy a house?'

'No, Jess, you've already done that. I want to wake up next to you every morning, see Ruby every day and put my savings to good use helping you to pay off this mortgage. You know. Be a family. I thought that's what you wanted too?'

'It is,' said Jess immediately. She didn't even have to think about that one. 'It's just it all seems so quick. And last time things happened so quick, look how that went.'

'You got a beautiful daughter?'

Jess frowned at Marshall.

'Don't throw that at me. You know what I meant. I meant I ended up with a broken family and permanently tied to a man I never loved.'

Marshall looked hurt for a moment and Jess cursed herself inwardly. Stupid woman. What a idiotic way to put it. 'I didn't mean it like that. I love you and I love what we have and I love the family we could become.'

'But you don't want that family yet?'

'I do. It's just... Wasn't this supposed to be a nice evening of good food and sex?'

Marshall sighed, moving the spaghetti around his plate.

'When won't be too soon, then? Six months? A year?'

Jess squirmed in her seat. Bubbles came over and forced her head onto Jess's lap, and Jess took some comfort in pushing her fingers through the puppy's fur as Bubbles sneakily sniffed her plate.

'Can we just stop talking about it tonight? Let me have a think about it. Can we just finish this wonderful meal you cooked for us and then go have amazing sex, and I'll think about it and we'll talk about it another time?'

'Okay. When?'

Jess sighed.

'I don't know.'

'My rental contract ends this month,' Marshall said.

'Okay, then we'll talk about it before then. I promise.'

'Okay.' There was a pause as they both settled back into their meals. 'What do you want for your birthday?' Marshall asked.

Jess laughed.

'Just you. Some alone time with you.'

Marshall grinned.

'I'll see what I can do.'

Jess sat back and took a sip of her beer, feeling her body relax. At the back of her thoughts somewhere, she was processing the idea of Marshall moving in. Was it too soon? Was it a bad idea? It didn't feel too soon. If anything, it felt like he already lived with them. She took a moment to consider how it would feel to wake up next to him every morning, to have him there every evening, to fall asleep every night next to him. To have someone to help when Ruby was acting up, someone else to walk Bubbles, someone to help pay the bills. Someone to hold her when she came back from work after a bad day.

Jess lifted her drink to her lips again and smiled.

In The Woods

They had to wait but trees are good at waiting. They can wait for centuries if they must. They didn't have to wait that long. Watching and feeling that girl being dragged up into the canopy, feeling her screams and fear and pain, made them realise they could wait no longer.

The trees sent out a message. Passing it from one to another until it reached the edge of the woods. They whispered it, in case *it* heard them. It was asleep and the trees it slept in kept it shielded, rustling their leaves in the breeze to hide the whispers.

Once the whispers reached the edge of the woods, the message was passed to trees further away. Across the road, into gardens, down verges. A couple of crows carried the message at one point.

So it went on and the trees in the woods could only wait as silence fell over it once more. The rustling stopped, the birds fell quiet and *it* slept on.

How far the message would go and whether anyone would listen to it were questions that plagued the trees. They stood tall, watching *it*, but there was nothing more they could do.

They had to wait.

9

Erica sat in her Mini Cooper and watched as the last but one police vehicle left the car park by the woods. She wasn't sure how she'd ended up here. She'd been at home, restless and unable to settle when her body had marched her to her car, started the ignition and driven her here.

The police were done for the day. The evening was getting late and soon the sun would be setting. There was still enough daylight for them to search the woods but evidently the woods had been searched. Had they found anything of the poor girl?

Erica sighed and looked down at her hands on the steering wheel.

Why was she here?

This missing girl, while sad and worrying, was nothing to do with her. She started the ignition again with the intention of going home but instead of going left at the roundabout, she turned right.

The road wound around the edge of the woods, carving out a spot of greenery for the residents of the town. Erica wasn't an expert on the woods. She only knew of that one entrance which Jess had shown to her as a place to walk Bubbles. Yet, somehow, Erica found a spot on a residential road to park and then a path leading back into the woods.

She stood on the edge of the tree line and frowned.

There was police tape across the entrance. She couldn't go in, not that she wanted to or knew what she was doing here in the first place.

A whispered voice made her look up. She studied the trees around her, shifting in the breeze. She could have sworn she'd heard a word. After a moment's pause there were no other noises and Erica looked back to the woodland path in front of her.

Movement ahead caught her eye and she squinted, as if that would help her focus. Walking up to the police tape, Erica studied the shadow ahead as best she could.

'Alfie?' she called.

The shape ahead stopped and then came closer.

Alfie appeared from the shadows, his hands deep in his jean pockets. He looked different and it took Erica a while to figure out what it was. He was wearing a loose shirt with the top button undone, but that wasn't unusual. He wore his normal boots and his hair was pushed back where he'd run a hand through it. Ah, that was it. He wasn't smiling.

Erica cocked her head at him. 'What are you doing here?'

'I could ask you the same question,' he said, but still he didn't smile. It was unnerving and Erica caught herself wondering if he simply didn't like her anymore. It came as a shock that she would miss his charming smile, or that she would miss it so quickly.

'You can ask me the same question. The answer is I have no idea. I was at home, happy, working, dinner being cooked and suddenly I'm in the car and I'm here. I didn't even know this led to the woods. What are you doing here?'

Alfie studied her.

'Something brought you here?'

Erica shrugged.

'Maybe. I don't know.'

A ghost of a smile appeared on Alfie's lips and Erica felt a glimmer of relief at the sight. 'Why are you here? I didn't think this was your...patch? Is that the right word?'

'You can use whatever word you like,' said Alfie. His smile dropped away and he looked up at the trees. 'I was also called here. Just like you.'

'You don't know why you're here either?'

For the first time, Alfie seemed to actually notice Erica. His gaze travelled up and down her until his piercing blue eyes landed on hers.

'I know why I'm here. I find it interesting that you don't. You haven't learned to listen yet. But you will.'

'Excuse me? I listen.'

'It takes practice to hear these things. Don't worry about it. You'll pick it up.'

'Pick what up?'

'Don't worry. And I'm here, so you don't need to be. You can go home.'

'You want me to go?' Erica looked from Alfie to behind him, into the woods. 'I'm pretty sure these woods are a crime scene. You shouldn't be in there.'

'Police tape is for humans. I'm allowed here. You should go home.'

'Alfie?' Erica's stomach twisted. 'You don't know anything about the missing girl, do you?'

'Hmm?' Alfie was looking behind him, between the trees.

'I've heard the stories. Of the fae seducing

teenage girls and whisking them away. Did you take her?'

Alfie snapped back to her.

'What would I want with a teenage girl?'

Erica raised an eyebrow and Alfie grinned. 'I'd rather have you,' he murmured and Erica was a little ashamed to admit that she softened at the tone of his voice.

'Then come away from the crime scene.'

Alfie considered Erica and then lifted up the police tape.

'You heard the message,' he told her. 'You're allowed in here too.'

'You just said I wasn't.'

'What do you think brought you here?'

Erica shrugged.

'Jess is worried about the girl that's gone missing. And then, it was strange, we've both walked Bubbles here recently—'

'Bubbles?'

'Jess's dog.'

'Ah, the big fluffy one.'

'Yeah. We've both walked her here in the last week and seen weird things.'

Alfie lowered the police tape and stepped closer.

'Like what?'

'Dead animals. Not weird, really. It's woods, with foxes and things. But there was a dead seagull. I've never seen a dead seagull, especially in woodland. Maybe in the city or by the side of the road, but in the woods? And then Jess found a mutilated fox. I mean, what would have done that? A fox might have killed a seagull, although that must have been quite a fight. But a mutilated fox? Only people could have done that. Right?'

Alfie studied her eyes and then lifted the police tape again.

'The trees called out for help and you heard them. That's what brought you here,' he told her. 'Come on. Come inside with me and let's see what's going on.'

Erica blinked at him.

'The trees called out for help?' Alfie nodded. 'Why?'

'I don't know, that's why I'm here. To figure it out. When trees put out a distress call, it's always to be taken seriously.'

'Okay,' said Erica slowly. 'And why did I hear it?'

'I don't know, daughter and granddaughter of witches, why do you think you heard it?'

Erica gave Alfie a look.

'If that's the case, why didn't Mum or Gran hear it?'

Alfie shrugged.

'I'm not a witch. I don't know how these things work. Are you coming with me, or not?'

Erica pursed her lips and looked over his shoulder to the trees.

'We could be contaminating a crime scene. Or if they catch us, they might think we're guilty of something.' She shook her head. 'And for what? Because you said the trees called for help? They probably called for help, whatever that means, because a girl's gone missing. Doesn't that happen all the time?'

'Nope. Been a long time since I've heard a cry for help and never from these trees.' Alfie dropped the police tape again. 'I don't know what's going on but I doubt it's something the police will be able to handle. Otherwise, why put out a cry for help?' Alfie turned his back on Erica and began walking into the woods.

'Well, now, hang on. Wait!' Erica shifted from one foot to another, watching him go. 'All right. Hang on.' Taking a quick glance around, Erica ducked under the police tape and ran to catch up with Alfie who's constant charming smile had returned.

The skin on Erica's arms tingled, the hairs standing up.

'We see any police, I'm out of here. Okay?' she whispered.

'The police are gone,' Alfie whispered back, holding his face close to hers and for a moment they stared into each other's eyes.

Erica snapped away from him and cleared her throat.

'Okay. So, can we find out why the trees cried out for help?'

'We can ask them,' said Alfie, moving away from her and leading the way down a path. 'Come on.'

They walked in silence for a while, Alfie looking up at the tree trunks and to the canopy, moving his head slightly as if listening to something. Erica watched closely, trying to listen, trying to hear what he could hear.

'Anything?' she murmured after a while.

'They seem reluctant to talk.' Alfie placed a hand on one tree trunk and flinched. 'They're afraid.'

'Of what? What could trees be afraid of? Oh.' Erica stopped and Alfie looked back to her. 'There was a fire engine heading this way yesterday. Were those kids lighting fires? That would scare the trees, right?'

'Sure, because no one ever lights fires in forests and woodland.' Alfie kept walking.

'Well, what then? They're not in danger. Developers aren't swooping in to chop them all down. So what are they scared of?'

'They can hear you, you know. You might want to choose your words carefully.'

Erica looked at the nearest tree trunk and brushed her fingers against it.

'Sorry,' she murmured, although she felt nothing but the rough bark beneath her skin. She sighed. 'I can't hear anything. I don't know what brought me here but I don't think it was the trees.' She looked at Alfie. 'Maybe it was you.'

Alfie raised an eyebrow at her but carried on walking.

'Oh? And why would I call you here?'

'I don't know. I haven't seen you in a while.'

'Because you keep avoiding me.'

'Yes, and you keep pestering my grandfather.'

'Pestering is a harsh word but you admit you've been avoiding me. And why's that?'

'I'm not getting into this in the middle of a crime scene.' Erica stopped walking. 'I think I should go back to the car.'

Alfie turned to her.

'Aren't you curious about the girl that's gone missing?'

'No more than anyone else. I want her to be safe, of course, but what can I do? If something horrible's happened, a human did it to her. Best to leave it to the police.'

'Ah, and maybe your detective husband will rush

from the future to come and save her? Is that what you're waiting for?'

Erica bit her lip. That hadn't even occurred to her, but now he mentioned it. 'How is your hunt for the detective going, by the way? Found him yet?'

The tone of Alfie's voice made Erica not want to answer. He knew the truth, she realised. She didn't know how, but he knew that she'd found Rick and that she wasn't contacting him.

'That's none of your business.'

'Oh, I don't know. It sort of is. Seeing as how if you decide against him, then perhaps there is a chance for me after all.'

Erica didn't reply. At the back of her mind an argument was being whispered about how much of a chance Alfie really had with her and the loudest voice wasn't one that Erica wanted to admit to just yet.

Alfie watched her struggling with her thoughts and shrugged, turning away to continue walking. 'I already told you, if this was a human thing, the trees wouldn't have called for help. And they not only called out to us, but they called out to you. You say you walked through here recently?'

'Yeah.' Erica slowly followed him.

'Maybe that's why you heard but your mother and Minerva didn't.'

Erica sighed again. Damn it, but that made sense.

'Fine. So, whatever happened to this girl wasn't because of a human?'

'Is that...it can't be.'

Erica looked up at Alfie.

'What? Can't be what?' She tried to follow his gaze as he narrowed his eyes, but all she saw were trees.

'There. You see it? Two trees, joined at the top.' Alfie pushed on, moving away from the wide path and down an overgrown stretch that had obviously been a well-walked pathway at some point. Erica followed, brambles catching at her clothes. She yanked her jacket free, searching ahead of them.

'I don't see it. Where are you going?'

'How can this be possible?' she heard Alfie mumble.

'How can what be possible? Two trees joined at the top? I don't know. Some weird growing mutation? Oh, that?' Erica finally spotted what Alfie was staring at. 'That's ivy, isn't it? It's grown up both trees and met in the middle. So what?' Although now that she studied it, it was strange how the trees bent towards each other at the top.

Alfie stopped, still some distance from the trees in question, and Erica almost collided with him.

'Get behind me,' he hissed. Erica did so without question. Alfie continued facing the trees in front of him. 'There's something here,' he said, his voice low. 'Something that shouldn't be.'

Erica peered around him but saw nothing out of the ordinary.

'What is it?'

'I'm not sure.'

A loud cracking noise sounded above them and Erica was pushed back. She fell down, her spine bouncing from a tree root and the impact of her landing sending shockwaves up her body.

'Ow,' she breathed as her back complained. Alfie stood over her, his back to her. A large branch lay across the path in front of them. Erica looked up and saw where it had been torn from the tree trunk and torn was the right word. The bark was stripped and what looked suspiciously like a claw mark was gouged into the wound on the trunk. 'What the hell?' she hissed.

'You do not belong here,' Alfie called out. 'Leave this place. Go back to where you came from.'

Erica pulled herself up and then grabbed onto Alfie as a laugh rang throughout the trees.

'What's that?'

Alfie took her hand and yanked her away, back down the path. He ran and she tried to keep up to avoid being dragged, through the woods and back out the way they'd come in.

'Alfie, stop! What's going on? What was that?'

Alfie stopped at the edge of the woods and looked back.

'You will not touch her,' he said. 'You will not even look at her. Leave this place or I will come back and you will feel our full wrath.' He spat onto the ground and then turned to push Erica further away from the trees. 'You're not to come back here, Ric. Don't go back in there until I say so. Am I clear? You must promise me.'

'What are you going on about? Alfie? Stop.' Erica tried to use her weight to stop him but Alfie ploughed on ahead, dragging her with him until they reached the road.

'Promise me,' he repeated, looking into her eyes.

The softness was gone, replaced with a hardness that simultaneously scared and intrigued Erica.

'You have to tell me why.'

Alfie shook his head.

'There is something in those woods and it means you harm. All of you. It's not safe, Ric. Promise you won't go in there. And you're not to go looking at those two trees that join at the top. Whatever you do, don't go to those trees or step between them. Promise me.'

'But—'

'We will deal with this,' Alfie told her. 'We will remove it. And you will stay away. Do you promise?'

Erica wanted to promise, her mouth was poised to respond but the words wouldn't come. Alfie relented a little.

'Please, Ric.'

'Ric?'

Alfie and Erica both turned to look up the road and saw Jess, Marshall and Bubbles heading their way. Bubbles strained at the end of her lead to Erica but Marshall easily held her back.

'What are you doing here?' Jess asked Erica, giving Alfie a look.

'Ah. Good. Jess. Can you please make Erica promise that she won't go into these woods at any point until I say so?'

'Why's that?' asked Marshall. Erica smiled. Both Jess and Marshall stood glaring at Alfie, Jess sidling protectively over to Erica.

'Because it isn't safe in there.'

Jess looked over to the woods.

'Because of the girl that's gone missing?' she murmured.

'There's a presence in there and it's dangerous. Please, Ric. Promise Jess, if not me. Please.'

'What sort of dangerous?' asked Marshall. 'Like, supernatural dangerous?'

Alfie looked Marshall up and down.

'Yes.'

Marshall gave him a nod.

'Then neither of you are allowed in there.'

'What?' Jess turned on Marshall.

'You heard me. If those woods are dangerous and some girl's already gone missing then neither of you are allowed in there. Especially if it's a supernatural type of dangerous. I know you, Jess. This isn't a case. You're not getting paid. There is no client. You're not going in until this fella says it's safe.'

'Alfie,' said Alfie.

'Oh, you're Alfie. Until Alfie says it's safe. When will it be safe?' Marshall asked. Jess stared at Marshall, opening and then closing her mouth.

'When we've dealt with it. I need to go and talk to the others about it, but first.' Alfie turned to Erica. 'Promise?'

'I promise not to go into those woods alone until you give the say so,' said Erica.

Alfie's eyes darkened.

'You're not to go in at all.'

'What if I'm with someone, though? Like Gran? Or Eolande?'

Alfie sighed.

'No. Unless I'm with you, you're not to go into those woods. Promise?'

Alfie watched Erica while Marshall stared down at Jess. The women exchanged a glance.

'Fine,' said Erica.

'Sure,' said Jess.

This time Alfie and Marshall glanced at one another.

'Good. Then I'll be on my way, and you're to go home. All right?' Alfie hesitated and Erica wonder-ed for a moment if he might kiss her on the cheek. If the thought had occurred to him, he seemed to think better of it and, saying goodbye to Marshall and Jess, ignoring the dog still straining at her lead, Alfie left.

'That was weird,' said Marshall, watching him go.

Erica leaned down and gave Bubbles a proper cuddle to say hello.

'I thought you two were having a romantic evening?' she asked. 'What're you doing out here?'

'It's hard to be romantic when there's a puppy between you crying and crying and crying. We thought a walk might wear her out so she'll shut up and go to sleep. I see there's police tape up. The woods are completely closed,' said Jess.

'Yeah. Alfie was in the woods when I found him. He talked me into sneaking in and then something, I don't know, threw a massive branch at us and Alfie pushed me out of the way and then dragged me out.'

'You what?' said Marshall, sliding an arm around Jess's shoulders. 'Yeah, you're not allowed in there. In fact, standing here is giving me the creeps. Come on.'

As they turned, a woman emerged from the woods. All three froze, Bubbles turning to look up at them.

Ten

'Everything all right?' the woman asked, shoving a hand into her pocket. It was the woman Jess had seen arriving in the car park in an old Mini. The woman in the suit.

'Yeah,' said Jess, squaring up.

'That's a crime scene, you know,' Erica told her. The woman looked back to the woods over her shoulder.

'Yeah. It's okay. I'm police.' The woman took her hand from her pocket and flashed what looked like a warrant card so fast that Jess couldn't tell if it was a library card or not, and that sparked off a memory.

'Woah,' she said, stepping forward. 'Can I take a proper look at that?'

The woman hesitated and Jess flashed Erica a smile.

'Remember when Rick showed us his warrant card?' she murmured. 'What if this is the same? Can I check the date on that?' she asked the woman.

The woman frowned.

'The date? Why?'

'Please ignore my friend. We were just leaving,' said Erica. Marshall held out a hand to Jess.

'Okay.'

'No, hang on. Seriously, can I take a proper look?' Jess pushed, ignoring Marshall.

Again, the woman hesitated.

'Sure,' she said, handing her warrant card to Jess. Jess couldn't hide her disappointment to find the warrant card in order and the date to be in the past rather than suspiciously in the future.

'Oh. Okay. Thanks.' She handed the card back.

'And what exactly had you been expecting?' the woman asked.

'Nothing. Just never seen a real one before, that's all.'

The woman accepted this and there was a pause as they each waited for the other to move.

'Well, as you said, this is a crime scene, so you really do need to move on,' the woman told them after it became clear that Erica, Marshall, Jess and the dog weren't moving.

'Yeah. Sorry.' Erica went to push Jess but Jess resisted.

'Are you normal police? Are you high up? A detective? Maybe you could help my friend here, she's looking for a police officer.'

'Jess,' warned Marshall.

'I suggest you try the local station,' said the woman.

'No, a particular officer.'

'That's enough, Jess. Come on. It'll be getting dark soon and we've got someplace to be,' Erica told Jess, moving to follow Marshall as he stepped away.

'I don't mean to pry,' said the woman as Erica and Jess turned to leave. 'But did I hear another man's voice a moment ago?' She looked up at Marshall and then down at the large puppy beside him.

'Yeah. A friend. He's gone now,' said Erica.

'And you were talking about something ripping a branch and chucking it at you?'

Erica, Jess and Marshall stopped and looked at the woman.

'You were listening to us?' Jess asked. What an invasion of privacy. She wished she'd remembered the number on the warrant card.

'Sorry about that. Occupational hazard.'

Jess and Erica exchanged a glance.

'I don't suppose you saw what ripped that branch?' the woman continued.

Erica shrugged.

'No. Chances are it just fell on its own. It was pretty high up. Nothing could have ripped it off.'

'Right. That branch off the path there?' The woman pointed. 'Where there's a claw mark ridiculously high up next to where the branch used to be?'

Jess looked between Erica and the woman as they stared at each other. 'You didn't see what did that?' the woman pushed.

'No,' said Erica, her voice tight.

The woman sighed.

'Emily,' she said, holding out her hand to Erica. 'Emily May. And you are?'

Erica glanced at Jess and Jess shrugged.

'Erica Murray. This is Jess Tidswell.' Erica shook Emily's hand.

'Marshall,' Marshall rumbled giving her a nod. 'Bubbles,' he added, pointing down at the dog.

'Can I ask why you were in the woods, Miss Murray?'

Erica groaned.

'Oh, okay. Look, I'm sorry. My friend was in there. He has it in his head that there's something supernatural going on and we're paranormal investigators and he convinced me to cross the police tape. But as soon as that branch fell, we left. We didn't touch anything other than a couple of tree trunks. I promise. And I'm sorry. Very sorry.'

Emily listened and nodded.

'Paranormal investigators, huh?'

'It's a serious business,' said Jess, waiting for Emily to laugh.

'Oh, don't I know it. I hate ghosts. I'm a were-wolf hunter, myself. It would seem like we're in the same line of business and it's always good to have contacts. Fancy a drink?'

Erica, Jess and Marshall stared wide-eyed at her.

'You what?' Jess blurted as her mind scrambled to make sense of those words. 'Werewolf hunter?'

'Werewolf?' Marshall nearly shouted, reaching out to Jess.

'Yeah. You hunt ghosts, right?'

There was a long pause as they processed this.

'I don't know if hunt is the right word,' said Erica. Jess checked out her friend. She seemed to having less of a problem with this than Jess.

'But still. Drink?' asked Emily.

Erica shrugged and looked at Jess.

'You're the one with something to go home to.'

They all looked up at Marshall who sighed.

'Fine. Go to the pub, let me know which one, and I'll take Bubbles home. Message me.'

'Thank you.' Jess stood up tiptoes and kissed him. 'I owe you one.'

Marshall raised an eyebrow.

'Yeah, you do owe me one.'

They watched as Marshall turned away, dragging Bubbles with him, and ambled back up the road.

Jess looked from Erica to Emily.

'Right. Fine. Let's go for a drink. With a were-wolf hunter.'

Emily led them up the road to the racing green vintage Mini Cooper. Erica stopped and stared.

'That's your car?'

'Yup.'

Erica stared adoringly at it.

'Erica's got a Mini, too,' said Jess. 'That one.' She pointed to Erica's new style sky blue Mini.

'Yeah, but it's not...this.'

Emily gave Erica a grin.

'Well, thank you. You need a lift?'

'Bit small for the three of us,' said Jess. 'Me and Ric will go together. We'll meet you there. Where are we going?'

'I saw a pub round the corner?' Emily suggested. 'But this is your patch, so I'll go wherever you like.'

Our patch, thought Jess. What did that mean? Their patch where they lived? Their patch where they...hunted? Where was Emily's patch? How many patches were there?

'That pub's fine. See you there.' Erica pulled out her keys and unlocked her large, curvy Mini with a beep while Emily slid into her own small car.

'Are you sure you want to be doing this? Marshall didn't seem happy.'

'Are you kidding? That woman said she's a werewolf hunter. What does that mean, Ric? Is she making money out of this? All this time we've been wondering if this type of business can work and then this woman appears and seems to be doing, what? The same thing? Think of what we could learn. Marshall understands.'

Erica started the car and pulled out. There was a roar and Jess saw in the wing mirror that Emily had pulled out behind them.

They found a quiet table in the corner of the bustling pub and Emily bought the drinks, which Erica tried to argue but it was a fight she instantly lost. Emily placed a pint of beer and two lemonades on the table and sat down. Erica pulled a lemonade over and sipped at it while Jess took a long sip of the other. She'd have preferred another beer but they'd be working tonight and she didn't particularly want alcohol impairing her judgement, or vision for that matter.

Emily looked between them.

'So,' she started. 'How long have you been in this line of work?'

Jess and Erica looked at one another.

'About two months,' said Erica.

'Although Ric comes from a long line of...this sort of thing,' Jess added. 'We sort of fell into it all when work got bad. That's how we met, through work.'

'What was the work?'

'Digital marketing agencies,' said Erica. 'We worked in marketing.'

Emily frowned.

'So, this is replacing your paid jobs? Have you turned the idea of hunting the supernatural into a business? Are people actually paying you?'

'Yes,' said Jess. 'Well, I mean, we've only just started, but so far, yes. You don't get paid?'

Emily sat back and there was a pause. Jess jumped as Emily laughed.

'No, I don't, dammit,' said Emily, sitting forward again, elbows on the table. 'I work all these crummy jobs to get enough money to survive and here I find out I could have been charging people.' Her exp-ression fell. 'Not sure who I would charge though.' She looked back up at Erica and Jess. 'What exactly do you hunt?'

'Hunt really isn't the right word,' said Erica. 'We're a paranormal investigation agency. We usually only deal with spirits, but it turns out there are other things out there—'

Emily laughed again, interrupting.

'Yeah. There are.'

Erica watched her.

'So, you're a werewolf hunter? Why are you here?'

Emily took a long gulp of her pint before she answered.

'Hang on,' said Jess. 'First of all, this question doesn't seem to faze anyone else here but me. Werewolves exist?' She glanced at Erica who gave her a small shrug. Turning back to Emily, there was faint smile playing on her lips as she watched Jess.

'What it says on the tin. I find werewolves and I kill them. Of course, it's more complicated than that. There are grey areas. Not all werewolves are out there killing people, and if they're not killing people then I'm not killing them.'

Jess and Erica stared at her.

'What gives you the right?' Jess asked finally. 'No offence meant. I'm curious.'

Erica sat back, allowing Jess to speak her mind.

'Like I said, it's more complex than all that,' Emily tried to reassure her. She wasn't doing a great job. 'Okay.' She sat back and sighed. 'What gives you the right to investigate ghosts? I'm guessing you exorcise them too, huh?'

Erica shifted in her seat.

'Not yet. I suppose we might if they won't leave and the client wants them gone, but I don't recommend it. To be fair, we haven't quite worked out our own rules or where our lines are yet. I suppose it'll depend on the situation. Out of our two clients so far, only one has turned out to be an actual spirit.'

Emily's eyes widened.

'Tell me you're not basing a whole business on one ghost.'

'Of course not,' Jess snapped. 'We're not idiots. Ric grew up around ghosts.'

Erica pursed her lips as Emily slowly looked at her.

'You know, I'd love to hear more about that,' Emily mused.

'You first,' said Erica, leaning forward on the table. 'Like you said, you're on our patch. What are you doing here?'

Emily gave her a knowing smile.

'I'm chasing a lead,' she said, stroking her half empty pint glass with the tips of her fingers. 'I read online that animal corpses were turning up in the woods around here. Dog walkers finding it strange.'

Erica looked at Jess who shrugged.

'I only reported the fox.'

'You found some?' Emily asked.

'Err, a mouse and a seagull and then a mutilated fox. All in the woods, on two separate walks.'

Emily nodded thoughtfully.

'Anything else?'

'Well...I mean, there's often something, isn't there. There are foxes in the woods and peoples cats go hunting in there. I've seen loads of them. So, sometimes we come across a rat or a mouse. Or a bird. But a small bird, you know? Or a pigeon. Not a seagull. The seagull was weird.'

'Well, you're not the only one finding them and other people are reporting them. Then I heard about this girl going missing, so I thought I'd come check it out. I happen to be passing through, on my way to Cornwall to chase another lead, so why not?'

'You think a werewolf could be killing these things?' Erica frowned. 'Wouldn't it eat them?'

Jess stared at her.

'You seem to be accepting this whole werewolf thing very easily,' said Jess. 'Did you know they existed?'

Erica looked down at her drink.

'Not exactly. But why not? Spirits are real. Fae are real. Why not werewolves?'

'Fae? As in fairies?' Emily grinned, looking between them.

'Don't call them that,' Erica told her.

'Not if you know what's good for you. They're not to be messed with,' said Jess, not taking her eyes from Erica.

'Wow. Okay, well. Good to know. Anyway, werewolves are real. Trust me. I've seen them, I've talked to them, I've chased them, I've killed them. Now, these bodies of animals you found,' Emily asked Jess. 'Were they drained of blood?'

'What? I don't know, how can you tell?'

'Any significant wounds?'

'I didn't look,' said Erica.

'Why not?'

'I just thought a fox got them.' Erica looked at Jess.

'The fox was mutilated. A leg torn off,' she told Emily.

'I thought you were investigators.'

'We are! But we're paranormal investigators,' said Jess, a little unsure of herself faced with the overbearing confidence of this woman. She straightened her back and took a deep breath.

'And you just mean ghosts?'

'Spirits,' Erica corrected.

Emily shrugged.

'Whatever.'

'Well. Yeah. Why? What else is there? Except fae and werewolves, of course.' Jess looked between Erica and Emily. There were unspoken things flying in the air between them and Jess wasn't having it. Erica cringed.

'There are other things,' she admitted. Jess glared at her. Why had she never mentioned this before?

'Like what?'

Emily sighed.

'Without wanting to sound cliché or stereo-typical,' she said, 'basically nearly everything you've ever heard of is real. Everything that can go bump in the night, suck your blood, haunt your nightmares. All of it. Well, about seventy per cent of it is real.'

Jess stared wide-eyed at Emily.

'What about the thirty per cent?'

Emily hesitated and gave Jess a small smile.

'Well, about ten per cent of that are the same creatures in the seventy per cent but with different names. Sometimes people think they've got a whole new creature on their hands when actually it's the same thing that was killing their livestock a generation ago, it just came out of hibernation.' Jess visibly shivered and sat back. 'The last twenty per cent of the time it's humans doing it. Humans think it's a matter of us and them. Humans versus these scary creatures that they don't understand and that can kill us. It's probably the only time they think of humans as being on the same side as the animals on this planet. You know, the animals versus the monsters. It never seems to occur to them that we're on the side of the monsters. To be fair, if it's just killing the local wildlife, then it's just surviving. I don't see a problem. We might just have to leave it.'

'A teenager's gone missing. What if whatever this is has killed her?' said Jess.

Emily shrugged.

'Local wildlife.'

Jess and Erica stared at her.

'But you kill werewolves that kill humans.' Erica pointed out.

'It's one kid. If a shark kills one human, it's an accident. The human shouldn't have been in the shark's world. If it is a werewolf and it kills again, that's when I'll get involved. But it's good to know what we're dealing with, so we can keep an eye on it.'

'So, you're just going to wait for someone else to die?' Erica asked pointedly.

Emily gave her a fierce look.

'You seem to be under the impression that I'm one of the good guys,' Emily said, her voice flat. 'I hate to break it to you girls, but there are no good guys in this. What we hunt has as much right to be here as we do and as much right to kill as we do.'

Erica put her lemonade to her lips while Jess tried hard to find an argument for that.

'Fine. So what else could this be?' Erica asked Emily after a long pause.

'Well, my first inclination was werewolf, as I say. But it could also be a chupacabra, they're nasty. They tend to kill livestock in Peru and Mexico, though. Be strange to find them in the west of England but stranger things have happened.'

'So, more likely werewolf then?' asked Erica.

Emily moved her head from side to side, as if weighing up the options.

'There are spirit creatures too. That might fall into your ball park.'

'Spirit creatures? Like what?' Jess asked.

'Depends on how you define spirit. A banshee, a wraith, a jikininki, arguably demons, wendigos. There are loads, from all around the world.'

'Don't look at me,' Erica said quickly as Jess opened her mouth while glaring at her. 'I didn't know about most of those either.'

'Most?' Jess's voice had gone up an octave.

'Well, I've heard of demons, so have you. And wendigos, but they're mostly in North America. I think.' Erica looked to Emily for help and the other woman gave a nod. 'Plus, you know, we've never talked about what else there is.'

'You mean, just because I never asked, "hey Ric what else other than ghosts are out there?" you didn't think to tell me?'

'I had no reason to tell you.'

'Well, you might have reason to now.'

Emily watched the conversation with a hint of fascination.

'Must be nice,' she murmured. 'To have some-one to work with.'

Jess couldn't tell if she was being sarcastic or

not.

'Do you travel a lot?' she asked, turning away from Erica.

'Yeah. I've been all over. I tend to follow the case instead of having my own patch. Everyone works differently and I don't have a family tying me to a specific place. I just have my favourite places. Lots of people like us have patches though, and I hate to intrude. So if this isn't a werewolf, I won't stay. Unless you'd like some help.'

'Help might be good,' Erica murmured, exchanging a glance with Jess. 'It seems like this might be something of a paranormal nature. Alfie was certain about that.'

'And Alfie's the bloke who was in the woods with you just now?'

'He's fae. So he can be trusted about these things, to a certain extent. Is there an easy way of narrowing down what we might be dealing with?'

Emily took a long gulp of her beer, nearly draining the glass and wiped her mouth with her sleeve.

'I wouldn't say easy, but there are signs. A body would be helpful, although unnecessary and obviously not ideal.'

'Well, maybe there are more animal bodies,' Jess suggested.

Erica studied her.

'You want to go back into the woods?'

'Not unless I have to. And Alfie forbade you to go back.'

'Look, I'll level with you,' said Emily. 'I don't want to have to go up against a spirit creature, of any kind.' Emily looked at Erica. 'I hate ghosts. Freak me out.' She leaned back and stretched her arms above her head. 'Don't suppose you have a card or something? In case I come across a ghost that maybe I could hand over to you?'

'Sure.' Jess started digging around in her bag.

'We usually work for clients,' Erica pointed out. 'For pay. We charge for our services.'

Emily shrugged.

'How much?'

'Depends on the case.'

'Well, we'll cross that bridge when we come to it, huh?'

'But, you don't charge?' Jess asked, handing a business card over. Emily took it and slid it into her jeans pocket.

'Nope. Unless someone offers.'

'How do you live? How do you pay bills?'

'I take on little jobs, usually. I find other ways,' said Emily dismissively. She leaned back and looked around the pub, continuing before Jess could ask any more questions. 'I tell you what. Seeing as how we don't know if this is a werewolf yet or not, let me do some more digging. I'll let you know what I find. Might be that I can just handle this. Trust me, you don't want to go after a werewolf.'

Jess took a gulp of her drink, feeling it churn in her stomach. It would be much better if someone else could handle this. They had a paying client to deal with and two businesses to run.

'Okay.'

'Great. I don't have a card, but I can give you my number. I'm staying at the Travelodge down the road.'

Erica unlocked her phone and set it up for Emily to put her number in. They waited quietly until Emily handed the phone back.

'I'll let you know what I find out and you let me know if you find out anything else. Nice to meet you girls.' Emily stood up.

'You too.' Erica stood and Jess followed suit. Emily gave them a nod and left.

Erica and Jess sat back down with a thump.

'That was odd,' said Erica.

'One word for it. I guess it's nice to know there are others like us, though. Or, rather, others who are more than us.'

'Not more, just a bit...different.'

'Whatever. Did you know there's so much more out there than ghosts?'

Erica hesitated.

'Only stories Gran told me when I was little.'

Jess sighed.

'Yeah, I guess it makes sense that if there are ghosts and fae then there are other things. Did you know werewolves are real?'

'No. I thought they were just stories. Gran used to talk about them sometimes.'

'Hmm. Do you think we can trust this Emily?'

'What's there not to trust? We're not getting paid, she's not after our money. If we wanted to, we could just walk away from all this. I don't see what she would get out of it if all that were lies.'

Jess considered this.

'True.'

'Look, I think Emily's right. We need more. Anecdotal evidence from a load of animal carcasses isn't enough. Maybe we should go back into the woods.'

'What? No. You can't do that. Alfie forbade you, and please don't go against him. He's...' Jess glanced around the pub as if he might be sat there, watching them. 'He's dangerous, Ric,' she whispered.

'No. He's not. And it's fine. He protected me. And I said I wouldn't go in alone. It'll be fine. Right.' Erica took a final gulp of her lemonade. 'Back to the hotel and work. I need to pop home first, I haven't had anything to eat yet. See you there?'

'Right,' Jess murmured, her mind still replaying the conversation with Emily.

Emily

So much for a normal case. It's never a normal case, is it? What is a normal case, anyway?

It's been that long since I had one of those.

Okay, so I didn't know if this was going to be easy or not. For all I knew, I'd come to this little town outside of Bristol, discover immediately that there's no werewolf and be on my merry way to Cornwall.

I still don't know if there's a werewolf, although it's not looking that way. I talked with the boyfriend of the victim. He's adamant. Something tall, long limbs and terrifying took the girl. Sounds like a werewolf to me. But then where's the victim? There should be remains, there should be a body.

The police don't seem to be holding anything back from me. I wonder how long they'll keep the woods shut for. The sooner they open them, the easier it'll be to investigate. But the sooner the teenagers will be back in there. Playing chicken with each other. Seeing who gets killed next. Idiots.

I can't say that, though, can I? I was that idiot once. Going into the woods, against my better judgement, so that my friends wouldn't think I was scared.

Maybe I should start doing workshops with schools. Why you're not a chicken if you don't want to go into the woods at night, or into woods where someone your age has vanished.

She has vanished, too. There's been no word about any clothes found, any body parts, any clue as to what could have happened to her.

Except for her boyfriend's account.

Anyway, the other important thing is that I've met two ghost hunters.

They do seem to come in packs. Little groups of paranormal investigators who swear blind they know how to find a ghost. Most of them over complicate it, but these two seem different. One doesn't have a clue but has all the enthusiasm, which makes me wonder if the other has all the experience. She seemed to know more than she was letting on.

I hope they are genuine ghost hunters. I could do with building my contacts.

Horrible things, ghosts. Always sad, usually angry, always creeping up on you and watching when you can't see them. There's a marked difference between being watched by a werewolf and being watched by a ghost. The werewolf brings out an instinctual fear of being prey, but a ghost is something else.

Plus, they can't be killed. You can shoot at them, sure, but it doesn't do much. Usually just makes them angrier.

If these two women can take on any ghost cases I find so I can get on with something else, then I'm all for it.

Which means that if this isn't a ghost and is something large, with claws and teeth, I should probably stick around and deal with it. At least then they'll owe me one. Right? Even if they're not the nice people they seem to be.

Also, the one who seems to know more than she's letting on, Erica, I think her name is, she knows fae. I've never met fae before.

Not sure how I feel about that.

In other news, this hotel is all right. Need to remember the details in case I have to come this way again.

11

The rain lashed against the windscreen as Erica pulled up in the hotel car park. It was going to be a long night. Jess's car wasn't there so Erica turned off the engine and sat with the radio on low. She could just make out the windows of the hotel through the rain and Erica studied each one in turn. There was no movement, no strange shadows or lights. Nothing out of the ordinary.

Erica checked her phone but there were no notifications and nothing from Jess saying that she'd be late. Sighing through her nose, Erica checked the weather app. It was due to be raining all night, she wondered if that would affect any of their technology. It also meant that any possible evidence in the woods could be washed away. Erica thought back through their conversation with Emily which led her back to the woods, which led her to Alfie. She'd visited her grandmother on the way home and explained everything that had happened. Minerva seemed strangely silent on the existence of were-wolves but had made encouraging noises about staying in touch with Emily. It was an interesting situation, she'd said, and one that should be followed through.

Which left the matter of Alfie. Given that Erica was struggling to make contact with Rick, should she be paying Alfie some attention? It was obvious he was still interested and, if she was honest, she might be a little interested in him.

She'd had a few boyfriends in her time but never one like Alfie. Never a confident charmer who was so cocksure that they should be together. Wasn't that part of what had drawn her to Rick when they'd first met? Not that they had met properly yet. Damn time travel.

Rick had been so sure about them, so certain, so in love. It had been difficult for her not to get swept up in it. The same could be said for Alfie, except that Jess was right. Alfie was dangerous, to a certain degree, and Erica was wary of that. She didn't want to get into something she then couldn't get out of, and she definitely didn't want to jeopardise her future relationship with Rick. If they ever did meet.

Of all of the possible things that Erica could regret at the end of her life, she had a strong suspicion that not giving in to Alfie's advances could be one of them.

Unlocking her phone again, Erica opened Facebook and typed into the search bar, "Rick Cavanagh".

Jess driving into the car park made Erica look up and then promptly close Facebook and lock her phone. Jess parked next to her and waved through the window. Erica waved back and then they waited. Jess gestured at the rain and Erica shrugged. They would just have to make a run for it.

Erica opened her door first, grabbing her laptop case and quickly slamming the door behind her, hitting lock on her key and then running for the hotel's main door. There was a slam behind her as Jess did the same.

They arrived at the porch damp but not quite

dripping and Jess rang the bell.

'Fun weather, huh?'

'Yeah,' said Erica.

'The police are back in the woods, I saw their cars as I drove past.'

Erica nodded, glad to hear it.

'I wonder if they'll find anything new in this weather. If they've found anything at all. Or if they have found things but don't know what to make of them.'

'Do you think it is a werewolf?' Jess whispered.

Before Erica could reply, the door opened to show Mrs Wilder who let them in with a smile.

'Coffee? Tea?' she offered as Erica went for the stairs.

'Oh, coffee would be lovely,' said Jess. 'Thank you.'

'I'll bring it up to you.' Mrs Wilder passed the room key to Jess and wandered off towards the kitchen.

Jess followed Erica up the stairs to the so-called haunted room and unlocked the door.

'Ready?'

Erica gave a nod and Jess opened the door. The room was empty. Erica wondered what they would have done if they'd opened the door to a spectre. Smiling at the thought, she stepped inside and was hit by a chill.

'Stop!' She held up a hand. Jess froze behind her. 'You feel that cold?'

'Yeah.' Jess rubbed her arms. 'It doesn't sit well with being wet.'

Erica looked around the room.

'Is there any reason why it would be so cold in here? The window's not open.' Erica took another couple of steps into the room and seemed to leave the cold patch, the room warming up to the same temperature as the hallway. She looked back to Jess. 'Are you still cold?'

'No. It seems to have shifted.'

Erica looked up at the walls.

'Is that you?' she asked the room. 'Are you here?' She paused but there was no response.

'So,' said Jess, wandering further into the room and placing her laptop on the bed. 'How do we do this?'

'Set up the rest of the equipment and try to make contact.' Erica turned around in the middle of the room, trying to feel something. Anything.

'So, no sleep at all then?'

Erica gave Jess a look.

'This was your idea.'

'No. Nope. This was your idea. I wanted to set up cameras and then go home to my nice big bed with a nice big man in it but you're the one who said we'd get better results spending the night in a cold, haunted hotel room on a rainy night.'

'To be fair, I didn't know it would be raining. And a night away from Marshall will do you good.'

Jess huffed at that and looked down at her laptop.

'What should I set up?'

'Camera feeds on both laptops,' said Erica. 'And I'll sort out the Dictaphone.'

A light tap on the door made them both jump and Mrs Wilder came in with a tray.

'I brought some biscuits too.'

'Thank you. That's lovely of you.' Erica told her, eyeing up the biscuits.

'I can't wait to see what you uncover. Is there

anything else I can get you?' Mrs Wilder smiled and then shivered. 'Oh, it's so cold in here. Shall I put the heating on?'

Frowning, Erica stepped closer to Mrs Wilder and felt the temperature suddenly drop. Goosebumps lifted on her arms and she rubbed at them.

'I don't think the heating will affect it,' Erica murmured. 'Come stand over here.' She gestured for Mrs Wilder to move where she had been standing before, further inside the room.

'Oh. It's warmed up,' said Mrs Wilder. 'Is that the ghost?' she whispered.

'Is there any reason you know of why the temperature in that part of the room would fluctuate?'

Mrs Wilder shook her head.

'But then, I'm not very good at that stuff.'

Erica nodded.

'Maybe we should get Marshall in to take a look,' she suggested to Jess. 'Just to rule things out.'

'Maybe. Let's see what tonight throws up first.'

Mrs Wilder left them to it.

'So, what did you think of Emily?' Jess asked after a moment as she fiddled with the laptop, trying to connect them to the cameras they'd installed. Erica fetched their coffee and Jess took hers gratefully.

'I'm not sure. I told Gran about her. She said she sounded interesting and we needed to stay in touch. Which is true, I guess. I guess I found her interesting too. What about you?'

'Weird,' said Jess. 'I found her weird. She was obviously watching us and listening when we were standing by the woods. How long had she been there? Long enough to hear Alfie's voice and hear about that branch nearly falling on you.'

'Not long enough to see me and Alfie in the woods, though. She saw the fallen branch but she didn't see it fall.'

'You think she's telling the truth?'

'I don't know why she'd lie.'

Jess looked up at Erica.

'Because she abducted and murdered that girl?'

Erica met Jess's gaze and took a sip of her coffee.

'Why is she still in the woods?'

'Maybe she's not human. Maybe she's the one who pulled down that branch. Maybe she's the one Alfie wants to protect you from.'

A chill ran over Erica.

'I hadn't thought of that.'

'Shit. Really? No smart comeback for why I'm wrong? Come on, Ric, that's terrifying. I can't be right about that.'

Erica shrugged.

'Sorry. I didn't get any bad vibes from her, but you know, I can't argue that. That is scary.'

'You need to introduce her to Alfie. That'll solve that one.'

Erica nodded.

'Yeah. Alfie.'

'Could it be her? Is there something out there that can pull a branch off a tree like that and then take human form?'

'I don't know,' said Erica, scanning her memory of the stories her Gran used to tell her. 'What type of creature can tear a massive branch off a tree that high up?'

Jess shook her head.

'You know, I'm not sure I want to know.' She glanced up at Erica. 'Maybe we should just leave this one to Emily.'

'Oh, so now she is a werewolf hunter and not some crazy, murdering monster?'

Jess sipped her coffee.

'How do you know those two things aren't the same?'

Erica smiled.

'Seriously, though, I think Emily was telling the truth. I didn't get any weird feelings about her. It all rang true. Did she send you any bad signals?'

Jess considered this and then sighed.

'I guess not. The whole thing just feels...wrong.'

'In what way?'

'I don't know. I don't know if it's Emily or the woods or what. Did you feel anything when you were in there?'

Erica sat down on the bed.

'I don't know. It wasn't the same feeling I get for a spirit.'

The light above their heads flickered. They both stared up at it.

'What's that?' Jess hissed.

Erica frowned and pressed record on her Dictaphone.

'Are the cameras set up?'

Jess nodded.

'I'm getting the feeds through.' She moved the laptops so they could both see the screens. The thermal camera showed darker than the other, with two red humanoid blobs of Jess and Erica sat on the bed.

'Hello? Are you here with us?' Erica called out into the room. They sat in silence for a moment and then Erica stopped recording, rewound the tape and played it. There was nothing but static. Erica sighed and sat back.

'Could have been a power surge. Maybe the kitchen turned on the ovens or something.'

'So, you didn't feel anything strange in the woods?'

'I don't think so.'

'So it could be anything, then, couldn't it.' Jess sipped at her coffee. 'I don't like that it's so close to home.'

Erica smiled and glanced at Jess.

'Steve and his wife lived fifteen minutes away from you.'

'Yeah, but this is different.'

'Different to having a murderer living fifteen minutes away?'

Jess shivered.

'Well, you don't have to put it that way. I just mean, I hadn't seen Steve in so long. But I walk the dog in those woods a lot. My daughter plays in those woods. It's different, you know? It feels more... personal. I just want whatever is in there to get out.'

'I get that,' said Erica, watching the laptop screens.

'And Alfie didn't want you in there, Ric. That means it's something really scary.'

'I know.'

'Have you heard from him?'

'No.' Erica's stomach turned. She chewed on the inside of her cheek and then took a deep breath. 'There was something else. I think I need to tell you, although I don't really get it.'

'What?' Jess shuffled closer. 'What is it?'

'When Alfie was leading me through the woods, he was heading for these two trees that are...joined at the top. Have you ever noticed them? They were hard to see, but it's ivy connecting them. Maybe it's easier to see them in winter.'

Jess frowned.

'I have no idea what you're talking about.'

'Okay, well, that's what Alfie saw and he seemed really confused by it. He was leading me to those trees when the branch fell. And then he—' Erica sighed and rubbed at the space between her eyes, '—it was really weird. He told me to not go back to those trees and to not step between them. He didn't want me stepping between the trees, I mean, what the hell does that mean?'

Jess blinked at her.

'Shit, Ric. You think it's all connected?'

'No idea. But I wanted to tell you. You know, once this is over and if you see two trees connected at the top by a load of ivy, don't go up to them. Or walk between them. Or whatever.'

'Don't suppose you can ask Alfie what the hell that's all about?'

Erica let another sigh out.

'I'll see what I can do. But he said he would figure it out. So both Alfie and Emily are working on this. I'm sure it'll get sorted.'

'Yeah. I guess. You're not going to go back into the woods, are you?'

Erica shocked herself by not answering at first. 'Ric? Tell me you're not going back into those woods.'

'I don't have a reason to,' she said, wondering what reason would take her back between the trees. 'Anyway, we're not here to discuss what may or may not be in the woods. We need to make contact with this spirit.'

The light above their heads went out, plunging them into darkness.

Twelve

'Ric?'

'Yeah.'

'You're still here, right?'

As their eyes became accustomed to the darkness, Jess could make out the screens of the laptops, still showing the room. At least that was something, although Jess's bowels loosened at the thought of seeing something on the screen sitting in the corner, hidden by the darkness, waiting for them. Eventually the glow of the street lights lit up parts of the room and soon it was only the corners that were truly terrifying. Jess tried not to look at them.

Erica was on her feet, gazing out of the window before crossing the room and opening the door, allowing in all of the light from the hallway. She closed the door and faced the room.

'It's just us,' she whispered, pressing record on the Dictaphone again. 'Hello? Can you hear me? Can you try talking to me? What's your name?'

Something rattled on the desk opposite the bed.

Jess couldn't move. She clutched at the sheets, balling her hands into fists so tight her knuckles hurt.

'Is that you? Are you trying to talk to us?' asked Erica.

A bowl next to the kettle shook and Jess gave a

high-pitched yelp as the bowl turned over. Trembling, her stomach rolling, she swallowed hard as her leg muscles prepared to propel her towards Erica and the door.

'Is it here?' asked Erica.

The sachets from the bowl, holding sugar and coffee, blew from the desk and Jess yelped again, instinctively holding up her legs, taking her feet off the floor.

On the carpet, the sachets moved in jerks, as if someone was prodding them. Erica stepped closer, cocking her head to watch what was happening. Jess took a deep, shuddering breath and tried to pay attention to what was going on rather than to her body screaming at her to run. She glanced at Erica, wishing she could be that calm. She closed her eyes. This was ridiculous. Whatever this was, it wasn't going to hurt her. Erica wasn't scared, she was curious. That was all this was. Someone trying to talk to them and all Jess had to do was try to listen. Opening her eyes, feeling steadier, she looked down at the sachets on the floor.

'Is that a "d"?' she asked.

'Or a "p"?' Erica suggested. 'Is that a "d"?' she asked the room, holding out the Dictaphone.

After a moment, she played the tape back.

'Is that a "d"?' came her voice.

'D.'

Jess jumped as the sharpness of the woman's voice, the clarity of the sound. She stared up at Erica in wonder.

'A spirit just said "D".'

Erica nodded and played it again.

Jess listened to the spirit's voice. It sounded forced or shouted. It was taking the spirit a lot of energy to communicate. She must be tired, Jess thought, moving a heavy bowl and then trying to talk to us.

'What's "D"?' asked Erica. 'What does that mean?' She held up the Dictaphone. 'Is it something to do with what's here? Oh, hang on.' She stopped the Dictaphone and turned to one of the boxes they had brought up that morning. Opening one, she pulled out a light with a motion sensor and fiddled to get the batteries in. Then she placed it on the desk. As she moved away from it, the light flickered on and then off as she climbed onto the bed.

'Right. This is a motion sensor light. It'll go on if you move near it or touch it. Okay? It should be easier for you. Do you understand?'

To Jess's horror and amazement, the light came on and then went off.

'Good,' said Erica. 'Is the "D" something to do with what's here?'

The light came on.

'Okay.' Erica glanced at Jess. 'Is "D" a name?'

The light remained off.

'Is it here, in the hotel?'

The light remained off.

Something nudged at Jess's mind.

'Oh God,' she murmured. 'Is it in the woods?'

The light came on and stayed on for a while before going off.

'Is "D" a supernatural creature?' asked Jess, images of werewolves floating in her mind.

The light came on and Jess held her breath.

'Shit,' she whispered. 'Is "D" a werewolf?'

The light remained off and both Jess and Erica sagged a little.

'Oh,' said Jess. 'What else could it be, then?'

Erica moved as if she would shuffle forward and then thought better of it.

'Is "D" a spirit?'

The light remained off.

'Does the word begin with "D"?' asked Jess. 'What begins with "D"?' She looked at Erica who was staring almost sadly at the box.

'Demon.'

The light came on and stayed on.

'It's a demon,' said Erica in a quiet voice. 'There's a demon in the woods.'

'What? How? What does a demon mean? Like, the devil?'

The light went off.

'The spirits can sense it as far away as Grandad's cemetery. It must be a strong one,' said Erica, watching the motion sensor box.

'Do you know much about demons?' Jess asked.

'No. But Gran might do. Alfie will. I need to talk to them.'

'No offence meant, I obviously don't know how this works, but how do we know this is real? How can we trust this spirit?' Jess whispered.

The light came on and immediately went off. Jess's gut twisted.

'Are you happy here?' Erica asked.

The light came on.

'Do you want to stay?'

The light came on.

'Did you used to live here?'

The light came on.

'Well, there you go. I think that's enough,' said Erica, sounding thoroughly downtrodden. 'Thank you,' she told the spirit. 'We may come back later to ask you more questions. Is that okay?'

The light came on, went off and didn't come on again for the rest of the night.

Jess sighed.

'This is huge,' she whispered.

'I think we need to go talk to Mrs Wilder. You want to do that, or should I? One of us can be packing up. I need to go find Alfie.'

'Do you have his number? You could call him now. Does he even have a phone?'

Erica shook her head.

'Nope. But he'll know. You want to talk to Mrs Wilder?'

Jess looked down at her hands in the darkness. In that moment, the light above their heads flickered back on and Jess blinked back the colours that danced across her eyes. Her hands were trembling, her chest tight. She didn't want to talk to Mrs Wilder. She wanted to go home. To crawl into bed with Marshall and lie, warm, in his arms. Erica watched her.

'You want to pack up and I'll go talk to her?'

That snapped Jess out of it. The idea of being alone in this room with a spirit that spoke of demons sent a violent shiver through her.

'I'll go,' she said, standing and shaking her hands to rid them of her nerves and adrenaline. She took a deep breath to steady herself. 'I'll go. You pack up. Meet you downstairs?'

Erica nodded and moved to take the cameras off the walls. 'Hey, reckon we got all that on film?'

'I hope so,' murmured Jess. 'Otherwise I'm pretty sure I imagined it.'

Erica actually smiled at that. Nausea crept into Jess's stomach and she left the room, gulping in air as she trotted down the stairs to see if Mrs Wilder was in reception.

She found the hotel manager in the back office and Mrs Wilder looked up at her as she entered.

'Ah, how's it going? Are you all right?' The woman's brow creased with concern and Jess wondered just how much of a mess she looked.

'Erm. Yeah, no, I'm fine. Just got a bit of, erm, scary news.' She gave a small laugh. Mrs Wilder offered her a chair, which she took, leaning forward in an attempt to make her stomach stop churning.

'What happened? Is there something evil up there?'

'Oh. No. There's nothing evil in your hotel. We spoke to the spirit. Hopefully we got it on tape, so we can show you, but we'll have to check through our equipment. For now, though, we know what the spirit is talking about, what's here, and it's not here in the hotel, so don't you worry about that. The spirit is happy here, she doesn't want to leave and I don't think she'll bother you much. I imagine,' said Jess, things starting to fall into place in her head. 'That the actual evil thing that has arrived has brought the spirit out into the open, as it were, so she can warn us. Well, she's done that now. She might go quiet again. Now, we can leave it here, now you know what's going on. Or we can try and find out who she is. She says she lived here once. What would you like to do? You can think about it, of course. Take your time.' Jess knew there should have been more gaps between those words but she reckoned she deserved one of Ruby's gold star stickers just for getting the words out coherently.

Mrs Wilder stared at her.

'Well...wow.'

'Yeah. I know. Sorry, it's a lot.'

'So, what is here? What was the ghost talking about?'

Jess hesitated and searched Mrs Wilder's eyes. Should she tell her?

'I can't say just yet. We need to look into it further.'

Mrs Wilder sat back and tapped her fingers on her desk.

'But, you will tell me? Even though it doesn't affect my hotel?'

Jess blinked.

'Yes. But not just yet.'

Mrs Wilder gave a singular nod.

'Very well. What happens now?'

'Erm, we need to investigate this further. So we'll be on our way now. We'll look over the footage and I'll write up a report for you. I'll be in contact to arrange a good time to come show you the report and hopefully the footage of what just happened. How does that sound?'

'Wonderful. Thank you.'

'And then you can decide if you'd like to go further and find out who this spirit is.'

'Yes. Okay.'

Jess stood up.

'I should go help my colleague.' She held out her hand. 'Thank you, Mrs Wilder, for sharing this with us and letting us in. I'll be in touch.'

Mrs Wilder shook her hand and flinched a little. Jess was cold, her fingers still trembling.

'Thank you,' Mrs Wilder murmured, concern hitting her eyes again. Jess ignored it. She needed fresh air.

She helped Erica carry everything out into the

rain and to her car, where they dumped everything in the boot before rushing to sit in the front.

Jess placed her forehead on the steering wheel.

'That was...something,' she mumbled. Erica's hand touched her back.

'Are you okay?'

'Not really.'

'What can I do?'

'Is it always that scary?' Jess looked up at her friend. 'Do you get used to it?'

Erica gave her a comforting smile and Jess relaxed a little.

'You get used to it. The more you do it, the easier it is. And not every case is going to involve a demon in the woods.'

Jess swallowed the sudden bile that rose up her throat.

'What do we do about that?' she asked in a quiet voice.

Erica sighed.

'I'll talk to Alfie, and Gran. Maybe Emily too? Now we know it's not a werewolf, she might leave. I have no idea what we do then. I've never heard of encountering a demon. Except in old stories. And even then, I don't really know how you get rid of them. Just what they can do.'

Jess didn't want to know what they could do, but she had to assume it included killing a seagull, mutilating a fox and making a teenage girl disappear. She clenched her eyes shut.

'That girl's dead, isn't she.'

There was a pause and Jess opened her eyes, filling slowly with tears, to look at Erica. Erica was chewing her lower lip.

'I think so.'

Jess took a shaky breath.

'Okay. Well. You do all the heavy lifting. If you don't mind, I think I'd like to go home now and get a hug from a man.'

'You do that.' Erica squeezed Jess's arm. 'No worries. I'll keep you in the loop.'

Jess nodded, wondering if Paul would keep Ruby for longer than the agreed couple of days. While her first reaction was to have Ruby with her, actually, when she thought about it, she wanted Ruby as far from those woods as possible.

'Go home,' said Erica, opening the car door. 'I'll let you know if I find out anything.' She climbed out and shut the door.

It took a moment for Jess to put her key in the ignition. By the time she was ready to pull out of the car park, Erica was in her car, engine on and waiting for her to go first.

She drove slowly, her mind whirring as the time ticked over to two o'clock. The roads were almost empty and on every corner were demons of all shapes and sizes, blood dribbling from their mouths and claws until Jess blinked them away.

In The Woods

It had thought this might be easy. The trees were so small in numbers compared to what it had seen before. All that lived there were badgers and foxes and birds and mice, and almost every evening young humans would make their way laughing loudly down the paths to light fires. It was a gift.

And then the fae had come.

The witch hadn't brought the fae, although it seemed apt that they knew each other. No, the trees had brought the fae.

For a moment, a small moment at that, it had forgotten the wisdom and strength of trees. That had been a mistake, but it would not be the end of it. No, it would fight back.

It had fought the fae before. It knew them. They were strong and crafty, yes, but they were stubborn and selfish as well. Much more suited to the world of humans than its own. Their tricks of seduction and magic may work on the humans and even the witches, but they would not work on it.

That was what it had thought to itself that evening, as it sat high in a tree, watching the sun setting over the woodland as uniformed men spoke to one another in huddles just below.

A female appeared, dressed differently. There was an air of authority about her but there was something amiss. Sniffing the air, it crawled down the trunk for a closer look.

She was an authority, yes, but she was also a liar. As the men pointed things out the woman made notes, taking out a contraption and pointing it at the trees.

It cocked its head curiously. Where were the lies? What was she hiding?

The woman looked up and it froze, worried for a moment that she might see it. Her gaze landed on it for a brief second and then moved on. It gave a soft growl. It did not like the feeling of worry. It was almost at full strength. The young human had given it so much, but it wasn't enough. Not yet. It needed more.

This woman's lies held so much energy that it began to drool, but it wouldn't take her. There was a strength about her.

A witch?

No. She was no witch. It was something else. She knew to look up into the trees when the others didn't. What else did she know?

She could become another problem, but she was only a human. Humans and witches, it could cope with, it would manage, if only it could find a little more strength.

The fae were the real problem. It dragged its claws through the bark of the tree trunk and listened to the tree scream. But the trees had brought this on themselves, bringing the fae here. They had to be punished, in time, when it had found the strength.

13

'How did it go?'

Erica jumped and spun round to find her grandmother standing in the kitchen doorway in the dark.

'What are you doing?' Erica hissed, holding a hand to her thumping heart. 'You scared the life out of me. What are you doing here?'

'I stayed after tea.' Minerva held her chin up. 'Why did I scare you? Did something happen?'

Erica took a slow breath, calmed her fluttering chest and ushered Minerva into the kitchen, turning on the light and blinking against the sudden brightness. Her family's two Labradors, an older golden and a black gangly puppy, walked sleepily over to say hello. Once both had been cuddled and had sniffed her, they went back to their beds in the corner of the kitchen. The youngest watched Minerva and Erica with half-closed eyes.

'Something happened. You remember I told you about the woods?' Erica sat at the large dining table and Minerva sat next to her. 'Well, it turns out that's what the spirit was talking about. It's here. That's what it means.'

'What what means? What's here?' Minerva frowned. 'It's very late, or very early, depending, my dear child, and I'm old. You're going to have to be clearer.'

Erica rubbed her face.

'The spirit saying, "it's here". She's talking about the thing that's in the woods, that took that girl.'

'And?' Minerva leaned forward on the table, her eyes wide.

'And it's a demon.'

Minerva sat back, sucking in her lower lip and shaking her head. Erica wasn't sure what she'd been expecting, but it wasn't that. 'It's bad, isn't it,' she whispered.

Minerva nodded.

'You say Alfie is talking to the fae?'

'Yes. I don't know how much he knows though, he wouldn't tell me. Apart from that strange thing about the trees.'

'What thing?'

'Oh, he saw something strange in the woods before that branch nearly fell on us. Two trees leaning into each other and ivy growing up them that joined at the top. He told me to never go up to those trees or walk between them. And then he just forbade me from going into the woods at all.'

Minerva narrowed her eyes and then gave a sharp nod.

'Good man. As well he should.'

'You're not going to do the same, are you?'

Minerva sighed and leaned forward again.

'This is a difficult one. On the one hand, this creature needs stopping and chances are it's powerful. It's going to need a lot to remove it from the woods. On the other hand, it's so dangerous, it's probably best left to the fae.'

'What do you think about those two trees? Why shouldn't I walk between them?'

Minerva stroked her chin and then shrugged.

'I could have a guess, but that's all it would be. I should talk to Eolande,' she decided, tapping her hands on the table.

'Alfie may have already talked to her. I thought I should ask him about it first?'

'Ask him about what?'

Minerva clenched her eyes shut and Erica turned at the sound of her mother's voice.

'Esther, love, we were just talking about—'

'About the fae and my daughter. I heard,' said Erica's mother, approaching while hugging herself. 'How did the job go?' she asked.

'Good,' Erica said. 'We made contact. And we know why the spirit is up, awake and making her presence known, as well as what "it" is and where "here" is.'

'A successful night then.' Esther sat down next to her mother.

'It's a demon, Mum,' said Erica. 'There's a demon in the woods. A demon killed those animals and that girl.'

Esther sat back and rubbed at her eyes, sighing hard.

'Shit,' she murmured.

'Yeah. Which is why I think I need to talk to Alfie. Before you get Eolande involved. Alfie's already involved.'

Erica and Minerva both looked at Esther, wondering what she'd say to that.

'Fine. That makes sense.' Esther gave Erica a look and Erica shrank back. She was fully expecting her mother to demand to be with her at all times when Alfie was there, but she didn't. Instead, that warning look was enough. Don't do anything stupid, it said, don't get involved.

Erica swallowed, her eyes aching. It was too late for this. She was too tired to think about demons and ghosts, never mind Alfie.

A knock at the door made them all jump and the youngest dog leapt to his feet to bark. Esther told him to be quiet.

'Who the hell is that?' Minerva asked. 'At this time of night.'

'They'll wake your dad up,' said Esther. 'He won't be happy.'

Erica jumped to her feet.

'I'll get it.' She headed for the door before they could argue.

She was hoping and expecting it to be Alfie, somehow hearing his name being spoken and appearing just as she needed him. Instead, she opened the door and found Emily on the front door step, giving her an apologetic smile.

'Hi. Sorry. I know it's late, but it's a demon. In the woods. There's a demon in the woods.'

Erica stared at her and then stood to the side.

'You better come in.'

The dogs got to Emily as soon as she set foot in the house and Erica stiffened. This was a woman who killed werewolves, what was she going to make of two over-friendly canines? To her delight and relief, Emily bent down to the dogs and made a fuss of each of them. The elder one then turned back to bed while the puppy followed at Emily's heels, happy to have made a new friend at any hour of the day or night.

Erica led Emily into the kitchen where Esther and Minerva were waiting. Emily stopped and gave a small wave.

'Hi.'

'This is Emily,' Erica told them.

'The one you told us about?' Minerva sniffed, looking Emily up and down. Emily didn't seem to notice, she was busy studying the kitchen. The puppy sniffed her boots until Esther shooed him away.

'Yes, the werewolf hunter.' Erica cleared her throat.

'Please, come in,' said Esther, gesturing to the chair opposite Minerva. 'Can I get you a drink?'

'Oh, a coffee would be lovely. Thank you.'

'Been a long time since I've heard of were-wolves,' Minerva said to Emily, studying her as she took a seat and Esther moved to the small coffee machine in the corner of the kitchen.

'Really? Does that mean you haven't heard of them around here? That's very lucky.'

'Do you find many?' Minerva asked.

'More than you'd expect, but not all are killers.'

Minerva softened, her curiosity getting the better of her.

'Oh? I didn't know that was possible.'

'Werewolves still have a human side. And anything's possible with humans.'

'Ain't that the truth.'

Erica watched, bewildered. Just like that, Emily had been accepted.

Esther placed a cup of coffee in front of their guest and took a seat.

'You're working on the same thing as Ric?' she asked. 'The girl who's gone missing in the woods.'

'I am,' said Emily, looking to Erica who sat back down.

'You said it's a demon?' Erica said. 'I know. We

know. We just found out. How do you know?'

Emily blinked.

'Me? How do you know? I've been in the woods, where have you been?'

Erica glanced at Minerva.

'Talking to a spirit.'

Emily grinned before sipping at her coffee.

'Nice. I guess you have to be able to talk to them, to hunt them properly.'

Minerva hissed through her teeth.

'Erica does not hunt spirits.'

'No? What do you call it, then?'

'She investigates paranormal activity and acts accordingly.'

'Bit of a mouthful,' said Emily, taking another gulp of coffee. 'And this ghost—'

'Spirit.'

'—Spirit told you it's a demon?'

'Yes. How do you know there's a demon?'

Again, Emily grinned.

'I saw how it got here.'

Erica, Minerva and Esther looked at one another and then all three turned back to Emily.

'What's that supposed to mean?' asked Minerva

'You seen the graffiti on the trees in those woods?' Emily asked Erica.

'Sure. A load of swear words and stupid pictures drawn on with spray paint or something.'

'Oh, okay. So, you haven't seen them recently?'

Erica frowned, thinking hard.

'I guess not?'

'Took me a while to find it. Got a lot in the boot of my car, but I managed to dig it out. I was worried I'd left it at home.' Emily opened her bag and pulled out a large book with pages half falling out. It

144

was a journal and as she leafed through the pages, Erica could make out doodles and scribbles.

'What's that?' asked Minerva, standing up to lean across the table for a better look.

'An old journal given to me by an old friend. He knew a thing or two about demons and those markings on the trees looked familiar. Here we go.' Emily found the page she was looking for and turned the book so they could all see the drawings. A shiver ran over Erica. It seemed wrong just looking at them.

'They're evil,' Esther murmured, instinctively pushing Minerva and Erica back.

'Yup,' said Emily. 'Satanic markings. Turns out they're used in summoning rituals.'

Erica looked up at Emily, thankful to rip her gaze from the symbols.

'You found these in the woods?'

'I was there today, chatting to the police, and guess what I saw when I looked up at the trees. I hadn't been to that particular spot. Apparently it's where some teenagers like to hang out and start fires, but it's a bit hidden away. Away from the main hang out place with most of the graffiti. Here, look.' Emily pulled out her phone and flicked through photos. She placed her phone on the table and showed them each photo in turn of the exact same symbols hastily drawn on the trunks of trees.

'Fuck,' breathed Minerva.

'Mum,' Esther chastised.

'Sorry, but...fuck.'

'Does it summon a particular type of demon?' Erica asked. 'Are there specific types?'

Emily nodded.

'My demon knowledge isn't great but I've spent

the evening researching. It's why I'm late. From what I can tell, these symbols summon something evil. Not one of the big powerful ones, which is a good thing, but still, something evil. Given that it's arrived in the woods, I wondered if it's some sort of ancient woodland demon. It seems at home there.'

'Oh, I don't know. Most creatures feel at home if they have enough food,' said Minerva.

'I feel sick,' Esther murmured, a hand at her mouth. 'What do we do? We need to get the fae involved. They can handle this, can't they? It's woodland. It's theirs, after all.'

Minerva and Erica stared at Esther, Minerva's mouth falling open.

'You *want* to get the fae involved?' she checked.

Esther nodded.

'You were right. And you are not allowed anywhere near those woods. Alfie was right. You're staying away. From those woods and from him.' She pointed at Erica.

Emily watched with a touch of amusement in her eyes.

'So, you don't want to come and investigate, then?'

'No, she doesn't,' Esther answered.

Erica sighed inwardly. She understood where her mother was coming from and there wasn't a part of her that wanted to go back inside those woods.

'No,' she said in a small voice.

'Because it's too scary. I get it, it's okay.' Emily closed the book.

'Because,' said Erica, glancing at her mother and grandmother for back-up. 'It's dark.'

'Tsh. Most things only come out in the dark,' Emily told her. 'It's the best time.'

'Even if this thing has better night vision than us? Why give it an advantage?'

'And you're not going in just the two of you. Ric needs to talk to Alfie,' said Minerva.

Emily gave a small growl of frustration, hidden by her placing her cup back on the table.

'Alfie? The bloke you were with outside the woods?'

'Yeah.'

'Why can't we find this Alfie now?'

'Because.' Again, Erica looked away. 'The cemetery is closed.'

Emily looked at each of them in turn but no one explained.

'Right,' she said, leaving a pause.

'I'd have thought he'd have given you his number,' Esther murmured to Erica who shifted uncomfortably.

'I don't think he has a phone.'

'He doesn't. Phones have a way of combusting as they move between planes. As I remember it, Alfie found that out the hard way. Last I heard, he lost five phones,' Minerva told them.

Erica caught herself smiling and looked down in an effort to shield it from her family. As she glanced up, Emily caught her eye and raised an eyebrow.

'I'll go find him in the morning,' Erica said carefully.

Esther looked at her mother.

'You can't get into the cemetery after dark?'

'Why are you looking at me?' Minerva asked, a hand on her chest.

'Because if anyone here has broken into that cemetery after dark, it's you.'

'That's very true, but I can't now.'

Erica knew she shouldn't ask, but she'd only forget later.

'Why not?'

'I may have...gotten caught last time.' Minerva had the decency to look just a touch ashamed and peered up at the ceiling.

Erica brushed her hand over her mouth, as if that would wipe off the smirk, and caught her mother's eye. Esther was smiling but gave her daughter a warning look.

Emily watched them each in turn.

'Okay,' she said, breaking the moment. 'Well, that thing is in the woods and chances are it'll be hungry again soon, so I reckon we should go in now. More chance of finding that girl and more chance of finding this demon before it gets stronger.'

'Sounds like it's already strong. I'm not sure what a couple of humans can do against it. That's why we need to talk to Alfie first.'

'Is Alfie powerful?'

'I guess,' said Erica. 'Depends on what you're comparing him to.'

'Us. Is he a danger to humans because of his strength?'

Erica risked a quick glance to her mother before she told Emily that he was.

'Then, if this thing isn't scared by a powerful fae, this thing, whatever it is, is damn scary and powerful.'

Erica took a shuddery breath.

'You make it sound like something that's settled into a new breeding ground,' said Minerva.

Emily shrugged.

148

'Maybe. There's a few tasty teenagers on the edge of the woods wanting to go looking for the thing that took their friend.' Emily looked down at the table and said deliberately but somehow also nonchalantly, 'And a few tasty police officers protecting them.'

Erica, her mother and grandmother stared at her.

'She has a point,' said Esther, unhappily.

Erica sighed.

'How do we get past those police, though? They'll notice us walking around in the woods, surely.'

'Oh, it's no problem, if you have the right I.D.'

'What?' Minerva frowned.

'I.D. A warrant card.' Emily shoved her hand into her pocket and pulled out a thick wallet. She rifled through cards inside and brought out the warrant card she'd originally shown Jess, sliding it across the table.

'You have a fake I.D.' Minerva laughed, clapping her hands as she sat back. 'You should get one of those.' She hit out at Erica's arm.

'Mum! No, she shouldn't. No, you won't,' Esther told her daughter. 'You're already getting into enough trouble with the police for getting in the way. You're not lying about who you are.'

Emily put her warrant card away and shrugged.

'You have to be careful how you use it. It's not like the movies or TV shows. You can't just flash it and head on into a crime scene. People might not think much of the British police, but they're not idiots. They're just underfunded. And a lack of funding doesn't mean they'll always let anyone into a crime scene without knowing who they are. I don't recommend a fake warrant card. What I do recommend is having someone on the inside, a police connection, but sometimes things get desperate, and when they do, a warrant card comes in useful. If nothing else, it acts as a distraction so you can run.'

Erica hadn't heard much past the mention of knowing someone on the inside.

Esther leaned forward on the table.

'You must get into trouble with the police a lot?' she asked.

Emily's reaction brought Erica back into the room. The shift in her expression was subtle but they all noticed it. Emily sucked on her teeth.

'I suppose if we have to wait for this fairy friend of yours, we have to wait until morning. I'll see you there, shall I?' She stood.

'Fae,' Minerva corrected.

Erica nodded.

'I guess.'

Emily hesitated.

'You think we should go now?'

Erica turned to Minerva.

'What do you think?'

'Me?' Minerva pursed her lips. 'I think you need more information, but the longer you wait, the more chance of someone else going missing. I don't think you should go without Alfie, and maybe Eolande, and that means waiting. But...'

'But?'

'But is there a chance this girl is still alive? Is there a chance you could save another person's life tonight? You know more than the police. You won't be looking where they're looking.'

'Where aren't they looking?' Esther asked. Minerva turned to her daughter.

'Up.'

'You don't know that,' Esther murmured.

'What human drags their victims up into tall trees?'

The women all looked down at the table.

'Not that I want you to go at all,' Esther started with a sigh. 'But if you have to go, then maybe Mum's right. Maybe you should be going now. How do you stop a demon?'

'There's a banishing ritual. It's worth a try,' said Minerva.

'Should we try the cemetery too?' Emily suggested. 'I could help us get in.'

'It's on the other side of the city.' Erica shook her head. 'About half an hour there at this time of night.'

'Depending on the state of roadworks in the city centre,' Esther added.

'We could go around the city centre.'

Minerva exhaled in a puff that immediately dismissed the idea.

'If we're going to the cemetery, we might as well wait to go to the woods in the morning.'

'Yeah.' Erica nodded. 'So, should we wait?'

Emily cleared her throat which was a poor cover up of another frustrated groan.

'You know what, you ladies can go in the morning but I actually have somewhere I need to be. I'm going now.' She stood. 'Up to you if you join me.'

'Woah, woah, hang on.' Erica stood but Minerva stopped her.

'I thought you came here to work as a team,' Minerva said to Emily. 'Why did you come here?'

'It's been a long time since I worked with

people,' Emily said. 'I thought it would be nice to work in a team, as you say, with this. Especially as I'm on your turf.' She looked at Erica. 'But we obviously do things differently and, if you have help from these fair—fae—or whatever, then maybe you don't need me. It's not a werewolf, is it.'

'No, but it's not exactly a spirit, as such, either,' Erica murmured. 'You know more about this than we do. We could use your help.'

Emily looked from Erica to Minerva.

Erica's grandmother shrugged.

'It's true. Our expertise are with spirits and the spiritual world, fae included. If this is something else, and it sounds like it is, then we need all the help we can get. We may have a big team.' She held her head up proudly. 'But our knowledge is limited in this regard. But then, if you have to go and you're not willing to wait...'

Emily chewed on her lip.

'In my experience, and vast knowledge, creatures like this don't often hunt in daylight.'

'But it's around in daylight,' Erica pointed out. 'It attacked me and Alfie in broad daylight. There's nothing to say we wouldn't find it.'

'And how many people have walked through those woods before that girl went missing? Even you walked through those woods completely oblivious before, remember. If this thing doesn't want to be found, it won't be found. But if it's hunting, or if it's feeding, it'll be easier to find. Especially if we know where to look.'

Erica wanted to argue with that but the words wouldn't come. She groaned, putting her face into her hands.

'I guess we have to, don't we. You're right. Now

is the best time. Even though it's terrifying.'

'We need to prepare,' said Emily, pulling out her car keys. 'I'll go get my stuff.'

'What stuff? What sort of preparation?' asked Esther.

Emily shot her a smile.

'Just the usual.' Her smile fell as they looked up at her blankly. 'Wait, how do you guys normally prepare?'

Minerva and Erica glanced at one another. Erica cleared her throat.

'Err, Jess does the research and I...go in...and...talk to the spirit. At least, that's the theory.' Erica sighed, avoiding Emily's eye as the werewolf hunter stared at her.

'Seriously? The theory? You're that new to this?'

Erica shrugged.

'No,' said Minerva. 'Ric has been talking to spirits since she was a child, as have I, as has Esther. How long have you been hunting were-wolves?'

'Since I was sixteen,' said Emily, not taking her eyes from Erica. 'Sounds like you and me deal with spirits differently too.'

Erica looked up, her stomach twisting sicken-ingly.

'How do you deal with them?'

Emily threw up her car keys and caught them.

'Find where they're buried and burn them, and if they come anywhere near me, I shoot them.'

Erica and Minerva glared at Emily as Esther gently murmured, 'What exactly are you getting out of your car?'

14

Jess took a sip from her wine glass and then lay back on the bed, curling up into Marshall as he wrapped his thick arms around her. She was cocooned in his safe world where there were no spirits, no demons, no scary creatures waiting to drag her or her daughter away. As long as Marshall was there, she was safe. She ran her fingers over his chest and then down to his naked thighs. He sighed contently into her hair.

'I think you should move in,' she said.

He held his breath. She waited for his chest to rise again and when it did, he answered her.

'You sure?'

She nodded, feeling the warmth of his skin brush against her cheek.

'Yes. Very sure. You're a part of this family and I want to make it official.' She held him tighter. Don't leave me, she thought.

He hugged her in response and kissed her head before releasing her and shuffling his position so he could look at her.

'You're not just saying this because of what happened tonight?'

Jess wondered how truthful to be.

'Maybe a little, but I've been thinking about it before. I do want to live with you. You're right, this living apart is silly. I was just scared. But tonight scared me more. The idea of not having you and Ruby with me scares me more. And I don't want to waste any more time.'

Marshall grinned and kissed her lips hard, his hands slipping down her body, over her hips and pulling her closer.

'There's another conversation there,' he murmured. 'About tonight. About what happened. And whether you should be doing this, but—' he added quickly as Jess drew breath, '—not tonight. Let's argue about that tomorrow. Yeah?'

Jess softened and shrugged. It was a conversation that had to happen. At least if it happened tomorrow, she would have time to think about how she felt and they could have some fun right now.

'Okay.' She kissed him, moving so that she sat on top, straddling him.

'If we're talking about making this more official, maybe we should get married,' said Marshall, cupping her breasts.

Jess stopped and slowly eased his hands away.

'Excuse me?'

Marshall faltered, searching her eyes for her true feelings. She wondered what he saw. Her stomach had flipped pleasurably at the words so she smiled at him and he relaxed, placing his hands back on her chest.

'It was just an idea,' he said.

Jess lowered herself to kiss his lips, imagining him as her husband, imagining herself as a wife. She smiled as their lips pressed together, her heart pounding.

'It's a good idea,' she murmured into the kiss.

With a moan, Marshall flipped her over so that he was on top and that's when there came a knock at the front door. Bubbles sprang to life downstairs, barking hysterically, and Marshall gave a soft growl, looking at Jess.

'Should we ignore it?'

'It's three in the morning. I don't think we can ignore it,' Jess whispered, scared whoever was at the door might hear her. Who knocked on the door at three in the morning? Either something awful had happened or there was someone unsavoury waiting for them downstairs. She had a sudden need to be fully clothed.

On the bedside table beside them, Jess's phone lit up. Marshall leaned over to check it.

'It's Ric,' he said, climbing off Jess. 'She's at the door.'

Jess gave an uncontrollable laugh.

'I'll kill her,' she murmured, rolling out of bed and reaching for her clothes.

Once downstairs, Jess grabbed Bubbles by the collar and opened the door. It wasn't just Erica stood on her doorstep. Minerva and Emily were there too, standing behind her.

'Erm. Hello. Do you know it's three in the morning?'

Erica took a deep breath.

'We're going into the woods to find the demon before it kills anyone else. We have to go now. Apparently. No, I haven't spoken to Alfie but Emily found Satanic symbols on the trees and we think that's how the demon got there.' Erica stopped just as she was running out of breath.

Jess's bowels loosened as the words sunk in.

'Wanna come?' asked Emily over Erica's shoulder.

Jess stared wide-eyed at Erica and then at Minerva who was stout-faced but broke the expression to give her a momentary apologetic smile.

'Erm. No?'

'Okay. It's okay. You don't have to,' Erica told her.

'Wait. No. Hang on. What? You're going into the woods? Now? Right now?'

'Right now,' said Minerva.

Jess turned as Marshall's heavy feet sounded on the stairs. He appeared beside her, wearing only his jeans, and looked out at the women. Emily eyed him up and then gave Jess a small knowing smile.

'No,' said Marshall, standing back and crossing his large arms against his bare chest. 'You're absolutely not going into the woods. Ever. And I thought you were banned too?' He turned to Erica.

Jess had to admit, there was something terribly attractive about Marshall standing topless in her house, smelling of sex and forbidding her from doing something dangerous. If she listened to him and said no, she could go back to bed with him...and spend the night worrying about Erica, get no sleep and be a mess in the morning. As opposed to going into the woods to face a terrifying demon and potentially death, leaving her daughter without her mother and never becoming Marshall's wife. Bubbles would be okay, she thought, looking down at the puppy. Erica's parents would have her if Marshall didn't. Jess frowned. The choice was an obvious one.

'Except, I kind of have to go,' she murmured.

Marshall blinked.

'What?'

'Tonight was scary but if we're going to make a business out of this, I need to get over the fear.'

'Of ghosts, not of demons or whatever the hell this is, and not at three in the morning.'

'Night is when these things feed,' came Emily's voice. 'There are police officers all around those woods. It wouldn't take much for one to become a meal.'

'Or for one of you to become a meal,' said Marshall. 'You're set on going?' he asked Jess.

'I think so.'

'Then I'll come with you.'

'No!'

Marshall raised his eyebrows at Jess's ferocity.

'No? Why not?'

'What if I die? Who will tell Ruby? Who will look after Bubbles?'

'Paul. Erica's parents. I love Ruby, you know I do, I'd do anything for her,—' Jess softened inside, '—and you know I love Bubbles. But neither of them need me if you're not here. Without you, I lose everything, Jess, and I don't want to lose you or them. If I come with you, I can protect you.'

Tears stung at Jess's eyes.

'Got any prior paranormal knowledge, Big Man?' asked Emily.

Marshall did a double take at her.

'No. Why?'

'Any special skills? Can you talk to the dead, like this one?' Emily gestured at Erica.

'No.'

'So, you're just big and in love?' Marshall glowered at her. 'Then you'll just be a distraction, for Jess and the rest of us.'

Jess frowned at Emily, stepping closer to Marshall.

'Now, hang on, I'm not bringing anything

special to this either. So why am I coming along? I'll just distract you, or whatever.'

Emily shrugged.

'These two were insistent.'

Jess looked at Minerva.

'I'll slow you down,' she told her.

Minerva gave a smile that somehow managed to shake Jess.

'My dear girl, you have never slowed us down, nor shall you ever. You are stronger and more capable than you know. Your man knows it, we know it but you haven't seen it yet. He's only worried because he loves you. He knows that you are capable of facing a demon with us.'

'I'm not a werewolf hunter or a witch,' said Jess.

'Pish! Who told you that?' Minerva turned around, ending the conversation. 'Come on. We're wasting time. The sooner we do this, the sooner we're back home and in bed.'

Marshall grabbed hold of Jess's wrist.

'What are you hoping to do? Find this thing and kill it?'

'We have a banishing spell and minor exorcism to try,' Erica told him. 'I'll look after her. That's if you really want to come,' she said to Jess. 'Honestly, you don't have to. It's okay.'

'But you're going. And what if something happens to you?' Jess murmured. 'What if I miss something important? I don't want to go, I'm terrified, but on the other hand.' Jess looked up at Marshall. 'I don't want to be the desk girl. Or client relations. Or any other boring shit like that. I want to be out in the field, I want to help. I can at least hold things while you do these spells or whatever it is. I want to help. And you have to let me go,' she added to Marshall. 'Trust that Ric and Minerva will bring me home.'

Marshall sighed but he didn't drop Jess's wrist.

'I trust them and I trust you. I don't know if I can trust the new girl. There's a weak link, Jess. Stay home with me.'

'My phone's on,' said Jess, easing her wrist form his grasp and reaching for her coat. 'And we won't be long. Three hours at the most, right?'

Erica gave a nod and a shrug in one.

'No idea.'

'Three hours at the most,' Jess repeated, going up on tip-toe to kiss Marshall. He didn't kiss her back. 'I love you. I love you so much it hurts and I can't wait for you to move in.'

Out of the corner of her eye she saw Erica's surprise.

Marshall searched Jess's eyes and then sighed through his nose. Pulling her close, he kissed her soft and deep.

'You come back to me or I'll go into those woods to find you.'

Jess nodded, smiling, her head spinning as she let go of Marshall and turned to join Erica.

'Three hours,' Marshall added to Erica. She held out her arms in another sort of shrug.

'We'll try our best. Maybe give it four.'

Jess glanced back to Marshall and Bubbles watching her walk down the driveway. Was this the right choice? She'd made bad choices so often, she should know how they felt by now. Why didn't she know how they felt? All she could tell, as of this moment, was that her body was screaming at her to go with Erica even if a clear and loud voice in her mind wanted nothing more than for her to run back into Marshall's arms.

'You've got a daughter,' she mumbled to herself. 'What the hell are you doing?' But she was doing this for Ruby. To make those woods safe again for Ruby to play in. To find out what happened to that girl and to make sure that never happened to her own baby girl.

Tears dripping down her cheeks, Jess squeezed into the back of Erica's Mini and watched Marshall's silhouette as they drove away from the warmth and safety of Jess's house and into the darkness towards the woods.

In The Woods

Sniffing the air, it froze, half way down a tree trunk and hovering over the uniformed man. They were coming. It could smell them. Not just the naïve witch but the strange woman he couldn't place, and someone stronger. It moved back up the tree. The determination and magic heading towards it gave it a headache.

Jumping from tree to tree, ignoring the branches flinching away, it stopped to watch the car pull up, the beams of headlights turn off. It held its breath as four humans climbed out of the vehicle. Four women.

There was the naïve witch. It spotted her first, standing up and stretching, her eyes gazing over the dark trees.

There was the strange woman. The strong one who wasn't a witch. What was she? She moved to the back of the car and lifted the lid. The others gathered around her.

There was a woman he recognised as a dog walker. What was she doing there?

And another woman. An old woman, stronger than the rest, casting a sharp eye over the trees and stopping where it sat. It studied her. Surely she couldn't see it. Surely the old woman's eyes were not that keen. The witch looked away, turning back to the others, and the soft sound of their low voices carried over to it.

Unable to make out the words, it sat and waited, not taking its eyes from the old witch.

15

Erica hugged herself as they huddled around the boot of her car. Emily had placed a couple of large duffle bags in there and now she unzipped each in turn.

'Here.' She pulled out something long and black and handed it to Erica. She took it and then shoved it back at Emily.

'It's a gun,' she said, stepping back. 'Where did you get a gun?'

Emily blinked, rubbing some imaginary dust from the barrel of the shotgun.

'I have a licence, don't worry. And I never put real shells in it. This is just to scare ghosts and it works a treat.'

'No, no, no.' said Minerva. 'That won't do. Put that dreadful thing away. We don't need it.'

Emily looked from Minerva to Erica to Jess and sighed, placing the shotgun back in the bag.

'Fine. We're on your turf and you're the ghost experts.'

She pulled out a brown leather holster and strapped it around her waist. Erica watched uncertainly.

'What are you doing?'

'I won't take the shotgun for ghosts but I will take my own weapons. Okay, so it's not a werewolf, but it's not exactly a ghost either, is it?'

'Demons are considered a form of spirit,' said

Minerva. 'They aren't necessarily corporeal like the creatures you say you hunt. You won't need a gun. A gun will be completely ineffective against a demon.'

'When was the last time you met a demon?' Emily asked.

Minerva pursed her lips.

'A long time ago, thankfully.'

'If you don't mind, I'll take my gun. Just in case. You never know.'

Minerva put a hand on Emily's wrist as the woman pulled out a silvery revolver from the bag.

'If anyone gets hurt by that gun, your life won't be worth living,' she hissed.

Erica started, staring at her grandmother. She'd never heard her talk like that, she'd never heard her use that tone. She hadn't known it possible for her grandmother to hiss so aggressively. Not for the first or last time, she had a stabbing moment of pride and relief that Minerva was not only on her side but related to her.

Jess seemed to share the moment, taking a shuddery breath beside Erica and moving closer to her friend. Erica took Jess's hand and squeezed.

Seemingly oblivious, Emily took some bullets and loaded the gun.

Erica frowned.

'Are those silver bullets?'

'Yeah. I don't actually have the normal kind. I make my own, so these will have to do. And don't worry,' Emily added to Minerva. 'I won't use it unless I feel I have to and it will never be pointed at you, Erica or Jess. Okay?'

'And if the demon gets hold of it?' asked Minerva.

A shadow passed over Emily's face.

'Then the demon won't know what's hit it. Are we ready?' She placed the revolver in her holster and pulled her jacket on to cover it up. Reaching back into the bag, she pulled out four torches, handing three out to the others. 'Let's go.'

Emily led the way down the path, towards the woods. They stopped just before the tree line and turned on the torches.

'Are you sure you want to do this?' Erica asked Jess. 'You could wait here for us. Be our back up?'

'Are you kidding me? You're not leaving me out here in the middle of the night, in the dark when there's a demon around.' Jess was still standing a little too close to Erica. 'I'm sticking with you guys. Just tell me what to do.'

Minerva was holding a small cotton bag which she passed to Jess without looking at her.

'Here. Hold this. Keep it safe.' She was looking up at the trees.

'Do you see anything?' Erica asked.

Minerva shook her head.

'No. But I can feel it. The trees aren't happy. They're calling out to us. Can you hear them?'

Erica cocked her head and then closed her eyes, trying to will her mind into silence but all she could hear was the soft rustle of leaves in the breeze and her friends breathing.

'No,' she muttered. 'Alfie said I must have heard them calling out before, he said it was why I ended up here the same time he did. But I couldn't hear them. Why can't I hear them?'

'You can.' Minerva patted her arm. 'And you will. Deep breaths, dear, and listen.' She pushed up to Emily and stepped ahead of the werewolf hunter.

'Come on, then. No point in hanging around here all night.' She stepped into the woods and placed a hand on the nearest tree trunk. 'I hear you,' she whispered. 'I'm here. While I am here, no harm will come to you.'

Erica followed her, brushing her fingers over the bark Minerva had just touched. She stopped and tried to listen but heard only the footsteps of Jess and Emily passing by, following Minerva into the woods. Taking a deep breath, Erica fell into step beside Emily.

'So, when you say you've killed werewolves, you mean you've shot them?' she whispered.

'Death is never easy or pretty,' Emily told her in a low voice, her eyes scanning the branches above them. 'Whether it's by knife or bullet. Bullet seems kinder. It's quicker for them and safer for me.'

Erica nodded, feeling a flash of fear as she was forced to step behind Emily as they followed a narrow dirt track between the trees. She didn't want to be left behind. In fact, if anyone was going to be at the back, where the demon could easily pick them off, surely it should be the person with the gun. Another deep breath and Erica focussed on Emily's back until the path widened and Erica could return to her side.

A crack of a branch above their heads made them stop, Minerva searching the treetops with narrowed eyes.

'See anything?' she murmured.

They all said they didn't and Erica looked back down quickly, aware that while they were all staring up, anything could grab them from the woodland floor. She half expected to see red eyes peering at her through the darkness, but there was nothing. She shone her torch this way and that but saw only leaves and brambles and ferns.

'Shouldn't there be rabbits or mice or something?' she whispered into the darkness. 'Don't animals come out at night to find food?'

They all searched around them, their torches picking out bits and pieces but mostly casting extra shadows.

'Not when there's a demon about, I guess,' said Emily.

Minerva nodded.

'The demon has silenced them. Poor things. They must be hungry. Which way were these strange trees, Ric?'

Erica gazed around them, trying to get her bearings.

'Over there, I think. Off the main path, over to the left.'

Minerva looked where Erica pointed and they continued walking, following the path further in. A burst of sudden cawing made them stop and all look up, shining their torches into the canopy.

The crows flapped their wings, peering down at them, calling out loud and clear. The sight and sound nudged at Erica.

'They did that when I was here walking Bubbles.' She glanced at Minerva. 'Were they trying to tell me then?'

'What can you hear?' Minerva asked her, infuriatingly. Erica bit the inside of her cheek and listened to the crows.

'I don't know. I hear crows.'

'You'll hear it soon enough,' her grandmother said, turning her back on them and continuing on. Emily and Jess followed but Erica hesitated, looking back up at the crows.

'Should I be able to understand you? Why can't I?'

Eventually, they walked into a small clearing and Emily led them over to the trees surrounding a fallen tree trunk.

'Look, here it is. This is where the kids light fires and here, here are the symbols.' She shone her torch from the blackened ground to the trees and the painted markings.

Minerva moved closer, studying the symbols.

Erica didn't know how she could bear it. The temperature had dropped, a chill sitting over the area, and the symbols, in-person, screamed. Oh, those I can hear, she thought bitterly.

Minerva pressed her fingers against one of the markings.

'Where did they learn this?' she murmured.

Erica narrowed her eyes against the screams. It was all getting a bit much. She couldn't think, her heart pounding against her chest and her breath becoming shorter.

'Can we move?' she managed to say before she had to sit down.

Minerva was on her immediately.

'What do you feel?' she asked, placing her palm on Erica's forehead.

'I can't breathe,' Erica gasped, fighting for another lungful as her chest tightened, as if someone was winding up her ribcage. 'I can't breathe. And the screaming.' She placed her hands over her ears but somehow that only made it worse.

'Screaming?' asked Jess, turning and shining her torch into the darkness. 'I can't hear screaming.'

She looked at Emily who shrugged back.

'The trees are screaming,' Minerva told them, holding Erica close. 'It's the trees.'

Erica shook her head. As she fought for another breath, her muscles tense, her hands at her chest fighting to loosen the tightness, a voice came through the screams.

Here.

Just like that, Erica's chest loosened and the air practically fell into her. She gasped and gulped it in, her muscles aching and tingling.

'What's going on?' asked Emily, her hand over her holster.

'What do you hear, Ric?' Minerva urged, holding her granddaughter close.

Erica looked up at the trees with the Satanic symbols.

'The trees hurt,' she said, a tear rolling down her cheek. Minerva nodded.

'They do. We need to clean the markings off. We will clean them off.'

Here.

Erica looked to the right as the voice sounded.

'Do you hear that?' she whispered. The other three stared at her.

'Hear what? What do you hear?' asked Minerva in a low, soothing voice.

'A woman. A woman saying "here". You don't hear it?'

Erica looked at Jess. Her friend was pale, her eyes wide, shaking her head, the bag she held at her chest trembling.

'I hear it,' Erica said, standing up. Minerva's arms fell from her and her grandmother waited, watching. 'I hear her.' Without thinking, Erica walked away from the clearing and back into the trees.

'Erica.' Minerva's voice came loud and clear, almost as a warning but Erica felt no threat. It wasn't a warning to her, she realised, but a warning to the demon. Erica glanced up and swore she saw movement above her head. A large dark mass moving from one tree to the next.

Here.

It was louder now. She was almost there. Erica pushed down a narrow, overgrown path, swiping brambles and branches out of her way and then stopped.

Emily and Jess crashed into the back of her, Minerva close behind.

'Holy hell,' Emily murmured in her ear.

In front of them, on the path, stood a girl. Arms by her sides, her clothes torn and bloodied, she looked straight into Erica's eyes. Erica opened her mouth to speak but no words came. Then the girl looked up and pointed.

Erica, Jess and Emily followed where the girl pointed with their torches, up into a tree, and all three shone light on a human body, twisted and hidden by leaves and branches.

Erica looked back down to the girl but she had gone.

Swallowing on her dry throat, Erica stepped forward to where the girl had stood but there was no sign of her. No prints, no sound of someone pushing through the leaves ahead of them. She shone her torch back up at the body above their heads.

'I think we found her,' she murmured.

'Ric!'

Erica looked down sharply at Jess who was

hiding behind Emily, shaking violently. Emily had drawn her gun and pointed it at Erica. No, not at Erica, she was aiming it behind her.

Erica's breath caught, a wave of cold air hitting her and making her teeth chatter.

Minerva pushed back Jess and Emily, her hand forcing Emily to lower her weapon.

'You do not belong here,' Minerva cried. 'Be gone from this place.'

Slowly, without any idea of why she would do such a thing, Erica turned around.

The demon was a good two feet taller than her and humanoid but its arms were too long, its claws reaching down to its knees. It was lanky, far too thin and its ribcage stuck out awkwardly. Its eyes were indeed red, glowing like embers as Erica stepped back. Its mouth opened to show rows of sharp teeth and then it reached out to Erica with one long arm, knobbly fingers stretching out until the claws almost touched her cheek.

A light came upon them in that moment, so blinding that Erica was forced to turn away and shield her face, hiding everything from view.

16

When Jess opened her eyes and blinked away the patches of colours, the creature had gone. She turned, shining her torch around them but didn't see it. Had she imagined it? Had the others seen it? Next to her, Emily groaned, rubbing at her face.

Jess looked up into the darkness and then shone her torch just enough onto the girl's body that she knew this was real, this was happening. She only caught sight of the girl's leg before she looked away. That was enough.

'I told you not to come.' A man's voice sounded. Jess pushed past Emily and saw Alfie approaching from where the creature had stood. He stopped in front of Erica, hands on his hips, glaring down at her. 'You promised me.'

Erica opened and closed her mouth, her eyes filling with tears. Jess didn't blame her. Her cheeks were soaked with the tears that had fallen since they'd entered these woods. She was still clutching Minerva's bag to her chest in some desperate hope that whatever was in it would protect her.

From behind Alfie came the tall, elegant figure of Eolande who only had eyes for Minerva.

'Shit,' Minerva murmured, moving past Erica and Alfie to meet her fae lover.

'What's going on? What happened?' asked Emily, shining her torch around them just as Jess had done.

'The fae are here,' Jess told her in a quiet voice. Emily stopped and watched Alfie and Eolande arguing with Erica and Minerva. Eolande said no words while Minerva tried to explain herself, pointing up at the tree.

Alfie, on the other hand, was still berating Erica.

'Don't you know what could have happened? It was about to kill you. If I hadn't been here, you'd be dead right now. Didn't you think this through? Why didn't you listen to me? I understand if you don't want me but could you at least listen to me when I'm trying to protect you?'

Erica blinked back at Alfie. How was she supposed to get a word in?

'What do we do?' Emily asked Jess in a whisper.

Jess sighed. Her body had relaxed, the trembling fully taking over and her knees weakening. Her eyelids were so heavy, she blinked in an effort to stay awake. The fae were here. Everything was going to be okay.

'I think we go home,' she said, glancing up into the tree above them. 'And we tell the police somehow about her.'

Emily followed her glance.

'Yeah. I'll do that. I'll make sure she's found.' Emily searched Jess's face. 'Where did the demon go?' she asked loudly, interrupting both fae arguments.

'It's gone,' growled Alfie, finally ripping his eyes from Erica. Erica kept her head bowed sheepishly.

'Gone where? Is it attached to any of us? Are we free to go, is what I'm asking,' said Emily wearily.

Alfie looked at each of them in turn.

'The demon is attached to the trees,' said Eolande in a voice like molten caramel. Somehow, the shadows around them lifted at the sound of her voice. 'You will leave now without fear and none of you will return until we have banished the demon.'

Minerva went to argue that but Eolande glared at her. Minerva slowly closed her mouth. 'There will be no further arguments,' she continued. 'You should have come to me.'

'I know. I know. I was going to, but it was late and the cemetery is locked up tight at night now,' said Minerva, brushing away Eolande's concern.

'There are other ways. You should have come to me.'

Minerva and Erica exchanged a glance that almost made Jess smile, if her knees hadn't given way at that moment. Emily caught her.

'I think it's time to go. I'll make sure the police find the girl.' Emily gestured upwards. 'Let's get out of here.'

'Finally, someone sensible,' Alfie muttered.

'She's the one with a gun,' Erica told him, following Eolande and Minerva down the path and away from the tree. Alfie caught up with Erica, his hand on her waist.

Jess and Emily watched them go.

'Oh, no, we're fine. Don't wait for us,' Emily grumbled, her arm around Jess. 'You okay?'

Jess nodded, summoning all of her strength to catch them up. There was no way she was letting the fae go out of sight until they were out of the woods.

The woods were silent as they walked. The only sounds were the low voices of Alfie and Erica, deep in conversation. It was something that Jess would ponder on later but at this moment, all she could concentrate on was putting one foot in front of the other and staying upright.

Where was the demon now?

'What did you mean? By what is it attached to?' she asked Emily quietly.

'It's what summoned demons do. Usually they attach themselves to the person who summoned them. Which begs the question, who the hell summoned this one? Who drew those symbols? It's not just about drawing the right pictures, there's a whole ritual around it. Words need to be said. Who did that? I wonder if they knew what they were doing? They were bloody lucky it didn't attach itself to them.'

'Maybe it was the girl,' Jess offered. Her head was beginning to ache, pain leeching into the sides and behind her eyes.

'Maybe. Anyway, if these fae say it's attached to the trees and you trust the fae, then we're okay, aren't we. I guess maybe that's why Erica said the trees were screaming.'

Jess shuddered.

'So, it's still in the woods.'

'Probably watching us leave,' said Emily. Jess glanced around them, nausea pulling at her throat at the thought of seeing those red eyes peering at them from the darkness.

They reached the tree line and left the woods, pausing to regroup.

'I'm sorry. Excuse me,' said Jess as they all turned to look at her. 'But if you can get rid of that thing, shouldn't you do it now? It killed that girl and left her in a tree. Can't you kill it before it does that again?'

Minerva shook her head.

'No. Now that we've seen it, I know our little exorcism won't work. It's been here too long, or at least, it's grown too strong.' She glanced at Eolande. 'But we could kill it together.'

Eolande was looking at the trees behind them.

'All of you are forbidden from entering these woods without us,' she declared. 'And there will be no further talk here. It can hear us.'

Jess shivered and stepped away from the woods, closer to Alfie and Erica. He still had an arm around her, standing between her and the trees. Jess was overwhelmed with the urge to have Marshall's arms around her. To be home and warm and safe. It competed with the violent urge to be sick.

Turning and shrugging Emily away from her, Jess vomited into the grass beside the path. Emily followed her, holding her hair away from her face. Erica joined them, gently rubbing Jess's back.

'You okay?' she whispered.

Jess wiped her mouth on her coat sleeve and nodded.

'Not really,' she said with a weak smile. 'I'd like to go home now, please. Where there aren't any demons. Please don't follow us,' she added almost silently.

Alfie watched her with interest as Erica led Jess up the path back to her car.

'It won't follow you,' he said . 'We'll make sure of it. You are safe, Jess.'

Jess gave him a grateful nod.

'You know,' she whispered to Erica, mindful of not breathing her vomit breath on her friend. 'I think I've changed my mind about him.'

Erica gave a quiet laugh and helped her into the

car.

'I'm taking Jess home first. Where can I drop you off?' she asked Emily.

'I'll go home with Eolande. We have too much to talk about,' said Minerva, giving Erica a kiss on the cheek and waving to Jess. 'Feel better, Jess. And I'm sorry.'

Jess nodded, waving to her. She was just happy to be sitting down. She closed the door and leaned her head against the seat's head rest, watching the others through the window. Their voices were muffled but clear enough. She refused to look back to the trees and for once was glad she couldn't afford that beautiful house she'd viewed on the edge of the woods. No, she would go a good distance from these woodlands and curl up in Marshall's arms, safe in the knowledge that Ruby was further away at her father's house, and she would sleep. She closed her eyes and the sight of the demon appeared in her mind's eye. Her eyes flew open.

Shit, she thought. How was she going to get to sleep?

'Okay. I'll take Jess home and then drop you off,' Erica told Emily. It didn't escape Jess's attention that Erica and Alfie exchanged a look. He still seemed angry, but none of it was directed at Erica anymore. Jess gave a small smile. She'd been wrong about him, she was sure. The charm was a little too much and he was too powerful for Jess to feel comfortable with, but Erica was safe with him and that was all Jess cared about when it came to Alfie. They were safe with him.

She closed her eyes again and this time the demon stayed away, although not completely. It rested on the edge of her dream as Jess settled between wakefulness and sleep, feeling the bumps and turns of Erica driving her home and back to Marshall.

Emily

Today I saw a demon.

It was different to the last one. This one almost looked human. Almost. But the proportions were off and the eyes were like fire. Like the fires of hell, I guess.

It never gets easier. Whether it's a werewolf or a ghost or something else. I see them, I look into their eyes and each time it's hard. It's terrifying.

I went with the new girls, Erica and Jess, and Erica's grandmother who happens to also be a witch. Poor Jess. She wants to bring more to the party and I don't blame her, but she was shaken to her core. Terror isn't the word. I wonder how she'll sleep tonight. I wonder how she'll cope in this business. Maybe she should stay behind the desk, as it were. Leave Erica to go out in the field.

And just before that demon touched Erica, bang! A flash of light and two fae appeared.

Demons I've seen before, but never have I ever seen a fae.

They looked human but more. Human but with some sort of charm about them. The woman was irresistibly beautiful and the man...well...less said about that the better. I'm glad I don't know them. For one thing, I doubt I'd get any work done.

I won't deny there's a part of me that's jealous of Erica and her gran though. Having the attention of those fae. You should have seen the male one kicking off at Erica. There was love there. Real love. And if I was her I wouldn't be leaving his bed for at least a week, if not a month, after that.

There's something else about them too. The fae. Something underneath all of it. Something strong. I stood there, between a demon and two fae, and I wanted to be near neither.

No, Erica and her gran can keep their fae. I'm sure they come in handy, when it comes to battling demons and satisfying urges but I've been getting on well without them.

The witches, on the other hand, are a different matter. They're much more useful. After years of dreading dealing with ghosts, who knew all I'd have to do was befriend a witch.

I admit, watching Erica in action, hearing trees screaming, was a little much. But she wasn't scared when the ghost of the dead girl appeared. They talked to each other, or communicated anyway. I wish I could do that. I wish I could be that calm.

Erica and her gran said I needed to leave the guns at home, and maybe they're right. Maybe guns aren't the right tool when it comes to ghosts. But they've never come across a werewolf.

So, we still have a demon to deal with. But now we know what we're dealing with. We've seen it, we know where it is, and I have two witches and two fae on the case.

You know, I might just sit back with Jess and let the others handle this one.

Oh, I spoke too soon. Erica's calling me. Looks like I might be chasing a demon after all.

17

Erica stood in reception, reading the posters on the walls about the breakfast available at the hotel, hugging herself tight. She gave a small smile as Emily appeared and nodded to her.

'All right?'

Erica nodded back and followed Emily through the corridor and up the stairs.

'Thanks for this. It seemed stupid to just sit in my car all alone. I just can't face going home yet.'

'It's all right. Not sure I can sleep after all that. Not sure how anyone can, to be honest. You'd think I'd be used to it by now. I know some people who just crash on any bed or chair after a night like that. They don't even dream,' said Emily quietly over her shoulder.

She stopped on the first floor and navigated through doors and around corners, Erica following closely.

'How many other people like us do you know?' she asked. How had this happened? Was the world full of those who dealt with paranormal incidences that most people simply didn't know about? How had she not known? Why hadn't her grandmother told her?

'A few. I think that happens when you travel around like I do. A lot of others probably don't know people like us exist. They think it's just them.

I just can't imagine that. How lonely that must be. At least you have your family, and Jess.'

Erica nodded. She would always be grateful for Jess.

'I'm not sure Jess feels that way now. This might have ruined everything. I'm the reason she was there. I'm the reason she probably won't sleep tonight. It'll serve me right if she takes her family and moves far away.'

Emily frowned.

'To where? These things happen all over. Trust me. I've seen them.'

'Where do you live, then? Do you have a base?'

'I do. It's in Scotland.'

Erica looked up at Emily sharply.

'Scotland? You've come a long way.'

Emily threw Erica a sly smile over her shoulder and pulled out a key card.

'Here we go.'

Erica followed Emily inside and shrugged off her coat, lying it across of the back of the unused chair, which she then sat on. Emily pulled out a bottle from her bag and nodded to the two cups on the table. 'Grab them.'

Erica did as she was told and Emily poured them both a dribble of whisky. Wrinkling her nose, Erica swirled hers around the cup while Emily downed hers and refilled.

'You don't like whisky? I might have something else. But whisky will help you sleep.'

'Will it stop me dreaming?' Erica asked. She wasn't a whisky drinker. She'd tried it only the once and the burning had stayed with her long after the vomit had left.

'Should do, but hey, I can't promise anything,'

said Emily, sitting on the foot of the bed and tucking her legs under her, nursing her cup.

Erica chewed on the inside of her cheek. She should be at home, in bed, getting some sleep. But every time she closed her eyes she saw the demon reaching out to touch her, she felt the spirit of the girl and her sadness, she heard the trees screaming. Perhaps she should have stayed with Jess, but Marshall had given her such a dark, angry look when she'd delivered Jess home that she wouldn't be surprised if Jess never spoke to her again.

'We really do things differently,' she murmured, staring down at the alcohol. She had to admit, it looked tempting. Emily looked at her sideways.

'Not in every case.'

'You carry guns and you shoot to kill.'

Emily stared down into her cup, swirled it twice and then downed it again, grimacing against the burn and exhaling through her teeth.

'You make it sound easy,' she said with a rough voice. 'It's never easy. I only do it if there's no other way. But if a werewolf is killing people, often the kindest thing to do is kill it. People often don't realise what they're doing and they don't take kindly to me telling them. Sometimes it's just too much. I've had people kill themselves before I get to that stage. I try my best, but a lot of the time death, one way or another, is the only realistic outcome. At least with you, they're already dead.'

Erica hadn't considered that.

'I guess.'

'But we still talk to them, right? I talk to the werewolves and you talk to the ghosts. That was pretty spectacular what you did in those woods. Finding that girl's body. Could you hear her in your head? What's that like?'

Erica shrugged.

'Nothing special. It's just a voice. Like I'm hearing you now, except I can't tell who the voice belongs to.'

'That's terrifying,' Emily said.

Erica frowned.

'It doesn't usually feel scary. I guess it depends on the voice, and on the spirit. She didn't scare me. She was just so...sad. Like, like it didn't have to be this way. She had so much to live for.'

'Yeah, well, don't we all. And then something comes along and messes it all up. That's life. Whether it's a demon, a werewolf, a ghost, a crappy boss or a lover who spins you round all wrong.'

Erica studied Emily.

'Which was it for you?'

Emily smiled down at her cup.

'Ah, well. Maybe you're lucky if it's just one of those things, huh? Guess.'

Erica leaned back in her chair, cup of whisky still in her hand.

'Werewolf.'

'Obviously. And?'

Erica tilted her head, watching Emily.

'A lover who spun you round wrong.'

Emily nodded, reaching forward to pour more whisky into her cup.

'A werewolf and a man. They both did this to me.' She gestured to herself and then downed the whisky, slamming the cup down on the table and sitting back on the bed.

'I'm sorry,' Erica murmured, wondering how much she could ask. Emily shrugged.

'What about you? What did this to you?'

'Nothing.'

'Oh, come on. How did you find yourself here? In this room with me, avoiding your bed and your dreams because you know there's a demon waiting for you there.'

Erica gave a soft smile.

'A crappy boss,' she said. 'I was doing okay. No spirits, even though I grew up with them. No fae. Nothing paranormal. Just me, Jess and a career. And then the crappy boss came along.' Erica looked up to find Emily smirking at her. 'What?'

'Speaking of which,' said Emily. 'That fae, the bloke, what's his name?'

'Alfie?'

'Yeah, Alfie. You sleeping with him?'

Erica blinked, her gut twisting in a panic.

'What? No!'

'Why not?' Erica looked down at her drink. 'You don't want to? Or is it weird, having sex with a fae? I got the feeling your gran and that other one were close enough to be doing it.'

Erica laughed and it brought her a little bit of joy to see Emily jump at the noise.

'Yes. My gran and Eolande, the lovers you didn't see coming. Or I didn't, anyway. It's not weird. Fae are incredibly sexual. It's generally what they do. Find someone, usually a human and usually a young one, seduce them, fall in love and have sex. That's what Gran says, anyway. It's not weird, it's just complicated with Alfie.'

'Why?'

Erica twisted her lips. She hadn't had anything to drink yet but the closeness of the hotel room made it seem easy to open up.

'I mean,' said Emily. 'Not that I would, because I

186

don't think I could with a fae, but that guy? I would. If you know what I mean. If a guy like that acted with me the way he does with you, I think I'd be in a bed with him right now instead of perching on a chair in a hotel room with the likes of me.'

Erica swirled her whisky.

'It's complicated,' she repeated. 'Because there's someone else.'

Emily leaned forward.

'Oh? Who?'

'I haven't met him yet.'

Emily blinked and then held her hand to her head.

'Nope. I've drunk too much, you need to explain that.'

'A couple of months ago, when I met Alfie, I also met this man who proclaimed to be from the future and my future husband.' Erica met Emily's eyes. 'He was a time traveller and he was mine and I loved him the moment I saw him, and then he disappeared back to his own time and made me promise to find him in this time, and I did, but then there's Alfie, and...' Erica swirled her whisky. 'And...I don't know what to do.'

Emily stared at her, mouth agape.

'You don't know whether to have lots of sex with a fae before you settle down with your husband? Sorry, you've lost me again. What does your future husband say about all this?'

'He doesn't know I exist yet. I found him online. I haven't contacted him yet.'

Emily laughed and sat back.

'Wow. Okay. So, what do you want to do?'

Erica took a deep breath and closed her eyes.

'What happens if I fall in love with Alfie and

want to be with him?'

The silence that followed forced her to open her eyes to find Emily staring thoughtfully at nothing.

'Ah. Yeah. I see your problem. You and Alfie make a fantastic couple. I can see you together. All loved up and happy, arguing because all he wants to do is protect you but you keep doing dangerous things.' Emily smiled to herself. 'I know the problem.' She met Erica's gaze. 'I've had an Alfie in my life. I mean, there's no future husband, but I've had an Alfie.'

A flicker of curious hope licked at Erica's insides.

'What did you do?' she asked, leaning forward. 'What happened?'

'He saved my life.' Emily sniffed, absent-mindedly stroking the bed beside her. 'He taught me to hunt, to shoot, to take care of myself. He was my first love. My first...well, everything.' She looked up at Erica. 'It was a mixture of things that drove us apart, I guess. I was so young when he found me that I wanted to see what life was like without him. You don't have that problem, though, and you know what? There's nothing wrong with having some fun. Anyway, who says you have to find this husband guy now? Who says you can't fall in love with Alfie first?'

'When fae fall in love, it tends to be for good. That's what Gran says.'

'And Alfie is in love with you.'

'But he's already let me go,' Erica murmured, half to herself. 'He's already told me to go after Rick.'

'So, why do you think he wouldn't let you go when you decided the relationship was over?'

Erica looked up again.

'What if I fall in love with Alfie and never fall out? What if I completely lose my chance with Rick?'

'Hang on. Rick? Doesn't Jess call you Ric? You'd be Ric and Rick.'

Erica squirmed in her chair.

'Yeah. Jess is already working on a theme song for us.'

Emily laughed.

'Okay. How about this.' She leaned forward again. 'What happens if you put all this thought into it and then you contact this Rick and he's not up for it? You could have just had Alfie all along?'

'You're saying I should contact Rick?'

'Hell, no,' said Emily. 'I'm saying you should do whatever your heart is telling you, and all the other mushy stuff. Ultimately, it sounds like you want Alfie. So, why not go after him with reckless abandon. See where it takes you. And then contact Rick, once you know what your heart really wants?'

Erica watched Emily for a moment. She looked down at her whisky and, after another moment of thought and decision-making, she downed the whisky in one go.

Emily whooped.

'Atta girl!'

The whisky burned down Erica's throat and into her belly, making her eyes water and sending blood rushing into her gut.

'Thanks,' she told Emily, standing.

'Anytime.' Emily grinned. 'I'll see you tomorrow, I guess. So we can sort this mess out in the woods. Use protection,' she added.

Erica nodded and said good night, letting herself

out.

She walked through the well-lit corridor as quietly as possible, down the stairs and out to reception where a stocky, tall man with brown hair curling around his ears, blue eyes and a charming smirk on his lips was reading the posters about breakfast.

'Hello, Ric,' he murmured when she stopped.

'How did you know?'

'I heard you calling to me,' said Alfie. 'At your house, on the way to the woods, inside the woods. I heard you.'

'No. No. I meant here. Now. How did you know?'

Alfie grinned and shrugged.

'All you have to do is want me there, really want it, and I'll hear it.' He approached her, holding out a hand. She took it immediately. Erica was done thinking. Follow her heart, they told her, and this was what her heart wanted. Not the man on Facebook, not yet. First, she wanted the fae.

Alfie kissed her knuckles softly before pulling her closer. She wrapped her arms around his neck and went up on tip-toes to kiss his lips. The feeling of him enveloping her, arms wrapping tightly around her waist, sent a warm thrill through her that could possibly have been the whisky.

Pulling away, Alfie produced a key card from a pocket and gave her a wink.

'Can I interest you in a night away from the bad dreams?'

Erica thought she should probably take a moment to really consider what he'd just said, what he knew. Had he been listening? How presumptuous of him to have gotten a hotel room. But she knew the whisky would wear off soon, and when it did the demon would return. The demon and her doubts.

'Yes, please,' she breathed, holding his hand tightly and letting him lead her through the hotel to their room where a large, comfortable bed waited for them. Abandoning rational thought, Erica allowed herself to succumb to Alfie's charms as he cocooned her away from the world and the horror that waited for them in the woods.

18

Jess didn't sleep. She tried to begin with. Climbing into bed with Marshall while he watched with concern plastered over his face. He'd held her tight, keeping her close and safe, but eventually he had drifted off to sleep, breathing deep, snoring lightly, and his grip had loosened. Jess hadn't moved. She'd stayed snuggled against him, feeling his warm skin against hers and trying to focus on the sensation. Anything to stop her from closing her eyes where the demon waited.

It soon became apparent that the demon was not leaving her thoughts. Terrified of what dreams lay waiting for her, Jess slid out of bed and silently left the room.

The house was full of shadows, so she turned the lights on as she went. Even though she knew Ruby wasn't in the house, she checked her daughter's bedroom, flicking on the light and leaving it on so that shadows had nowhere to hide. Bubbles followed her sleepily from room to room as Jess checked each corner, turning on lights as she made her way downstairs.

She found herself in the kitchen, in the dark so that she could see through the large patio windows into the garden.

The security light wasn't strong enough to light up the whole garden. Jess didn't like going against nature. There was the one light that Marshall had fitted and it lit up just enough to see what Bubbles was doing on those dark winter evenings. The light created more shadows which would dance as the trees and shrubs moved in the breeze, or as the dog passed. But with the light off, standing in the dark, Jess could see every inch of her garden. She stared into the plum tree growing at the back, wondering what lurked amongst the branches and leaves. Had she brought it home with her? How would she know?

A hand landed on her shoulder and Jess screamed, turning and hitting out.

'Woah, it's me! It's me.' Marshall grabbed her wrist before she could hit him. Jess looked up into his eyes and growled.

'Don't do that to me. Don't creep up on me. What were you thinking?' She snatched her wrist away and smacked him on the arm. He flinched but she guessed that was more at her tone than the force of her hit.

'I'm sorry. I'm sorry. I didn't mean to scare you. I woke up and you weren't there and I panicked. What are you doing?' Marshall rubbed his eyes, looking past her and into the garden. 'Did you see something?'

'No.' Jess sat down at the kitchen table. What would she have done if she had seen something? Got straight on the phone to Erica, that's what. She shuddered, running her hands over her face. 'I didn't think this...,' she murmured.

Marshall sat next to her, leaning close.

'What?'

'That this would happen. That it would affect me like this. I thought it would be like those shows, you know? Like our new client. You go to a hotel, spend the night, talking and using gadgets and maybe you see a ghost but it's okay because Erica's in control. We get paid and we move on. I didn't know about demons or werewolves or evil things attaching themselves to us. Erica never mentioned any of that. None of her family did.' Jess, vision blurred with tears, looked up at Marshall. 'I can't do this,' she told him, the tears coming fast. 'I can't do this to Ruby, or you. I can't do this to me.'

Marshall pulled Jess up and onto his lap, holding her tight and rocking her as she cried into his neck.

'I know it's scary. I'm scared too. But I'm not going anywhere and Ruby is safe. Erica and her family would never put you or Ruby in harm's way. You know you're part of their family, right? I see how they are with you. How they were with me when we first met. You're one of them. You said they checked nothing was attached. I think you need to trust them. That's the only way this will work.'

Jess nodded, not lifting her face. He was right. He was always right.

'Don't give up on it all yet. This isn't going to be the norm, is it? Maybe you can tell Erica that you'll only deal with the client and ghost side of things, anything else is up to her? Yeah? Sleep on it, at least. You've checked the house. Nothing's here but us.' Marshall paused to kiss her shoulder. 'Come back to bed and get some sleep. Things will feel different in the morning. Yeah?'

Again, Jess nodded. Marshall wiped away her tears as she lifted her head and she studied his face. His kind, soft, weathered face. What would she be doing if he wasn't in her life right now? Probably sat at the table with a knife in her fist going deeper into an anxiety attack. She kissed his cheek and then his lips. She kissed him again, harder.

His grip on her tightened and he searched her eyes.

'What can I do to make this easier?' he murmured, a husk in his tone that suggested he knew exactly what Jess wanted in that moment. Wiping her eyes with her thumb, Jess climbed off his lap and pulled on his arm, making him stand. Without looking back, she led him back to bed and climbed on top of the sheet.

'I need you,' she whispered. 'I just need you to be close.' She knelt up and beckoned for him. He moved over to her, hands on her hips, kissing her softly. Soft was no good, she realised, it allowed her mind to wander as her eyes closed. She pulled him closer and kissed him back hard, pulling him down onto the bed.

𝕾ℭ𝕽

They woke the next morning still entangled. Marshall freed his arm and checked the time. They'd been asleep for only a few hours. No wonder his head was pounding. He lay back and tried to remember what day it was and what his plans were. What could he cancel? All of it, he realised. There was nothing urgent to do. He'd get up, make them coffee and call the customers he was supposed to be seeing today. They'd understand. One of them, Mrs Becker, had been so thrilled that he'd found himself not just a woman but a daughter as well that she'd started paying him more, telling him to treat Ruby.

He looked over at Jess and smiled. The night's activities flashed through his mind, making him hard again. She was pretty when she slept, but that wasn't difficult. She was always pretty, even when she was terrified and sobbing into his chest. Something inside him fluttered and his erection went down. There was nothing arousing about the early part of last night. Jess had been physically shaking when Erica had dropped her home. Marshall had wanted nothing more than to tell Erica she was never to see Jess again, but he couldn't do that. It wasn't his decision to make, and he knew that if he made Jess choose, she would choose Erica. All he could do was be here for her, in whatever way she needed. And if she needed rough sex to take her mind off the night's horrors, then he was happy to help.

He ran a finger over her shoulder and down her arm, relishing her soft skin. She gave a light moan and shifted position. He took the opportunity to free himself completely and then rolled over to watch her.

He needed to be here for her today. Not only to see how she felt when she woke but because Ruby was coming home today. In a couple of hours, in fact. He wondered whether he should wake her. She might need time to process everything. Marshall didn't move. If he was honest, part of him was hoping she'd wake up in the mood for more sex. That had been the plan, to have as much of it as possible while Ruby was away. Loud, freeing sex, the kind they couldn't have when the four-year-old was under the same roof. This demon and Erica had ruined that somewhat. It wasn't the romantic few days that Marshall had planned but there was always a chance that Jess would wake up feeling better and up for making the most of the alone time they had left.

Jess's eyes opened slowly and she looked back at him.

'Good morning, beautiful,' he murmured. She smiled and stretched and then the memories from the night before seemed to crash down on her. Marshall sagged a little.

'What time is it?' she asked sleepily.

'About half seven.'

Jess rubbed her eyes and groaned.

'Rubes will be home in a couple of hours.'

'Why don't you stay in bed. Get some more sleep,' Marshall offered. Jess shook her head.

'No. No, I need to think.' She looked over at him and smiled, giving him back a tiny bit of hope. 'Thank you for last night. I don't know what I would have done without you.' She kissed him and then rolled out of bed. Marshall watched her go with a sigh, hearing the bathroom door click.

He made his way downstairs, Bubbles following him closely, and kicked the coffee machine into action before letting the dog out. Leaning his back against the kitchen counter, arms crossed against his bare chest, he looked out at the garden. The morning light filtered through the plum tree leaves, dappling the lawn. As always, his attention was drawn to the fence panel he'd fixed when he'd first met Jess, remembering seeing her through the broken slats and thinking how beautiful she was. He smiled at the memory of passing buckets of worms through to Ruby. Anything that meant he could keep talking to Jess.

He made his way back to the bedroom with two cups of coffee, Bubbles leading the way, and found Jess sitting on the bed naked. His hope reignited, he placed the cups down and sat beside her.

'How's it going?' he asked, moving her hair from her face and kissing her shoulder. She leaned into him, a hand on his thigh.

'I don't know. You're right. Things look different in the morning. But I don't know how I feel yet.' Jess looked up at him. 'Ruby will be here soon and I need to get my head straight.'

Marshall nodded, the last of his hope fading.

'Okay. I'll take Bubbles for a walk, let you think.'

Bubbles, hearing her name, jumped up, putting her front paws on the bed and shoving her large head into Marshall's lap. He ruffled her ears.

'No. Hang on.'

Marshall stopped moving and Jess ran her fingers down his chest. He knew what that meant. It was something she'd always done and something that never failed to make him hard. He waited a moment, in case he'd read the situation wrong. Jess kissed him and then kindly called Bubbles out of the room, closing the door. He hadn't read it wrong. Grinning, he pulled Jess to him and kissed her hard.

They let the coffee go cold.

෨ ෬

Jess sat at the kitchen table watching Bubbles sniffing the grass in the garden. She was on her second cup of coffee and Paul was running late. Not that she minded. It gave her more time to think, and it meant that either they were having a good time or Ruby was putting up a fight about putting her shoes on. Jess smiled. Of course she wanted Ruby to have a good time, but if that good time could coincide with Paul experiencing the reality of parenthood, all the better.

Marshall came downstairs in a fresh t-shirt and his old jeans, staring at his phone. He blew her a kiss, putting the phone to his ear and disappearing through the patio doors and into the garden with Bubbles.

Jess took a deep breath. Demon aside, life was good. Was she really going to let one terrifying night change everything? No. But the demon couldn't be ignored.

Erica hadn't responded to the message she'd sent yet, which was strange but it had been a strange night. Maybe she was still asleep.

How had she done it? Jess wondered. Had she just fallen asleep? How had she gotten through the night without the sex? Without someone to look after her? Jess was certain she wouldn't have slept at all, she would have spent the night wandering room to room, seeing demons in every shadow. Maybe Erica's mother had stayed up with her, reassuring her, talking things through with her.

Jess checked her phone again but there were no messages.

Bubbles heard Paul and Ruby before Jess did and came running through the kitchen and to the front door before she gave a bark. Marshall looked through, catching Jess's eye and she gestured that she had this. It always took him time to speak to his customers. They often wanted a chat.

Jess grabbed Bubbles' collar and opened the door. The dog leapt forward but Jess held her back.

'Bubbles!' Ruby threw herself at the dog and Bubbles licked at the girl's hands.

'Oh, I see. The dog's more important than me?'

Jess chided. Ruby looked up at her mother and nodded.

'Yes. Mummy!' Ruby threw herself into Jess's arms and Jess gripped her daughter tight, breathing her in. She smelt a little of Paul, as she always did after time away with her dad. Ruby went to go into the house but Jess stopped her. 'Marshall's on the phone. Leave him be.'

'Hey, kid.'

'Marshall!' Ruby ran full pelt at Marshall as he appeared in the kitchen doorway. He caught her and swung her up, giving her a quick hug before putting her down.

'You been good?' he asked.

She nodded.

'Yup.'

'Eaten all your vegetables?'

Ruby pulled a face but nodded.

'How did it go? Was she good?' Jess asked Paul while Ruby was distracted.

Paul nodded, staring at Marshall.

'Yeah. It was fun.' He handed over Ruby's bag and then another bag. 'Here. A birthday present.'

Jess started and blinked down at the bag before slowly taking it. She'd managed to completely forget her birthday was only a couple of days away.

'Oh. Thank you. You really didn't have to.'

'It's nothing much. Got anything planned?'

'Erm, yeah. Just a little gathering. Nothing much.'

'There's going to be cake!' Ruby shouted. Jess glanced back to her.

'Yes. Yes, there will be cake.'

'And I'm allowed to stay up.' Ruby held her chin up.

'Only if you're good between now and then.'

Ruby pouted, resisting the urge to stick out her tongue.

'You okay? You're quieter than normal,' asked Paul as Marshall started asking Ruby how school had been.

'Hmm? No. I'm okay. Just work stuff, is all.'

'Well, not long now until your birthday. You can let your hair down.'

Jess blinked up at Paul and then nodded. She didn't want to question anything, but she wasn't used to him being this nice to her.

'What are we doing today?' Ruby asked, arms around Bubbles' neck.

'Not sure yet, sweetheart,' said Jess. 'But I think you'll be spending the day with Marshall. How does that sound?'

In answer, Ruby gave a whoop of joy and ran into the kitchen and out into the garden, Bubbles following her. Marshall, smiling, said goodbye to Paul and followed the child and dog.

'So,' said Jess, turning back to Paul. 'What's going on with you?'

'What? What have I done?'

Jess struggled. She could hardly call him out on being nice to her.

'Back to normal now?' Jess changed the subject. 'You'll have her again in a couple of weeks?'

'Yeah. Okay. Have a good day,' said Paul. Jess fidgeted as Paul hesitated.

'I'll call you later,' she told him, moving to close the door. 'When work's done and we'll work out plans. Yeah?'

'Okay.'

Jess closed the door before Paul had turned

around to head back to his car. It was rude and it wasn't like her to not be polite about his life and what he and Ruby got up to, but she needed to talk to Erica and as she closed the door, her phone beeped.

Marshall was in the kitchen, sipping a cup of coffee and watching Ruby and Bubbles running around the garden.

'You sure you're okay to have her for today?' Jess asked, reading Erica's message on her phone.

'Of course. Whatever you need.'

Jess glanced up at Marshall.

'I love you,' she murmured. Marshall turned to her.

'Love you too.'

'Thank you for last night. For being what I needed. For being here for me. You know, I was thinking this morning.'

'It still is morning.' Marshall smiled as Jess wrapped her arms around him.

'Yeah. I was thinking of what I'd have done if you weren't here and it doesn't bear thinking about. Move in with me. Move in with us. Today. Now.'

Marshall laughed.

'Now? Right now?'

'Yeah.'

'While you're in the woods doing terrifying things?'

'Ruby can help you.'

Marshall laughed again, giving Jess a squeeze.

'I'm not going anywhere,' he told her, kissing her head.

'I know. But I want to make sure. I want us to be a proper family,' Jess murmured. 'And if you do want to put a ring on my finger, I just want you to know my answer will be yes.'

Marshall didn't reply, so Jess gave him another hug. 'I have to call Ric,' she told him, taking her phone and coffee into the living room.

In The Woods

The demon sat high up in the tree, listening to the footsteps and voices of humans entering the woods. With a snort, it scrambled down the trunk, peering through the leaves. It knew that voice now. While it still didn't know quite what she was, she was aligned with the witches and the fae, and she was back in the woods. She walked down the path, glancing up at the trees, her gaze just missing the demon, leading a group of humans behind her.

'We've checked down here,' said one.

'The dogs have been down here too,' said another. 'They didn't find anything.'

'Did they react at all?' asked the woman. There was a tinge of apprehension about her. The scent wasn't the sort of fear that the demon desired but there was a small hint of it there, beneath her demeanour. She kept looking up while the other humans looked down.

'Yes, but there wasn't anything there.'

'I think we need to accept that we're not going to find a body,' said another human.

'Try telling the parents that,' said the woman. She was leading them to the remains of the girl. The demon followed, leaping from tree to tree, and beneath it the woman listened.

'Squirrels,' explained one of the humans with her. She didn't respond.

'What about the markings on the tree?' she asked, turning left to go down the narrow, overgrown path that led to the body. 'Any news on who made them?'

'We've asked around. The markings are meaningless, of course, but we might have the boy who drew them. Turns out he enjoys drawing Satanic symbols. We found notebooks of them. One of our liaison officers is talking to his parents.'

'Good,' said the woman. 'Can I have his name?'

The demon hesitated and sniffed. The humans were suspicious. It peered at them curiously. They were suspicious, not of it, but of the woman.

'Thing is, we asked after you,' said one carefully. 'And no one's heard of you.'

The woman didn't miss a step. She carried on leading them through the woods.

'Any idea why that might be?' the human continued.

'Obviously you're talking to the wrong people,' said the woman, stopping. 'Here. Look. Down there, you see? A little opening and a tree trunk. People come here and light fires. See the blackened wood? There's more symbols here, on the trees. Have the dogs been around here?' The woman purposefully looked up, hands on her hips, as if simply gazing up at the canopy and sky or stretching her back. For a moment, as she gazed up, her eyes narrowed, curiosity clouding her features, and then just as quickly, it was gone.

'Yeah. We had some reactions. This is where the girl went missing. Her scent was all over this place. We've searched here a number of times.'

The demon hopped into the tree where the girl was decomposing. It stood over her, waiting for the woman to find the body. When she did, they locked eyes and stared at one another.

After a moment, the woman pointed directly at it.

'What's that?' she asked.

All of the humans looked up and the demon growled before relenting and moving away. The humans gathered, gasping, shielding their eyes and searching the branches of the tree above their heads.

Soon, there would be more. Climbing up the tree trunk to recover the corpse, but for now the demon waited and watched. A hunger grew in its belly.

This wasn't over. The woman had claimed the empty body of the girl, but she would be back and she wouldn't be alone. The witches and the fae would be with her. The trees groaned and swayed with the certainty.

It needed strength. It wasn't yet at full capacity but it was so close. Another meal, perhaps two, but they needed to be big. Foxes and birds wouldn't do the job. No, it had to be human. One of these adult humans would make a good meal, and now that they'd found the body high up in the tree, they were afraid. The demon licked its lips, tasting the fear as it spread through the air.

Yes, one of these humans. Not the woman. She would fight back, she would be troublesome. One of the others, an unsuspecting one. One who had caught sight of it when they'd looked up.

There. A man, hands by his sides, standing away from the others as they busied themselves organising the recovery of the girl's body. He was staring up the tree, not at the girl but at where the demon at been, and the terror surging from his body tasted delicious.

19

Erica was back in the small café of the Victorian cemetery, waiting for the coffees and brownies she'd ordered to be loaded onto a tray. Alfie sat outside, face up to the sunshine, eyes closed. Watching him, Erica allowed herself a smile. Why hadn't she done this earlier? This felt right. Not just right, but like she belonged. A sense of belonging to Alfie, with Alfie.

Not that she was done chasing Rick, but Rick could wait. If they were destined to find one another, the universe would introduce them. In the meantime, Erica could get used to being with Alfie.

As she carried the tray of coffee cups and brownies on plates to Alfie's table, he opened his eyes and looked to the gravel parking area.

'They're here,' he murmured. He turned his attention back to Erica, his gaze lingering, that charming smile playing on his face as his fingers caught her hand and he pressed it to his lips. Erica felt the heat of her cheeks burning, spreading down to her chest. She cleared her throat, wishing she could dislodge the redness.

'All right?' said Emily. 'Look who I found.'

Jess approached the café and table behind Emily, doing a double take at Alfie.

'Everyone okay?' she asked, giving Erica a meaningful look.

'Yup. Here. I got everyone a coffee and a brownie.' Erica avoided Jess's gaze, arranging everything on the table. Jess narrowed her eyes at her friend.

'Ooh. The perfect breakfast,' said Emily, taking a brownie.

'You haven't had breakfast yet?' asked Erica.

'I've had breakfast, second breakfast, brunch and lunch,' said Jess, taking a coffee and eyeing up a brownie. They all watched as she took one.

'Lunch? It's not even eleven yet.'

'A four-year-old will do that to you,' Jess explained, taking a big bite.

Alfie laughed, his hand finding Erica's under the table. Erica allowed it, relishing his secret touch.

'So, are we okay to talk here?' asked Emily, looking around the café. There was a family sitting inside and a couple sat at a table outside with them.

'It's safe to talk here,' said Alfie, sipping his coffee. 'When we get to the juicer stuff, we'll move on.'

'I don't know what that means, but sure. Why not.' Emily bit into her brownie.

'So, does anyone have any updates? Anyone else get no sleep last night?' Jess asked with a sigh.

Erica and Alfie exchanged a glance and a smile.

'I helped the police find the body,' said Emily quietly, taking another bite of her brownie. 'So that's sorted. And the police have found the kid that drew the symbols. I'll follow that up.'

'What are you going to do?' Erica asked.

'I mostly plan on scaring the shit out of him enough to stop him doing such stupid things. It'd be nice to find out if he knew what he was doing, though.'

'Sounds good,' said Jess. 'So, that's all the loose

ends, right?'

'Pretty much. Just the demon to deal with.' Emily glanced back to the couple sitting nearby but they were ignoring them.

'We'll get rid of the demon,' said Alfie. 'There's no need for you girls to step foot in those woods until it's done.'

Emily chewed her brownie slowly, studying him, and swallowed.

'I disagree.'

Erica pulled her hand away from Alfie's.

'I think my gran might have something to say about that.'

He studied her and shrugged.

'Fine. That's up to Eolande. I'm not one to say no to Minerva about anything, but you're not going into those woods until that demon's gone and I've checked it's gone.'

Torn, Erica prodded her brownie.

'That's sweet of you,' she said slowly. 'And I understand where you're coming from.' Alfie raised an eyebrow at her. 'But no one, not even Eolande, tells my grandmother what to do and no man, not even you, tells me what to do,' she continued gently. 'But I guess, if there's no reason for us to be in the woods and you and Eolande can handle it, then we should stay out.' She looked at Jess. 'I imagine Marshall feels the same way?'

Jess nodded.

'And I agree with you. He can't tell me what I can and can't do, but it's coming from a place of love. He'll agree if I have to go in.'

'Well, aren't I lucky I don't have a man in my life,' said Emily, taking a gulp of coffee and sitting back.

'Did you get any sleep last night?' asked Erica. Emily nodded.

'No less than usual.'

Jess shook her head.

'I ended up sat in the kitchen in the dark staring out at the garden and wishing I had one of Emily's guns.' She squirmed in her chair. 'Good thing Marshall was there. He dragged me back to bed. I wouldn't have gotten any sleep at all without him there.'

Jess and Erica stared at one another a moment.

'Did you sleep?' Jess asked carefully.

Erica's cheeks burned again.

'Yeah.'

Jess frowned.

'You didn't see demons when you closed your eyes?'

'Well, yeah.'

'I helped a little with that,' said Emily. 'She came back with me after we dropped you off and I gave her some of my finest whisky. It's how I slept. I had a lot more than you but I guess you don't drink much, huh?'

Erica hesitated.

'Yeah. That must have been it.'

Alfie stifled a laugh and Erica gritted her teeth as Jess looked between the two of them.

'So, how're you going to kill the demon?' Emily asked Alfie.

He looked her in the eye, his ever-present smile still on his lips.

'We have our ways. Better than anything you can do.'

Erica's brow creased.

'You don't know that.'

'Yes. I do,' Alfie told her. 'Because we're capable of things that you aren't. Just leave it to us. Come on. Let's go find Eolande and Minerva, they'll tell you.' He drained his coffee and stood up, waiting for Erica to join him. She looked from him to the others, drinking the last dregs in her cup and wrapping her brownie in a napkin.

'Come on, then.'

'Where're we going now?' Emily asked, gathering her stuff.

'To where the fae live,' said Erica.

Jess waited for Emily and the two followed Alfie and Erica through the cemetery, down winding paths, to the wooden door in the wall. Emily hesitated.

'Is that staff only?'

'No. But everyone assumes it is, so most people don't venture in,' Erica explained. 'The staff call it the Secret Garden. The public are allowed in, they just don't normally see it or think they can venture inside.'

'Yeah, because they think they're not allowed.' Alfie rolled his eyes. 'It has nothing to do with the fae living in the trees on the other side of this door.'

Erica looked to him.

'That's why?'

'That hadn't occurred to you?' Alfie gave her a kind smile, his eyes softening and the love on his face took her immediately back to last night.

She shrugged.

'Yeah. A few times. Never really gave it much thought though.'

Alfie laughed and opened the door, leading them through.

On the other side was a patch of grass, left to

grow long for the wildlife. In the centre of the lawn was a tree with a bench over to the left against the wall. In front of them and filling the rest of the space were tall, thin trees growing close together.

The Secret Garden was empty.

'Where are they then?' asked Emily. 'The fae?'

'He says they live in the trees, but they don't. The door to their world is between the trees. Is that right?' Erica asked Alfie. He gave a nod and then slipped between the nearest trunks and disappeared.

'Oh. Okay. Bye,' said Emily.

'Did you spend the night with him?' Jess hissed in Erica's ear. Erica's stomach flipped, her mouth drying.

'Erm.'

'Of course she did,' said Emily. 'You went straight to him after you left mine, didn't you?'

Erica chewed on the inside of her cheek.

'You had sex with him?' Jess whispered.

Erica sighed and gazed at the trees, checking there was no one there.

'Yes,' she said. Jess widened her eyes and opened her arms. 'Why? Because I wanted to, Jess. Because I like him. Because we nearly died in those woods, that damn demon nearly touched me and I just needed someone last night.'

'You don't have to explain yourself,' said Emily. 'I would have done the same. Hell, she did do the same.' She gestured at Jess. 'You're telling me you didn't spend the night naked with that hunk of a man in your house?'

Jess opened and closed her mouth.

'That's different. We're in a relationship. We're moving in together.'

'Yes! You mentioned that last night, as if

everyone already knew,' Erica was aware she had raised her voice. She took a moment to breathe before continuing quietly, 'When did that happen?'

Jess shrugged.

'I know it hasn't been long but it feels like it has. It feels like he's always been there, like I've known him all my life, and he wants to move in and I want him to move in.'

'Look at you guys. Two ghost hunters playing happy families.' Emily grinned.

'She's not playing happy families. She's shacking up with a fae. A powerful, dangerous, scary fae,' Jess accused.

'He's not dangerous,' said Erica. 'And can we stop this now, please?'

'I really don't think you guys realise how lucky you are,' said Emily. 'Most people who do what we do can't have healthy relationships, never mind a family. I can't do that,' she told Jess. 'I'm too screwed up. And sleeping with someone who's not human, well, that comes with the job. But you know that. Your gran knows that. And there's nothing wrong with it,' she added to Erica.

Erica nodded.

'Thank you. It's my life and I can sleep with who I like.'

'Who are you sleeping with?'

The three women turned to find Erica's mother closing the door to the Secret Garden behind her.

'Shit,' murmured Emily.

'Sorry, I shouldn't ask. It's none of my business,' said Esther, studying her daughter. 'It's Alfie, isn't it?'

Erica stared at her mother and just as she opened her mouth to reply, Eolande, Minerva and Alfie appeared from the trees.

Alfie hesitated when he saw Esther.

'Mrs Murray,' h e said, nodding to her. She glared at him and then gave her daughter a look. Erica avoided her, trying to catch Alfie's eye.

Please don't do anything stupid, she willed. Please just be normal.

Alfie, whether he understood her look or not, gave her a subtle wink.

'Esther,' said Minerva. 'I thought you might change your mind. Thanks for coming.'

'My mother and my daughter want to go up against a demon. Of course I'm here. I brought the things you wanted. What can I do?' Esther handed her bag to Minerva who took it and checked the contents.

'Fabulous,' she declared, letting Eolande see inside. The fae approved with a nod.

'What's in the bag?' asked Emily.

'You'll see. Shall we get started?'

20

Minerva and Esther sat on the bench with the others forming a circle from either side, sitting where the grass had been cut short. Eolande sat beside Minerva on the grass, her legs crossed. Alfie sat beside Erica, his knees bent, one hand resting a little too close to her. Jess had allowed Erica to position her between herself and her mother and much to Erica's delight, Emily had then sat beside Jess.

'So, we're all going in together, right?' Emily asked. 'I don't want to be sat in the mud for no good reason.'

'It is not muddy,' Eolande told her.

'Really? 'Cause my arse is feeling damp.'

Eolande and Emily had a short stare off before Minerva brought the conversation back.

'It's been a long time since I've faced a demon and a long time since the fae here have dealt with a demon.'

'It must be removed from the woods. The trees are in pain, the animals are too afraid to go about their lives. The best method is to either kill the demon or remove it from this plane, otherwise it will simply move on and cause more pain,' said Eolande.

'Killing it sounds good,' Jess agreed. She wanted it gone and unable to come back.

'It may be easier to send it back where it came

from,' Minerva told her. 'We've spent much of the night researching how to send this particular demon back, or how to kill it.'

'Sending it back where it came from would certainly be easier. It seems to have been summoned close to the gateway. We can open the gateway and send it back through,' Eolande explained.

'Gateway?' Erica glanced at Alfie.

'Those two trees that meet at the top. You remember? I told you not to go near them so you went in the dead of night, straight to them and faced off with a demon.'

'What? I didn't—'

'The girl's body was in a tree like that,' Emily mused.

Erica looked between them.

'The girl's body was in the trees that meet at the top?'

'Yeah. I thought it was different. Never seen anything like it, but I don't frequent woods as often as you'd think I would.' Emily shrugged.

'That's a gateway?' Erica looked back to Alfie who nodded.

'To another plane, where this demon came from. Where a lot of demons are still residing. That's why you shouldn't walk between them. We have no idea if the gateway is open or closed. We'll have to ensure it's closed once the demon is gone,' Alfie added to Eolande. 'I didn't know there was a gateway in those woods. I wonder how long it's been there.'

'That's for another time,' Eolande told him. 'An oversight, yes, but gateways are not necessary for the summoning of demons. They merely help things along. We'll close it once we're done. First, we need to send this creature back through it. It's a specific type of demon that thrives among the forests.'

'It's old. Ancient. It probably came here when the first humans were hunting among the trees,' Minerva added.

'A lot of the ancient forest spirits were protective,' continued Eolande. 'They looked after the trees and cared for the animals that lived among them.'

'So, like you,' Erica murmured.

Alfie grinned.

'Yeah. Like us.'

Eolande nodded.

'The fae, or what would become the fae, were among those spirits, yes.'

'So, what, the demon came here from hell? It can go back and forth?'

'Hell's existence is arguable,' said Minerva.

'But it's likely that places like it exist, surely?' Esther asked.

'Exactly.'

'So it's old. That means it's strong,' Emily said, hugging her knees to her chest and rocking back.

'It'll take time to get to its full strength. The more it feeds, the stronger it will become,' Eolande explained.

'That's why you girls found the dead animals to begin with. It was building its strength,' Minerva told Jess and Erica.

'Makes sense,' said Jess.

'And now it's eating humans,' Erica murmured.

'And it will continue to eat humans from now on, is our guess.' Minerva nodded.

'Shit. There are police officers still in those woods. I showed them where that girl's body was. They have a whole heap of new evidence now. And the demon was there,' Emily told them. 'It was watching us. It stood over the girl's body when I pointed it out, tried to stare me down. Like I've never had to stare down a monster. But I bet some of the officers saw it too, even if they don't know what they saw.'

'It won't attack in broad daylight, will it?' Esther looked from Minerva to Eolande.

'Actually, I think it might. It challenged me,' said Emily. 'The way it looked at me. I could hear it following us, listening to us.'

'It's threatened by us,' Minerva told them. 'It knows there are fae in the woods now and that they're going to come for it.'

'Not to mention witches,' said Alfie, flashing Erica a smile.

Jess watched the two of them. That smile of Alfie's was just a touch more happy and the rosy heat on Erica's cheeks was just a touch warmer. She ground her teeth. Of course she wanted Erica to be happy, but why couldn't she be happy finding a handsome police officer to settle down with? Why did she have to choose a fae? Alfie could be trusted, she knew that. He obviously loved Erica, he always had done, but what would happen when she decided she wanted the detective instead? What would happen when she changed her mind?

Alfie's gaze lingered on Erica the way that Marshall's lingered on Jess. Maybe this wasn't that bad, she realised. Maybe Erica had changed her mind about the detective. Jess turned her attention to Minerva and Eolande and spotted the same look hidden in Eolande's eyes as she listened to Minerva speak.

There was a chance that falling in love with fae ran in the family. It was in Erica's blood.

Jess studied Esther. The one woman in the family who had resisted the fae. There was certainly no denying the glares she was giving Alfie. Alfie acted as if he didn't see them, but how could he not?

Jess tried to concentrate on the demon. That was the immediate problem. The trouble with fae relationships could be tackled once the demon was dead or gone.

'The point is,' said Minerva. 'It's likely to act rashly. It'll need to feed and it doesn't know when we're coming.'

A silence settled over the group.

'We need to go in now and hard,' said Emily eventually, shifting her position with a grimace. 'So, how do we kill it or whatever?'

'Ritual and magic brought it into this world and ritual and magic can send it back,' said Minerva. 'The problem is that it likely wanted to come into this world to feed and grow strong. It's not going to want to go back. Which is why it was easy for whoever allowed the thing into our world but it'll be hard for us to send it away.'

'What do you need for the ritual?' asked Emily. Her tone had changed, along with her expression. She was all business. Jess watched, fascinated. This was what she needed to learn how to do. How to view these things as business rather than personal. How to deal with them head on rather than letting her emotions and fear get in the way. But then, Emily didn't have a little girl waiting at home for her. Did she have anyone waiting at home for her? Not by the sounds of it, but that didn't mean there was no one at all.

'Esther's brought everything I need,' said Minerva, gesturing to the bag Esther had handed her. 'Everything else Eolande has.'

'So...you don't need us?' Jess asked, looking between the two.

'Surely only the fae need to go into the woods,' said Esther, glancing at Alfie. 'There's no need for anyone else to go in. You've handled demons before, you can handle this one. Right?'

'If there are humans in there, someone will need to get them out,' said Eolande.

'And it depends if the demon has fed again or not. If it's stronger, we might need more power,' Alfie conceded with a sigh.

'There are more than two of you back there,' said Esther, gesturing to the trees with her head. 'I can feel them watching us.'

The hair on the back of Jess's neck stood up and she looked past the others to the trees beyond. For a moment, she imagined seeing two bright eyes staring back. Then she blinked and was back in the quiet of the Secret Garden. Somewhere, a robin was singing.

'Alfie and I will go,' Eolande declared. 'Minerva, Erica and Esther, it would be helpful if you could join us.'

Jess breathed slowly, full of relief at not being asked and once again filled with a sense of helplessness.

'What can we do?' she asked.

Eolande looked from her to Emily.

'Nothing.'

Jess sagged. At least that meant she could go home to Marshall and Ruby. Maybe they could go to Marshall's flat and help him pack his things. No, Ruby would be a nightmare in that situation. Jess would end up going home and sitting with them, worrying and fretting about Erica until her phone rang with the outcome.

'Oh, come on. I haven't stayed here all this time just to be left out at the last minute,' said Emily. 'I'm useful. I'm experienced. Use me.'

Eolande studied her.

'It might be good to have more hands,' Minerva murmured to her. Eolande looked Emily up and down.

'I suppose. If you and Jess protect whatever humans are in the woods, Esther and Erica can help us with the ritual.'

Alfie cleared his throat.

'Except that I don't want Erica in those woods.'

Erica and Esther both shot Alfie a look and Jess caught herself watching Esther instead of Erica. The woman's features softened. If she came around to Alfie, then maybe Jess could too.

Alfie turned his attention to Esther.

'Yes, I love your daughter. I always have, since the moment I saw her in your belly and saw who she would be. I know you don't approve, but it is what it is.' He turned to Eolande. 'And I won't have her in those woods.'

Erica looked between the fae.

'Don't I get a say in this?'

'No, you don't,' said her mother. 'For the first and maybe the last time, I agree with Alfie.'

Jess half expected Alfie to take Erica's hand and it was possible he considered it as his fingers twitched, but he held back. Neither of them gave any sign of the intimacy between them.

Erica sighed.

'I'm sick of having this argument,' she murmured. 'You said I could go into the woods if you were there and you're going to be there,' she told Alfie.

'Yes, but your mother wants you safe too.'

Jess smiled. So that was his game. He was trying to win Esther over.

'We would keep her safe, Esther,' Minerva argued.

'And on that note, I'm not happy about you going either,' Esther told her mother. Minerva looked down her nose at her daughter. 'But I know that there's no arguing with you.'

Erica held up her hands.

'But there's arguing with me?'

'Yes.'

Erica sat back and looked to Jess for help but Jess simply smiled at her and gave a slight shrug. It was nothing to do with her.

'Enough!' cried Eolande. 'This is getting us nowhere. Alfie and I will go into the woods with Minerva and at least one other witch. It is up to you whether that is Erica or Esther, but we must have two witches. These two will come along as our assistants and to help any humans out of the woods.' Eolande gestured to Emily and Jess. Emily raised her eyebrows and shot Jess a look.

Don't, thought Jess. Don't argue with her.

'Assistants,' Emily mumbled under her breath.

'Well, that's sorted,' said Minerva before Esther could argue. 'Now, who's going with who? How many cars do we have?'

'We're going now?' said Esther, leaning back on the bench.

'When do you propose we go?' her mother asked. 'When it's dark? When someone else has been killed?'

'I know, I know. Now just seems very...immediate.'

'That's the point.' Minerva clapped her hands. 'Do you have your car, Ric?'

'Yup.'

'Excellent. And we have Esther's and...' She looked at Emily and Jess.

'I have mine,' said Jess, glancing at Esther. If they were going now, she needed to know who was staying behind.

'Excellent. And you have your tiny car?' Minerva asked Emily.

'Sure do.'

Erica and Esther were watching each other.

'I don't want you there,' Esther said gently, just to her daughter. 'If you get hurt, or killed...'

'I'll be with Gran and Eolande and Alfie. I'll be fine,' Erica murmured.

Esther shook her head.

Alfie sighed.

'Fine. You can come but only if you stay with me at all times,' he told Erica. 'And I'll protect her with my life,' he added to Esther.

Esther searched Erica's eyes and then gave a nod, her eyes wet.

'I suppose I don't have much of a choice.'

'In that case,' said Jess, unable to hold the question in any longer. 'Could I ask a huge favour?' Esther waited for her to continue. 'Could you look after Marshall and Ruby and Bubbles? I don't want them just at home waiting for me alone. If you know what I mean.'

Esther smiled a smile so warm that Jess immediately relaxed.

'Of course. They're always welcome.'

Relief washed over Jess and came out as a laugh.

'Thank you,' she managed.

'And you.' Esther turned on Alfie. 'I don't like you but I know you have genuine feelings for my daughter and it would appear she feels the same. I'm not going to say I'm happy about that, because I'm not. She is under your protection in those woods. If anything, and I mean *anything*, happens to her I will hunt you down and make you pay.'

Jess expected Alfie to laugh that off. What possible threat could Esther be to him? But instead he remained serious. He bowed his head, placing a hand over his heart.

'I swear to you, Esther Murray, daughter of Minerva Warner, you have my word and honour that I will protect Erica with my heart and my life.'

Jess snapped to look at Erica. Marshall had said some sweet things to her but never anything like that. Erica was staring at Alfie, as well she may, a smile blooming. She reached out and took his hand.

'Oh. Well. That's a turn up for the books.' Minerva grinned, breaking the mood. 'Fantastic. Let's go, shall we?'

Emily

Assistant, indeed. I am no one's assistant.

Damn fae.

Although, if I'm honest, I will admit it's nice working in a team again. It's been far too long. No, wait. I actually don't think I've ever worked in a team this large. It's usually just me and someone else, if there ever is a someone else. For so long, it's just been me.

Still, fancy calling me an assistant. Just because I'm not a witch or a fae.

Fancy calling Jess an assistant too.

She's so much more. I'm so much more. We can bring things to this that those witches and fae can't.

Admittedly, and I want to make this clear, I'm not angry with the witches. I'm actually a little jealous. Three women all from the same family having little family disputes and arguments. Oh, the drama!

Erica's shacked up with Alfie, which I could see coming a mile off, and her mother's not happy but her grandmother seems practically giddy about it. I imagine because she's shacked up with a fae herself.

I wonder why Erica's mother is so against it. Is it just because he's a fae? Is it just because she's trying to protect her daughter?

Whatever. Maybe I'll get a chance to ask Erica,

if we all make it through this. I kind of hope for Alfie's sake that Erica makes it through without a scratch. Her mother seems harmless enough but then people say that about me.

I need to make a note of this cemetery, though. It's Victorian and it's beautiful. So unexpected. Nature has truly taken over and there's a damn café here. It's a tourist destination or a community venue, or whatever, and I bloody love it.

You can feel the ghosts too. There must be so many. I wonder how many were listening to us. Do ghosts like the fae? Do they get on?

No wonder the fae like it here, too. And the witches. But then the witches would like it here. The birds, the trees, the ghosts. Not to mention the brownies. If I was local, I'd spend so much time here, just for the coffee and brownies.

The ghosts might put me off. I can feel them glaring at me, like they see through me, know what I am. But actually, it isn't quite so threatening with three witches here. I actually experimented when we were all walking back to the car. I felt the ghosts gathering closer so I stepped up to Erica, just to be near her, and the ghosts backed off.

There's power in befriending witches.

I'll keep a note of this place, make sure I visit again next time I'm down this way.

For now, though, we're off to slay a demon. Or send it back where it came from, or something.

And I'm the sodding assistant.

Assistant, my arse.

21

Erica drove with Alfie to her house first. Minerva said they had everything they needed but as a group they had too many cars. Emily was meeting them there and Jess was leaving her car at Erica's, as soon as she got off the phone to Marshall.

By the looks of it, Marshall hadn't been keen on the idea. Jess had flinched and grimaced her way through the conversation. That was love, Erica thought. If Paul had put up that argument all those years ago, Jess would have given him a piece of her mind or ignored him completely. She didn't want to upset Marshall.

Erica and Alfie drove in silence to begin with, until they'd gone a fair distance from the cemetery and her mother's car in front, with Esther, Minerva and Eolande, had vanished thanks to a red light splitting them up.

'So, you're going to protect me with your heart and your life, huh?' Erica broke the silence, glancing at Alfie out of the corner of her eye.

He grinned.

'I meant it,' he told her. 'I'm as happy about you going into those woods as your mother. If I can do anything that makes both you and her happy, I'll count that as a win.'

'You have one night of sex and suddenly you're having to work to make the womenfolk happy.'

Erica shook her head, feeling Alfie watching her as she kept her eyes on the road.

'I've been trying to make your mother happy ever since I screwed up,' Alfie told her softly. 'I knew she'd keep you from me. Nothing's worked though. Maybe this will.'

Erica frowned.

'You haven't been doing anything. I hadn't even heard of you until a couple of months ago. What have you been doing to try and make mum happy and like you?'

'Staying away from her. What else is there? I don't think a bunch of flowers would do it.'

Erica laughed.

'And what about you?' she asked after a pause, glancing at him again. Even out of the corner of her eye, he was handsome in a rugged, country way. 'What makes you happy?'

'You do,' Alfie told her. She caught him smiling to himself.

'You mean, last night did?'

'No. Just you.'

Erica gripped the steering wheel and tried to hold off the grin.

'We are going to do that again, though, yes? Spend more nights together? Don't tell me that was it.'

'Oh, I think there'll be a lot more of that,' Erica murmured.

At Erica's family home, Esther sat Erica's father down and explained the situation and what was going to happen. Alfie hid behind Erica, stroking the older golden Labrador, as Erica's father's heavy stare found him. Erica watched, bemused. It had never occurred to her that she would get into her thirties and still have the problem of her parents not liking her boyfriends.

Jess fretted by the front door and, tired of fighting the glaring, Alfie succumbed and joined her on the door step. Erica made sure she had everything she needed and followed him, breathing in the fresh air.

Jess and Alfie stopped talking as she approached them.

'You don't have to stop talking about me just because I'm here,' she told them.

'Cor, the ego on you,' tutted Jess, giving her friend a smile. 'Hey, remember when we were just looking for ghosts?'

Erica sighed and crossed her arms.

'It's been a long two months, hasn't it.'

Jess nodded and straightened as a van pulled into the driveway.

'I'm not sure I want to do this again, Ric,' she said gently. 'Ghosts are one thing but this?'

'I know, I know. Never again.'

Erica and Alfie watched as Jess went to the van's passenger door and gave Ruby a hug. Bubbles bounded out and ran straight past Erica and Alfie, into the house.

'He's been here before,' said Alfie, watching the dog go.

'She and yes. Mum and Dad keep threatening to steal her.'

Erica pulled Alfie back into the house as Marshall got out of the van. He needed some space with Jess. Erica led Alfie back to the kitchen where the others were waiting.

'Marshall and Ruby are here. In case Bubbles

hadn't told you.'

Bubbles was moving from one person to the next, tail wagging as the Murray's own black Labrador puppy bounded around her. Emily stood in the corner, leaning back against a worktop, arms crossed against her chest. Her expression lightened as Bubbles said hello to her. When the puppy reached Erica's father, she leapt up placing her large front paws on his lap.

'Good. I'll get them settled.' Esther pushed past Erica, giving Alfie a look, and went to greet her guests.

'Are we ready then?' said Minerva. 'I think it's time to get this done.'

'Give Jess a moment,' Erica told her.

'Fine. Well, she's with Emily anyway. So, we should all get going.' Without waiting for an answer, Minerva led Eolande through the house and out onto the driveway where Erica's Mini waited.

'Everything okay?' Erica asked Emily. She could tell it wasn't.

'Yeah. No. It's fine. Family dynamics, huh? Tell Jess I'm waiting in the car for her, whenever she's ready.'

'Will do.'

'I'll go with Minerva and Eolande,' Alfie whispered to her, pausing to kiss her cheek quickly.

Blushing, Erica avoided eye contact with her father and went to find Jess.

Esther was making a fuss of Ruby, pulling out a box of colouring pens, pencils and paper and leading the way back to the kitchen and the large dining table.

'Where's Jess?'

'I'm here.' Jess appeared with Marshall in tow.

Her eyes were red but she seemed to have gathered herself. 'Ready when you are.'

Erica gave her a nod.

'Emily's waiting in her car for you. And, erm, the others are waiting for me,' she told her mother.

Esther looked from Ruby to Erica and then gathered her daughter in her arms.

'Come back to me. Come back alive and in one piece. And, I can't believe I'm saying this, stay close to Alfie. And Gran. And Eolande. And look after Jess. Okay?'

'Okay. To all of those things.'

Erica kissed her mother and then went to get the same lecture from her father.

It was time to go find the demon.

They met in silence by the woods, where Erica and Jess had first met Emily, and followed Minerva to the tree line, leaving the two Minis parked one behind the other on the road.

'It'll know we're here,' Minerva whispered, turning to face the group. 'It'll attack if it spots a chance, so let's not give it a chance until we're ready. Keep your eyes peeled. Emily and Jess, I want you both in the middle.'

Emily's features darkened and Erica winced inside. Still, Emily didn't argue, sticking close to Jess who was already looking up and breathing hard, clutching the bag of Minerva's things to her chest.

'Where are the police?' Erica asked. 'They found the body this morning. Shouldn't this place be crawling with them?'

No one had an answer for that.

'I guess we'll find out. Everyone know what

they're doing? Ready?' Minerva asked.

Erica, Jess and Emily nodded. Beside her, Alfie took Erica's hand and squeezed.

'Stay close,' he murmured.

They entered the woods, Eolande leading the way, her fingers trailing on the tree trunks as she passed.

Erica looked above them as they walked. Alfie still had her hand and walked in front, leading her along. She couldn't see anything. Only the sunlight through the leaves which rustled in the breeze, and glimpses of the blue sky patched with white clouds.

Where was it?

'Can you see it?' she whispered.

'No,' murmured Jess, in front of Alfie.

'It's not here,' said Alfie in a normal voice. Eolande stopped and looked back.

'It's here,' she told them. 'It's just not with us.' She looked around, searching between the trees.

Emily pulled out her revolver.

'Well, if it's not here, that means it's elsewhere. And what's more important than the people trying to kill it? Food.'

'Put that thing away,' Minerva demanded.

'Look. You do things your way but I have my own way. And my way works pretty damn well,' Emily hissed. 'The bullets in this gun are only for that thing and only if needed. I don't waste my bullets. I know what I'm doing. You want me to respect your ways, you have to respect mine.'

It had been a long time since anyone had spoken to Minerva like that. Anyone other than Eolande, that is. Erica held her breath, waiting for her grandmother's reaction.

'You shoot no one but that demon,' she told

Emily in a tone so serious and low that it made Erica quiver, sending her straight back to her childhood when her grandmother had chastised her for stepping on the flowers or being rude to a spirit. Erica blinked. She'd spent so long blocking out the memories of the spirits inside her grandmother's old house that sometimes they took her by surprise.

Emily mumbled something under her breath as Minerva turned back to Eolande.

'What do we do now? We need to find it.'

'There was just the one police car in the car park,' said Emily. 'Did anyone else notice? There can't be much of a presence. Maybe that's where it is. Watching them. Waiting for them to get close enough.'

'No. It would be here, with us, by now,' said Eolande. 'Why would it wait?'

'Then it's hunting something else. Or it's feeding,' said Emily.

'You don't know that.'

Emily sighed.

'Yeah. What the hell do I know about hunting predators?'

Minerva didn't have a response for that. She looked back to Erica who shrugged. Emily had a point.

'We shall see where it is,' said Eolande. She folded her hands together and bowed her head. When she parted her hands, a ball of light floated before her. 'Find the demon,' she told it. The ball of light seemed to think for a moment and then it moved past Eolande and down the path.

'What the hell?' breathed Emily.

'A will o' the wisp,' Minerva told them, beaming.

They followed the wisp a short way as it bathed the brambles and trees around it with a soft blue glow. It was almost comforting, if not for the fact that it was leading them to the demon.

As Erica strained to see and hear anything out of the ordinary, voices found her. The trees, she realised, were whispering to one another.

The witches are here. The fae are here. We are saved.

The words were passed along, from tree to tree, animal to animal, as the crows landed on a branch above them, peering down to watch them walk. Erica looked up at them, wondering how she could talk back to them.

A loud scream sounded through the woods. The wisp faded away. Erica tightened her grip on Alfie, her heart pounding hard against her ribs, wishing she could do the same as the wisp.

'This way.' Emily overtook Minerva and Eolande and ran off down the path. Erica went to follow but Alfie held her back until Eolande nodded at him.

'Go.'

Erica, Jess and Alfie followed Emily, with Eolande and Minerva taking up the rear as fast as Minerva could go, which was fast for a woman of eighty-nine—something she wasn't afraid to tell people.

Alfie still had hold of Erica's hand which made it hard to run without colliding with trees and brambles. She yanked her wrist and pulled herself free. He glanced back to her and then, deciding that she was okay, continued to run after Emily.

They found her in the small clearing where the girl's body had been found, in front of the trees that met at the top forming the gateway to other worlds. It was hard to fit so many people into the clearing, especially as it was already crowded. Erica counted five teenagers, three boys and two girls, one of whom was in the process of running away. Then there were four. The scream had come from one of the boys, standing where a fire had once been. He backed up against Alfie, jumped and turned to face the fae. He blinked up at him, trying to decide in his panic if Alfie was friend or foe.

One boy stood near the tree where the girl had been found. While his chest heaved, his face remained calm as he looked up into the red eyes of the demon standing over him.

'You took her from me,' he whispered, tears falling down his cheeks. 'Either leave me alone or take me too.'

The creature reached out a long arm and claws to the boy and snatched at his wrist. The boy didn't fight back.

'This isn't real,' he whispered.

Erica caught her breath.

'Do something!' screamed the remaining girl, backing away. 'Help!'

There was a whistle, low and fast, and then the sound of a gunshot.

22

The first silver bullet from Emily's revolver entered the demon's chest and the woods seemed to pause and wait. The teenagers fell silent, the boy falling back as the demon released him. Erica and Jess waited and Alfie squared up to the demon. Emily lowered her weapon and the demon looked down at itself, then back up at Emily and made a noise that Jess could only describe as a breathy laugh.

Emily aimed and fired again, and this time the bullet hit the demon between the eyes.

Jess forgot herself for a moment, raising her eyebrows. What a shot. Emily really did know what she was doing.

Again, the woods seemed to hold its breath.

They all watched as the demon, clenching its red eyes shut, pushed the bullet from its skull, through the bone and flesh. The bullet dropped to the soft woodland floor and this time the demon didn't laugh. It growled. The sound sent a rumble through the ground and Jess couldn't catch her breath.

She ended up stepping closer to Erica and Alfie, and Alfie grabbed her before she toppled. Putting an arm around her, holding her up.

'Can you run?' he whispered.

'I don't know.'

Minerva and Eolande were behind them, Eolande towering over the crowd as she pushed through, placing herself between them and the demon.

'You do not belong here,' said Eolande. 'Do you know what I am?'

The demon hissed at her and stood tall, shifting so that it faced only her.

Minerva pulled on Jess, taking the bag from her.

'Get the kids out of here,' she told her. 'You and Emily. Quick.'

Jess didn't tell her legs to move, but perhaps they didn't need telling. She grabbed Emily and then moved around to the side to try and gather the teenagers.

'It killed her,' said the boy, still gasping for breath, his skin pale.

'We need to get you out,' said Jess in her best mothering voice. 'Out. Now.'

One of the boys turned and ran. Apparently, he just needed permission to go, or perhaps direction. But the remaining two boys and girl stayed put.

'My ancestors forced you away centuries ago,' Eolande told the demon. 'Now, I will do the same.'

The demon laughed, a choking hiss that bounced around the trees.

'Your ancestors are dead, fae-ling,' came the demon's voice. Just the sound was enough to put pressure on Jess's bladder, and the sight of the creature's mouth moving brought bile up into her throat. 'You are too weak. I am stronger now.'

Eolande actually smiled.

'Strong, yes, but not strong enough, and I am not alone. You came into our world and that was a mistake. Now, you will go back where you came from.'

'I was invited into this world,' said the demon,

its eyes shifting to the teenagers. 'By one of the humans. You have no power to make me leave.'

'We're human,' shouted Minerva. 'And we have the power.'

The demon looked at her, then at Erica and finally at Jess and Emily. Jess's mind went blank as the demon's eyes locked onto hers, and then her chest became tight. She couldn't breathe. Stumbling back a step, reaching out for Emily, Jess tried to force in a breath.

'Pathetic, weak humans,' the demon spat.

'Release her!' cried Minerva.

Something hit the demon then and Eolande and Minerva both glanced at Alfie who had seemingly only waved a hand. The demon stepped back and immediately the pressure was relieved from Jess's chest. She sucked in a large lungful of air, a hand over her heart.

'I think we should go,' she murmured.

Emily's hand was on her arm.

'Come on. Let's get you out of here,' she said to the teenagers.

'No one is leaving,' declared the demon. 'I will devour you all.'

Jess, tears in her eyes, glared at the creature. She turned, grabbed the nearest teenager who happened to be one of the boys, and yanked him away into what felt like a brick wall.

The boy fell back and Jess held her face. There was blood on her fingers.

'You may not leave,' the demon repeated.

'Well. Shit,' muttered Emily, looking at Jess's nose.

'I call upon you, demon!' cried Minerva. She stood beside Eolande now, pulling sage from her bag which she lit with a lighter from her pocket. The demon hissed. 'To tell me your name.'

The demon seemed unsure for a moment.

'Your name!' Minerva screeched. 'Speak your name.'

The demon twisted and growled as the burning sage reached it.

'Malarbor,' it groaned.

'Demon Malarbor,' said Minerva, handing the sage to Erica and taking a crystal from her bag, which she held out. 'You do not belong here. You are not welcome here. Go back to where you came from.'

Malarbor snarled and laughed, although this time it sounded painful. Then, with sudden, jerking movements, it swiped out at Erica.

Alfie stepped forward and a bright light from his hands pushed the demon back. Malarbor cried out.

'You do not belong here, demon Malarbor. You are not welcome here. Go back to where you came from,' Minerva chanted, passing the crystal to Erica. Erica held both the sage and crystal up high.

Jess felt for the barrier that had given her a bloody nose. It was weakening. Not enough for them to push through, but whatever Minerva was doing, it was working. Emily had let go of her and now gripped the clothes of the two teenage boys, ready to pull them through.

'You do not belong here. You are not welcome here. Go back to where you came from.'

Minerva pulled from the bag an old glass bottle with a clear liquid inside. Jess only glanced at it. There wasn't the time or the space to wonder what the liquid was. Minerva showed the bottle to the demon who gave a hiss and readied to pounce on her.

Eolande spoke softly, opening her palms and the demon writhed, falling back.

'I have given you enough opportunity to go, demon. You leave me with no choice. Regna terrae, cantata Deo, psallite Cernunnos.'

The demon screamed and Jess automatically put her hands on her ears. It didn't stop her hearing the horrific noise, a strange twisted scream as if there were two voices, one low and one high, being tortured together. It was almost as if Jess could feel her brain recording the sound. It would be the thing to wake her up, drenched in sweat, for nights to come. The thing that would haunt her at her lowest moments. The thing she would hear during the darkness when her and Erica were working a job and trying to speak to the kindest and gentlest of spirits. Whenever the shadows would creep up, whenever Jess would feel the doubt creep in, there would be that noise.

There was no more space for fear inside Jess and just like that, her stomach settled and her legs grew stronger. She could run now, if only the demon would let them. She could fight now, if only she were any match.

This creature had hurt so many and in that moment, a second of time although it felt much longer, Jess decided that she would not be among them. Not anymore. This demon could not hurt her. It would not hurt her.

She watched Erica, her friend standing in front of the creature, helping her grandmother, and wished she could do more.

Behind her, the boy murmured, talking to himself but Jess couldn't make out the words.

'Regna terrae, cantata Dea psallite Aradia,' Minerva continued. Jess tuned it out, which was easy enough when she didn't understand a word of it, and the demon continued to roar and hiss as she spoke. With every word, it seemed to anger more until the trees around them began to quiver and the ground beneath them tremble.

'Protect her!' cried Eolande as the demon lashed out. 'She must finish the incantation.'

Alfie stepped forward as Eolande fell back, exhausted. The scent of sage filled Jess's nose. Still, the invisible wall did not give.

As the demon wretched and screamed, Emily pulled the three teenagers close and Jess stepped between them and the battle. All five crouched low, Emily keeping one hand and some weight on the invisible wall.

'As soon as we can, we run,' she told them. 'You hear me? You can't do any good here.'

'I couldn't stop seeing it,' the boy murmured. He was closest to Jess and she turned to study him. Anything to avoid looking at the demon.

'In your dreams?'

The boy nodded.

'In my room, by my bed. I saw it taking her, over and over. Pulling her away.' He clenched his eyes shut.

Jess swallowed hard.

'It'll be over soon. He won't be able to hurt anyone else. Don't you worry.'

'Why is this happening?' the boy whispered.

Jess wanted to give him an answer, so she did the best she could.

'I don't know,' she told him. 'I'm sorry.' She held onto him, putting her arm around his shoulders and hugging him while keeping herself between him and the demon.

'Omnis fallaciae, libera nos, dominates,' Minerva shouted as the creature roared and was thrown back again by Alfie.

Minerva didn't stop, she didn't hesitate. It was as if she couldn't hear the screams.

In The Woods

It remembered once, a long time ago, many centuries before these witches were born, being stabbed through the stomach with a silver blade. Those humans had been as foolish as the woman who had shot two silver bullets into it. Silver did nothing but sting. The feel of the blade slicing through its flesh was a pinch compared to the agony of the witch's spell.

Each word was pain, tearing at a new part of it. From its claws and eyes to its legs and arms to its heart and liver. It roared and screamed but nothing seemed to ease the torture, and each time it reached towards the witch to cease her chanting, the fae would push it back.

Alone, the fae were too weak and the witches too ignorant. Together they were strong but not strong enough. It was determined. They would not be strong enough to send it back.

It didn't want to go back.

Back to the silence and monotony and boredom.

It hadn't asked for the door to open, for the light to enter its life. It hadn't asked to come here, but it had been invited. The invitation of new sensations. Sensations it had long forgotten.

Here was colour, filled with new noises and smells and tastes. It wanted more. It hadn't had nearly enough of the fear of humans. It wanted to be satiated. To be satisfied. To be filled.

It lent its head back to the sky and screamed in frustration.

This wasn't the first time this had happened. It knew those words, it knew their order. If it could just make the witch miss one word, if it could just close her mouth, remove her tongue, even just a swipe to the head to make her falter, the spell would be undone.

The pain would stop.

It would be able to stay and feed and rejoice in the terror it could bring to the humans and animals in this wood.

It could go beyond the wood. It just needed one more meal. Maybe two. Just a little more strength.

It howled as the fae pushed it back yet again. Every step forward was rewarded with two steps back, and each step was agony.

Last time it had been too weak. It hadn't fed quick enough and the fae had pushed it back before it had a chance to realise what a lush world this was. It hadn't known what it had.

This time it was stronger.

It pushed forward.

Witches and fae would not get the better of it. It was older now and filled with the fear and blood of humans. It had tasted this world and it was not going back.

23

Erica growled with the effort of keeping the sage and crystal aloft as the demon pawed the ground, hissing and spitting.

'Form a circle!' Eolande yelled as Alfie was forced back a step. 'Quickly now.' Eolande gestured to Jess and Emily. 'Form a circle around it.' She stepped round the creature and the demon was allowed to fall forward a few steps to make space.

Erica placed the crystal on the ground in front of her and Alfie gripped her wrist as she held the sage up. With her free hand, Erica took Minerva's. Her grandmother was still chanting, although the words came slow and carefully. She was running out of breath, the effort of holding off the demon and keeping the magic flowing was exhausting. Erica could feel the energy coming off her in waves.

On the other side, Emily took Minerva's hand and Jess took Emily's on one side and the teenage boy's on the other. The other two teenagers connected up with Eolande until they formed a large circle around the demon.

Eolande closed her eyes, face tilted up to the sunshine. Alfie squeezed on Erica's wrist and focussed his attention on the demon. A bolt shot around the circle, sending dirt flying up as it moved down their legs and into the ground.

'It must not touch Minerva,' said Eolande, not

opening her eyes.

Within the circle, the demon held its head and whimpered. When it lowered its arms, it glared at Minerva and roared, jumping forward. Tendrils of light whipped out of Eolande and wrapped around the demon's arms and legs, holding it back.

'You cannot stop me,' came the demon's voice. 'I will not be quietened. I will not go back. I am anger and rage and I am hungry.'

All too soon, Eolande had to let the demon go, unable to hold on any longer. She exhaled in a rush, opening her eyes before steadying herself once more.

'Come on,' Erica murmured without thinking.

The demon glared at her, red eyes glowing the same shade as the sage's embers. Then, with speed that wasn't natural, especially given the pain it was in, the demon lashed out a claw at Erica.

Alfie stepped forward in front of her, a light shining from him. It blinded her and she blinked it away, her senses screaming that she could no longer see the demon. When the light dissipated, the demon was back in the centre of the circle as Eolande held it with what power she had left. On the ground in front of Erica kneeled Alfie, holding his head.

'Alfie?' Erica screamed. 'Alfie? Are you okay?' She let go of Minerva and lowered the sage.

'Erica!' Eolande cried but Erica didn't hear her properly. Not enough to pay attention. She bent to Alfie, a hand on his back, and he looked up at her.

'Get back in the circle,' he growled.

There was a deep cut, a slash, running from his chin up diagonally across his face to his scalp. It had missed his eye, thankfully, but the blood was coming thick and fast. 'Get back.' He pushed Erica back into place. 'Form the circle.' He managed to get to his feet, grabbing her wrist in a trembling, slick hand and taking Eolande's with the other. He swayed a little and Erica watched the blood dripping from his chin down his white shirt.

Her eyes must have filled with tears but they only felt hot. Searing heat that tipped down her cheeks, wetting her whole face. Her throat closed and in her belly, an anger built and raged, demanding to be let out.

She took Minerva's hand, held up the sage high and closed her eyes, imagining the rage in her belly travelling up her body, through her right arm and into her grandmother.

Minerva's voice changed. Not only did it become stronger and louder, the words coming a little faster, but now it was as if there were two voices. Minerva's and another, only a little different, speaking the incantation in harmony.

'Ut coven tuam secura tibi libertate servire facias,' the voices shouted from Minerva's mouth to the demon.

The demon roared and fell to a knee, claws over its head.

Erica didn't know the incantation. It had taken Minerva months to learn it by heart and she had been worried she would be rusty. Perhaps that was why she had slowed, trying to dredge the words from her memory, despite having gone over and over them throughout the night and morning. There was so much to learn, so much to remember, and the words had to be said with such determination without pause or break. Each word was magic, each word was power and each one cut through the demon.

It's happening. It's coming.

Erica closed her eyes again as the whispers sounded in her ears. Minerva's voice wavered but only for a moment as Erica focussed again on the anger inside her, of the vision of Alfie covered in his own blood, his face torn open. She had only just allowed herself to love that face and this demon had ruined it.

Keep going. Keep going.

The whispers were softer this time, as if the trees were afraid of distracting them.

The demon looked from Minerva to Erica to Alfie.

'Love,' it spat in an eerily calm voice, as if accepting the pain. 'It does not taste good.'

'There's only love here,' shouted Emily from the other side of the circle. Alfie's grip tightened on Erica and she wished she could drop the sage and hold him.

'There is also anger,' said the demon, watching Erica as its body flinched and trembled with each of Minerva's words. 'Such anger.'

'You have no power over us,' Erica recited. 'You do not belong here. Leave this place.'

'Oh, if I could shape and twist that anger.'

'This anger is mine and mine alone,' said Erica. 'It is not yours. I am not yours. You do not belong here.'

'The chaos we could cause together.'

'You do not belong here.'

Erica felt the invisible tendrils of the demon fluttering over her body, searching and prodding for a way in.

'Think of what that anger could do.'

Erica looked the demon in the eye.

'This anger is aimed at you, Malarbor, and all that you have done. All it can do is rip you limb from limb, tear you open and apart, and send you back from where you came. You don't belong here. You have no power over me. You are not allowed in,' Erica spat.

The demon flinched, removing its invisible tendrils and falling back a step as Minerva spoke with more force.

If only more of them knew the incantation, they could all chant it. The demon would not be able to stop all of them. They would be able to finish it quickly and completely and this would be over.

As it was, even with Erica's strength added to Minerva's, the words came slower, taking more breath, as Minerva swayed a little.

'Eolande,' Erica called out. 'We need more.'

Just one more push, she thought. She glanced at Alfie. His skin was an unhealthy pale, the blood congealing on his face while fresh blood still seeped from the wound. He blinked slowly. He was no more use to them. All of his power, all of his strength was going into keeping him upright and part of the circle.

Guilt nudged away at the anger in Erica's belly but she pushed it down and away. Not yet. The guilt could come later as she replayed the moment over and over in her mind, trying to work out what she should have done differently. How she could have stopped it.

He's still alive, she thought. That's all that's important. He's breathing. He lives. We can deal with the blood loss, we can deal with the wound. All that matters is that he stays with me.

The demon growled and roared at Erica and then he turned, away from Minerva, its back on Erica. She almost fell forward as something in front of her was removed. She gripped the sage and Minerva as Alfie almost fell forward with her.

'Stay with me,' she told him. 'Don't you dare leave me.'

He closed his eyes and smiled through the blood on his lips.

'Over there is love and anger but here,' the demon sniffed, clutching its abdomen, holding itself together. 'Over here is anger and hate.' It focussed on Emily and she glared back, breathing hard as the presence of the demon fell over her.

'Stay strong,' Erica called to her. 'Don't let it in.'

'They are stronger than you. They have no need of your weapons. And why? They have not felt your trauma. Your pain. Your anguish. Why should you be weak when they are strong?' The demon stepped closer to Emily and Eolande growled with the effort of trying to keep it back. 'I can make you strong.'

'You do not belong here,' Emily told it. 'And you can't come in.'

The demon bared its teeth and threw back its head, screaming as if getting the pain out in one go.

'I can help you,' it told Emily, a hint of a whimper in its voice. 'I can make the pain stop.'

'Yeah, and the rest of it. You don't belong here. Back off,' Emily spat.

'You will be undefeatable. No creature will touch you.'

'I said no!'

'Cernunnos ipse truderit virtutem plebi Suae,' came Minerva's voice mixed with Erica's. Erica wondered briefly if she should be unnerved by that. The low sound of her own voice coming from her grandmother's mouth. Yet, somehow it seemed right. There was power in it, strength in sharing the anger that still raged inside her with her grandmother.

Was it her imagination, though, or was her voice becoming louder than Minerva's? Erica looked to her grandmother.

'Keep going,' she whispered at the same time as the trees. 'Keep going. Nearly there.'

'I will give you such strength,' the demon cooed to Emily.

'I've been touched by creatures before,' she told the demon. 'Been there. Done that. And you, Malarbor, have no power over me.'

The demon growled, gnashing its teeth.

The teenagers between Jess and Emily whimpered, the girl holding Emily's hand taking a step back.

'Don't move!' Eolande screamed. 'Keep the circle! It can't hurt you.'

The demon's eyes flicked over the girl.

'Your friend tasted delicious,' it told her. 'Her fear was ripe the moment I ripped the flesh from her bones. Her pain was fleeting but the taste of fear lingered. You humans die too easy.'

The girl cried out, her face wet with tears, and she stepped back but she didn't break the circle. Erica stared at her, willing her hands to stay connected.

'If we die too easy then you really should move on. Go back to where you came from,' shouted Emily, drawing the demon's attention back to her. 'Go back to your little demon friends and tell them how a few witches and fae beat your arse.'

The demon growled.

'And don't forget about the few little humans with no powers. Don't forget how they kicked you back to where you belong, you weak, pathetic shit.' Emily spat on the ground in front of her.

The demon's growl came from within the pit of its gut, the ground beneath them trembling with its rage as it lashed out a claw, striking Emily.

'Silence!'

24

Emily screamed.

Jess had expected that. If the demon made contact, she'd expected Emily to fall, perhaps for the circle to break, but Emily held on tight, screaming and then breathing hard through her teeth as she summoned her strength.

The demon retreated as Eolande threw more tendrils of light at it and then Minerva finished the incantation.

'Benedictus Dea, Matri gloria!'

From behind Eolande, between the trees that were joined together by ivy, grew a bright white light. Jess gripped the hands in hers, determined that this wouldn't fail because of her. The light grew as the demon roared and then there was a flash. A weight pushed against Jess as she was blinded and her hands slipped as she fell backwards. There was a dull pain as she landed on her back, crashing against a tree and the sting on her arms that must have been nettles and the thorns of brambles. Jess tried to pull herself away, scrambling forward but the light forced her to keep her eyes clenched shut. Using her arms as a shield, she called out, 'Emily?'

There was no response.

Still, the demon screamed which Jess had to take as a good sign. If the broken circle meant it hadn't worked, surely it would have gone quiet. Surely the light would have gone.

The screaming intensified as the light made a strange rushing noise and then disappeared with a pop.

Jess lowered her arms carefully, blinking hard and fast. The colours that danced in front of her refused to go but she could see enough. She hadn't been the only one to be pushed back. In fact, all of them had been thrown to the ground, the circle well and truly broken. Minerva was sitting up, holding her head but looking around. Erica was already leaning over Alfie, studying the wound across his face and talking in a low voice.

'Emily?' Jess murmured. She managed to get on-to all fours and then stopped at the sound of a new voice.

'What the hell was that?'

It was male, booming and echoing around them, and it hurt Jess's head. Grimacing, she looked over her shoulder. What now?

On the path behind them, surveying the scene, were around ten police officers and standing at the front was a man in a suit. He glanced down at her.

'Is everyone all right?' he asked.

Jess laughed and then continued crawling over to Emily who was lying in the dirt. The teenagers had already made it back to their feet, holding each other as a uniformed officer went to them. Collapsing next to Emily, Jess belatedly searched for the demon.

'It's gone,' she murmured.

Emily whimpered and Jess searched her face.

'Did it get you? I can't see.'

'Well, that's something,' Emily mumbled through gritted teeth. 'Guess I've always been lucky like that.' Gripping her arm, her knuckles white, Emily sat up and pulled down her top to reveal her shoulder. She tried to look at the back of her arm but whistled in pain. 'Can you see it?'

What Jess could see were three silver jagged lines running down Emily's right shoulder blade. They were old scars, withered in places. Jess blinked and looked away, examining the rest of the exposed skin.

'Yes.'

At the top of Emily's arm was a fresh wound, a slash similar the one across Alfie's face. It pulsed and throbbed as blood pumped from it. 'You need to put pressure on it. It's bleeding.'

'It's burning,' said Emily, still breathing through her teeth.

Jess leaned in closer. Along the edges of the wound the skin was turning silver.

'Help!' Jess shouted. 'I need water! She's been burned. Help!'

Two uniformed officers ran to her, one taking out his personal bottle of water. Surveying the wound, he undid the bottle and gently poured the water over it.

'Steady,' he murmured as Emily cried out.

'Ambulances are on the way!' came a voice from the other side of the clearing. It sounded so far away which was impossible, the clearing wasn't that big.

As the last of the water dripped onto Emily's arm, she sat up straighter and thanked the man, putting her hand over the wound.

'We need to cover it,' he said.

'I'm always saying I should carry bandages with me,' Emily scoffed, her voice becoming a little easier. 'At least the burning's stopped. Thanks.'

'Good,' said the officer, patting himself down in case a bandage had miraculously appeared on him.

Without thinking, Jess peered up at him and studied his features. Wouldn't it have been amazing, she thought, if he had been Rick Cavanagh. But no. She didn't recognise him. Of course, Erica would be the better judge, but Jess thought she'd know him if she saw him, even a younger version of him.

The officers moved away. The teenagers were talking in hurried gasps over to the side and Minerva was shouting at an officer, daring him to arrest her. A couple were crouched over Alfie, next to Erica, examining his wound.

'I guess the demon's gone,' Jess murmured, looking up at the scorched trees.

'Better have done. Otherwise I'll kick its arse back to hell,' Emily growled. Jess glanced at her.

'This isn't the first time this has happened, is it?' she asked.

Emily have her a long sideways look.

'You mean that other scar? That wasn't a demon. That was a werewolf. The first one I ever met, before I knew what to do. When I was like them.' She nodded to the teenagers. 'Young and stupid and no idea of how dangerous the woods could be. Or how dangerous anywhere can be. That's what started all this.' Emily's gaze flickered away. 'Don't be like me, Jess,' she murmured. 'You've got a kid and a dog and a good man. Don't follow the darkness. Kids and dogs and good men don't belong there. Keep hold of them. Hold onto them tight.'

Jess blinked, her stomach twisting.

'You think I should walk away?' she whispered.

Emily looked her in the eye.

'I get that you're tired of the normal life, but the abnormal life has brought me misery and grief. It's too late for me now. I don't know anything else. I'll never have the kid. Don't think I'll ever get the good man, not like yours. But you've already got it. Don't lose them.'

Jess shook her head, her throat constricting, tears blurring her vision.

A paramedic pushed past her to sit beside Emily and began talking to her. The eye contact was broken, the moment was gone.

Jess sat back, trying to blink away the tears.

She should have looked for Erica, but all she wanted in that moment was to go home to Marshall's warm arms, Ruby's sticky smile and Bubbles' wet nose.

In The Woods

Around the bustling humans, the trees breathed. They relaxed, their aches and pains easing as the tension across the woods lifted. Yes, there were blackened trunks and the fear still hung heavy among those branches, but it would soon drift away. Quietly, softly the birds began to sing. Mice and foxes and badgers stuck their noses from their holes and sniffed at the air only to find the heavy presence of evil gone. The trees beckoned them forward. *It's safe now*, they said, *it's safe*.

The memories would stay but the pain would go.

The trees would pass down the story of the demon to the saplings that grew around them and to the animals who would pass the tale to trees further away.

The lessons would be learned. The demon would not be allowed to return and if it did, they now knew how to banish it.

Witches, the trees whispered. *Fae.*

The old oaks would nod and smile if they could. They already knew this from stories passed down when they were tiny saplings decades and centuries ago.

All through the woods, the message passed through.

The demon is gone.

The witches and fae saved us.

Through the branches and canopy, a sigh of relief could be heard.

Deep inside the woods, the two trees that joined at the top by strangling ivy flashed blue for a moment. The only ones who noticed were the crows.

25

The whole group was eventually led by the police and paramedics out of the woods, along the narrow dirt paths strewn with roots they had to avoid tripping over, and into the main car park. Police cars and two ambulances were parked up waiting and a couple of officers were talking to the bystanders.

'Is this over yet?' Jess murmured. 'It's my birthday tomorrow. I'd quite like this to be over now, please.'

'It's over.' Erica took her hand and squeezed it. 'We'll be partying in no time.'

'Yeah. I think I need a party after all that.'

The detective in charge, the suited man with the booming voice, turned on Erica, Minerva and Jess, and sighed.

'You've got nothing on us,' said Minerva, holding her chin up.

'Police obstruction,' he told her. 'The woods are a crime scene.'

Minerva opened and closed her mouth and then held her chin up again.

'Can't go around arresting eighty-nine-year-old women for that. I didn't know.'

'Yeah. Right.' The detective raised an eyebrow at her and then looked at Erica and Jess. 'And what are your excuses?'

'There were teenagers in there. They were there before we were,' Minerva told him.

'And we'll deal with them. But what I saw was you all standing in a circle chanting something. In a crime scene. Where we'd just found the mutilated body of a missing girl,' he told them, lowering his voice.

'That does look bad,' Erica murmured. Her mouth was so dry it ached. She was only half paying attention to the detective, scanning the crowd in the car park and the paramedics, searching for Alfie. She couldn't see him. Come to think of it, she didn't remember seeing him leave with the group at all.

'It does.'

'And you didn't see what was in the middle of the circle, by any chance?' Jess asked.

A police officer in the distance caught Erica's eye.

The detective hesitated, narrowing his eyes.

'I might have done. That might be why I haven't arrested you yet.'

On Erica's left, Jess looked to Minerva on Erica's right. Erica was staring beyond the detective, to a uniformed officer talking to one of the teenagers.

'Well, that thing you're not sure if you saw is why we were there,' Minerva told the detective. 'That thing killed that poor girl and it was going to kill again. We had to break into your crime scene or someone else would have died.'

'I know,' said the detective.

'What?' Jess and Minerva nearly shouted in unison. Erica felt Jess's gaze on her then. She hadn't shouted with them. She'd only just made out the detective's words, his voice morphing into a hum at the back of her head as she watched the police officer beyond him.

'Oh,' murmured Jess, following Erica's gaze.

'What do you mean you know?' Minerva demanded.

'It attacked one of my officers. Thankfully he made it to edge of the woods to his colleague. He saw it too. Two eye witnesses. And now I've seen it. Look.' The detective leaned closer. 'I don't know what that thing was but I also don't know if you were involved.'

'We got rid of that thing!' cried Minerva. 'It's gone.'

'Sergeant Cavanagh!' the detective shouted over his shoulder. Erica jumped, her heart pounding as the officer she was watching made his way over. He was younger than she remembered but older than his Facebook profile picture. That was a mercy.

He stopped beside the detective and looked at each of the women in turn. His gaze didn't linger on Erica. He didn't seem to hear her pounding heart, or her breath catch as just for a moment their eyes met. There was no recognition from him this time, there was no love.

'The thing that attacked Levy,' the detective was saying. 'Can you describe it?'

Rick struggled for a moment.

'Tall, black, long arms, Sir. It had...red eyes. It wasn't...'

'Human,' Minerva finished for him. The detective shot her a look.

'Did you see the clearing? These ladies stood in the circle?'

'Yes, Sir.'

'Was the thing you saw that attacked Levy

there?'

'Yes, Sir. Inside the circle.'

Minerva crossed her arms with a smug smile.

'And have there been any reports of people inside the woods since that girl went missing? Any reports of these women in the woods?'

'No, Sir. No reports.'

'Thank you, Cavanagh.'

Rick nodded and walked away without even a fleeting glance at Erica. She frowned.

'So, the girl's family didn't mention anyone like you, neither did the girl's boyfriend. In fact, he says he's never seen you before today.' He gestured to the teenage boy talking to another officer. 'Normally, I would arrest you for obstruction but...but...' The detective sighed. 'I can't explain that thing. I saw it with my own eyes but I can't believe it. I have evidence that it killed the girl and attacked my officer. And you say it's gone now?'

'It is,' said Minerva.

The detective sighed again.

'One of my officers will take your details. We pick you up again, you'll be arrested. Okay?'

'Fair enough,' Jess murmured. 'I for one have no intention of doing anything like this ever again.'

Erica nodded, staring at the ground, her eyes burning.

Minerva made a whining noise.

'I suppose.'

'Good. Stay there, I'll get someone to talk to you.'

The detective walked away, calling an officer to his side.

'You okay?' Jess whispered. 'That was him, wasn't it?'

'Who?' Minerva hissed in Erica's other ear.

'Rick,' she mumbled. 'That was Rick Cavanagh.'

'Your Rick? From the future?' her grandmother asked, looking around wildly for the sergeant who had vanished into the crowd.

'Only in the present,' said Jess, nodding.

'Oh. That's good isn't it? You've found him.' Minerva nudged Erica with her elbow.

'There wasn't anything there,' she murmured. 'He didn't know me.'

Jess frowned.

'Of course he didn't. Future him said he'd be crap. He said you'd have to ask him out, that present Rick wouldn't realise. You have to go fight for him, Ric.'

Erica looked up, finding Rick again.

'I guess.'

'Where did Eolande and Alfie go?' Jess asked, searching the car park.

'Away. They don't want to get caught up in the police and systems. They need to shut that gateway, now the demon's gone. Maybe they're still in there, waiting for everyone to clear out. And Eolande will need to try and heal Alfie's face.' Minerva looked at Erica out of the corner of her eye. 'His poor handsome face.'

Erica's lips twitched.

'That happened because he was protecting me,' she murmured.

'Because he loves you. No matter what you decide and who you choose.' Minerva took Erica's hand and squeezed. 'And it is your choice.'

It was supposed to be comforting and it was, a little bit, but Erica found it only raised more

264

questions than she'd had before. Now wasn't the time to ask them, however, as a police officer came to take them to the station.

The morning had turned to late afternoon and it looked like it was going to be a long day.

As they reached a police car, another suited man approached them. He was younger than the other detective with dark hair and blue eyes. Erica caught herself staring before snapping away. The stare caught his attention, though, so it was to her that he directed his question.

'Excuse me, ladies. I'm looking for a Miss Emily May. Do you know her?'

An alarm seemed to go off in Erica's head.

'No,' she said before Minerva could open her mouth. The detective looked at her, then at Jess and Minerva. 'Should we have?'

'I'm led to understand she was here and seen talking to you.'

Erica shook her head.

'I don't know anyone called Emily.'

'Okay. She may have been using an alias. Caucasian, long black hair, brown eyes, about your height.' The detective gestured at Jess. 'I'm told she was in the woods with you. She was injured.'

'Doesn't ring any bells,' said Minerva.

'Maybe she was there with the teenagers. It was all very chaotic,' said Jess. 'If she was injured, wouldn't she be with the paramedics?'

The detective looked between them again and then handed them each a card.

'If she gets in touch with any of you, I'd appreciate it if you could let me know. It's very important that I find her.'

'Why's that?' asked Minerva, squinting at the

card.

"Detective Chief Inspector Murphy", it read, along with a mobile number. Jess flipped it over but that was the only information.

'She's a dangerous individual,' he told them. 'Wanted for murder. You see her or hear from her, don't engage, let me know straight away. Okay?'

The women stared at him.

'Okay,' Jess murmured.

'Right you are,' said Minerva.

'Sure.' Erica nodded.

They watched as the detective moved away.

'Murder?' Minerva whispered.

'Because it isn't black and white,' Jess muttered under her breath. 'Because sometimes humans are the monsters. Because she hunts and kills were-wolves.'

Emily

Another scar to add to my collection.

By hell this one stings.

I should probably get it looked at but that means hospitals and doctors, which could also mean police. I've had my fill of the police for this month. I haven't even had a chance to look at the wound. I can't see it properly, I need a mirror, which means waiting until I find somewhere to stop for the night.

I feel bad not saying goodbye to Jess and Erica, but they'll understand, I'm sure. I'll get in touch at some point, see how things are going. I know it looks suspicious that I turn up in their lives at the same time as that demon and then vanish about an hour after that thing did, but I can explain myself. They'll understand.

I just can't be near the police, given what I do. Day in, day out. Night in, night out. And that place was crawling with police.

As always, I am forever grateful for paramedics. I don't know what they did to my arm, but the pain has stopped. Yeah, it's throbbing, but it's bearable. I can still drive.

So, that was the demon in the woods. A small detour from the plan but sometimes they are the most fun. I've not just made new contacts but witchy contacts. Witches who can talk to ghosts. I just know that'll come in handy.

And now I know how to banish demons. Another thing that might come in handy. I might have to ask Erica for a transcript of whatever her grandmother was chanting. Never know when I might need that.

Especially as that damn demon touched me. It's always a scary thing when a monster makes contact. It's terrifying when there's blood. What does that mean? You don't turn into a werewolf if one scratches you, I know that. But if a demon scratches you? What if it didn't go back from whence it came. What if it's attached to me? The fae said it was gone, but how much can I trust them?

But then, they were touched too. Alfie was caught right across the face. Poor bloke. I feel for him. At least my scars can be hidden away.

Life goes on.

Despite the scratches and bites and fears.

I'm back on the road and back to the original plan. The next stop is Cornwall where something's been killing the sheep in strange ways. I thought it sounded like a werewolf but I thought this demon was a wolf. A nice reminder that I need to stay open-minded.

Open-minded and maybe take a little moment to appreciate the ocean and small Cornish villages with little to no wi-fi.

What could go wrong.

Famous last words.

26

Erica sat in her Mini outside Jess's house staring down at her phone and Rick Cavanagh's Facebook profile picture on the screen. The picture didn't do him justice. He wasn't bad looking but he wasn't an Alfie. He wasn't even who she had met two months ago.

There had been no choir or ringing of bells when their eyes had met. There had been no rush of blood or pang of something connecting. Had she been stupid for expecting that?

No, she thought.

That had all happened when Rick had looked into her eyes two months ago. When Rick from the future had bustled around her, not knowing whether to avoid her or kiss her. Her heart had pounded and her blood had rushed and her mind had panicked and somehow stilled at the same time.

That hadn't happened with present day Rick, but it had happened with Alfie.

Erica sighed.

More than anything at that moment, she wanted future Rick to come back.

'Come back,' she whispered, closing her eyes. 'Come back and take me away from here.'

A knock on the window beside her head made Erica jump and yelp. Heart pounding against her ribcage she looked up into Alfie's eyes. He waved at her and she quickly closed her phone and opened the car door.

'Sorry to interrupt,' he said. The slash across his face was no more than a silver scar now. Eolande, whatever she had done, had done a good job.

She smiled up at him, getting out of the car as he brushed his fingers self-consciously over the scar.

'Damn demon,' he murmured.

'I think it looks good,' she told him, moving his hands away. 'It makes you look distinguished.' She frowned. 'Does it still hurt?'

'No. And there shouldn't be any more damage. Thank the moon for Eolande.'

'She's not with you?'

'She's coming with Minerva.'

'Of course she is.' Erica smiled up at Alfie's face, feeling her blood rush as he studied her. There was a pang in her gut as their eyes connected and the world around them stilled.

'Is the gateway...?' she drifted off, unable to find her voice.

'Closed and locked. Only the fae now hold the key.'

Erica gave him a curious look.

'What does that mean?'

Alfie gave a half-hearted shrug.

'We have doors all over the world. It's fairly easy to turn a gateway to other worlds into one that only moves between this world and ours. It's no longer a threat. Demons may still be summoned, but not so easily.'

Erica smiled, searching his eyes.

'Thank you,' she murmured. 'For saving me.' She ran a finger down the scar on his cheek.

Alfie took her wrist and pressed his lips against

it.

'I told you. I will protect you with my heart and my life.' He glanced down at the phone in her hand. 'Whatever you choose.'

Erica's smile faltered.

'I saw him.' The words spilled from her. 'In the car park. After you left and we were trying to not get arrested. He was there.'

Alfie nodded and waited for her to continue. She watched him swallow and look away, up at the stars above their heads.

'I didn't feel anything.'

Alfie looked back to her. 'I thought I'd feel something. I don't know, anything. A rush or a connection or something. And I didn't. He didn't even look at me twice. I felt nothing. But you know what?'

'What?' Alfie murmured, looking down at her with soft eyes.

'I feel all of that when I'm with you.' She met his gaze. 'What did you do to me?'

Alfie smiled but it wasn't his usual cock-sure charming smile. This one was real, it had depth, it was him.

'Nothing,' he murmured. 'Just what you wanted me to do.'

Erica took those words and checked them. Yes. He'd backed off when she'd asked and come forward when she'd wanted him, he'd hesitated when she had and allowed her to make her own decisions. Just as he'd promised.

'You said it was my choice.'

'I did.'

'And I'm allowed to change my mind.'

'Of course.'

'I choose you.'

This time Alfie's smile was sad.

'Your heart doesn't belong to me, Ric,' he murmured.

'That's not for you to say,' she told him. 'Right now, as of this minute, I choose you. I want you.' She went up on tiptoe and kissed his lips lightly.

'What about your mother?' he murmured, his eyes turning hungry.

Erica shrugged.

'Are you kidding? You saved my life. She can hardly say anything about this.'

Alfie laughed. 'Anyway, she's inside already so we'll find out, won't we.' Erica held out her hand and after a moment Alfie took it. Erica looked him over, in his usual loose shirt and blue jeans. 'You didn't bring a present for Jess?'

'You don't know that.' Alfie squeezed her hand and then moved forward to kiss her.

They made their way up the driveway and Erica knocked on Jess's door. Marshall answered. Ruby, sitting on his shoulders, squealed when she saw Erica. Music filled the house behind them.

'Ric!' She held out her arms and Marshall grabbed onto her.

'Stay still, Rubes! Come in, come in.' Marshall eyed Alfie but said nothing.

Inside the house the party was getting started. There were balloons in every corner and a banner along the wall in the hallway that read, "HAPPY BIRTHDAY!".

'We haven't missed the dinner, have we? Or the cake?' Erica asked.

'Of course not. Plenty of time for cake.'

Ruby squealed again and Marshall flinched at

the noise.

'Jess is in the kitchen.'

'Cheers.' Erica pulled Alfie after her, finding not just Jess but her parents and Bubbles in the kitchen too.

Esther blinked at Alfie and then gave him a nod. Erica's father shook his hand, taking Erica's breath away.

'Thank you, for what you did,' he told him. Alfie, equally speechless, could only nod.

'Yes. Thank you. But you ever hurt my daughter or break her heart and I'll break you,' Esther murmured. Alfie laughed.

'That's more what I was expecting.' He went serious. 'You have my promise, Esther. No harm will come to your daughter while I'm around, whether I have her heart or not.'

Erica squeezed his hand and then let go to approach Jess.

'Happy birthday.'

Jess paused pouring a large glass of wine to hug her.

'You brought Alfie.'

'Well, no. I came alone but we met outside the front door.'

'Close enough.' Jess grinned, her eyes already tipsy. 'Look. Before this so-called-dinner-turned-party goes any further, I've been thinking.'

'Yeah?'

Jess pulled Erica closer.

'After that demon went and the police came, Emily said something to me. About Marshall and Ruby and Bubbles.'

Erica frowned. What now?

'What did she say?'

'Basically to put them first. Not to go down this road. And she's right, Ric. I don't want to go down the path she went down. I don't want that life.'

Erica blinked.

'What are you saying? You want to close the paranormal agency?'

To her great relief, Jess shook her head.

'Oh, no. No, no, no. I found that fascinating. Now, the demon's gone? And that gateway is closed, right? It's all over? I can get drunk without worrying about a demon and teenagers getting killed and if we're safe?'

'It's over. We're safe. Alfie says they've turned the gateway into a fae door. Which I didn't know was a thing.'

'Good.' Jess held up her drink in celebration and then took a gulp. 'Right. So, we're going back? To the hotel to talk to the spirit some more?'

'I thought so.'

'Good. No, I like that bit. And I like that you do the scary stuff and I deal with the clients. But nothing else. I don't want to go through this again, Ric. Spirits are one thing but I can't do demons again. Ever. And I don't want to know about were-wolves or whatever else Emily mentioned. I don't want to know about them and I definitely don't want to meet them. Just spirits, yeah? Is that okay?'

Erica grinned.

'Of course. Just spirits. Nothing else. And you know what? You haven't called them ghosts yet. You've just called them spirits.'

Jess's eyes lightened and she opened her arms.

'It's happened! I'm finally a paranormal invest-igator.' She toasted herself and took a sip of wine.

'I don't think that's what it means,' said Erica

but Jess shrugged.

'Whatever. I'm taking it. It's my birthday. Oh, and I got something this morning, it was left on the front doorstep. It's from Emily. We still have her number, so how about anything too scary comes along, we just pass it onto her?'

'Deal.' Erica looked around at the gathering guests as Marshall opened the front door to more people. 'What about that detective guy who was asking after her?'

'Pfft. He's not getting her number or anything else about her. Not from me,' Jess told her. 'I know it's a grey area and I don't want the life she leads, but she helped us and she got hurt. I saw her wound, Ric. It was awful. There was silver around it. What does that mean? Is that a demon thing or is it because she shot it with silver bullets? No, she does what she has to do. She takes down creatures that kill. And I can't in my right mind give her away. Don't you think?'

Erica agreed.

'Absolutely. I'm with you.'

Jess poured another glass of wine and handed it to Erica. They clinked their glasses.

'To business.'

They each sipped their wine as Jess's eyes found Alfie on the other side of the kitchen, talking to Marshall.

'What about Rick?' she murmured. 'Are you going to contact him?'

'No,' said Erica gently. 'No. Future Rick was...different to that guy near the woods. I didn't want to get to know that guy. It didn't feel right, you know? It's hard to explain. But Alfie.' Erica smiled over at the fae as their eyes met across the kitchen. 'There's something there and I want to know what.'

'There was something there with Rick, though.'

'Future Rick. But he's gone.'

'He just hasn't become who he's going to be, yet. Maybe you're the person who makes him that man.'

Erica sighed.

'Sounds like a lot of hard work.'

Jess nodded.

'Yeah. So, you and Alfie.'

'Me and Alfie. And you and Marshall.'

Jess grinned.

'He moved half of his stuff over today and we're getting the rest tomorrow. I've got my family together.' Jess took a deep breath and hugged herself. 'Everything just feels right, you know?'

Erica nodded and put an arm around her friend.

'I do know.'

27

Jess moved through her house, weaving between her friends and family with her wine glass that never seemed to empty, and grinned until her cheeks hurt.

The day had been a busy one, filled with hugs and laughter and kisses from Ruby, and kisses and moving boxes with Marshall. They'd already had a private celebration, just the three of them and the dog. Ruby had brought her a cupcake that they'd purchased when Ruby went to help Marshall pack some boxes and Marshall had stuck a candle in it and lit it.

'Make a wish,' he'd said but Jess couldn't think of anything to wish for. She already had everything she wanted.

To keep my happy, healthy family, she'd wished before blowing out the candle.

The demon was not forgotten but for today it no longer haunted her when she closed her eyes. For now, at least, there were no red eyes in the shadows, no dark forms in the corners. There was just light and laughter and love.

Jess sipped her wine.

This is happiness, she thought. As long as she kept a tight control of her thoughts, this was happiness.

'Jess! My dear girl.' Minerva approached her

with open arms and they hugged. 'How are you? Have you had a good day?'

'I have. And I'm good. Actually, I'm very good.'

'Good.' Minerva beamed. 'Because I want to give you a couple of gifts.'

'Oh, you didn't have to get me anything.'

'Yes. I did. I had to get you these. Here we are.' Minerva produced a wrapped box and on top lay a black charm of swirls.

'Oh, Minerva. This is beautiful,' said Jess, lifting up the charm. 'You really shouldn't have.'

'Yes, I should have. This isn't really your gift but I need you to have it. It's a protection charm imbued with...' Minerva glanced around the room and then whispered, 'magic.'

Jess's stomach sank.

'Oh?'

'Put this one above your front door. Marshall can help with that. It'll ward off evil spirits and demons.'

Jess swallowed hard.

'Oh. Thank you.'

'I've got a pendant and chain as well, for you to wear if you're ever feeling unsure or unsafe. When you and Erica are working or whenever.'

'Thanks.'

Jess didn't want the charm or the pendant. Still, she politely took them and pocketed both. It was a lovely thought. Minerva wanted to protect her, but Jess didn't want reminders of the demon on her person or in her home. No, that episode was over, to be forgotten and never repeated.

'I'd like to do a cleanse of your house too. You know, I've been meaning to do that since you moved in.'

'Yes. That would be good. Maybe when Marshall's moved in properly.'

'Excellent idea. Just let me know when.' Minerva offered Jess the wrapped box. 'Now, here is your proper present.'

Jess relaxed a little and put her wine glass down on the nearest table. She carefully unwrapped the box and lifted the lid.

'Are these...Tarot cards?'

'You're a witch, Jess Tidswell. You just haven't realised it yet. And I know your talents don't lie in speaking with spirits and you have no interest in herbs, so I wondered if maybe you could read the cards. It's a modern pack. Beautiful artwork. Erica helped me find them. I'm no good at cards myself and Erica's awful at them. Esther used to read them when she was younger, so she might be able to help. I understand the internet might be good for learning, too.'

Jess grinned.

'I love them,' she said with complete honesty. 'Thank you.' She wrapped her arms around Minerva's frail frame and kissed her cheek. 'I'm going to go look at them now. Thank you.'

Minerva hugged her back.

'You're a part of this family, child. You and your girls and now your man. Remember we're here for you, whenever you need us.'

Jess nodded, her eyes welling.

She took the box of Tarot cards and her glass of wine into the kitchen and placed them on the counter. Unpacking the box, she looked through the cards and accompanying book. Minerva was right, the artwork was beautiful. She put everything back, taking care not to put finger smudges on the cards and set them far back on the counter where wine wouldn't be spilled on them and four-year-old fingers couldn't reach them.

As she turned to go back to the party, she remembered the package that had been delivered that morning from Emily. Jess had opened the card but had left the gift. She found it now, waiting for her on the kitchen table and sat down to open it.

Another box and inside, on a bed of velvet, was a small silver knife. The breath caught in Jess's throat. On the one hand, Emily had sent her a weapon and a reminder of the life she didn't want. On the other hand, it was beautiful.

There was a small card next to the knife.

Jess.
I know, I know. I told you to leave this life behind.
But in case you don't, this is a silver letter opener.
For when you're going into a dangerous situation
and for when you need it. Don't be afraid to protect
yourself.
You have my number. Get in touch whenever you
like, even if it's just to say hi.
Happy birthday and love to you and yours.
Emily.

Jess held the card to her heart and studied the knife. It would be a shame to let it go to waste. She would have to send Emily a thank you message. Delving into her pocket, Jess pulled out the protection charms from Minerva and placed them on the velvet next to the knife before closing the box and putting it with the Tarot cards.

As she stood back she heard a faint buzzing noise. Lifting some discarded wrapping paper on the worktop, she discovered Erica's phone and the screen lit up with a message.

She didn't mean to read it but the words were right in front of her.

Hi. It's Rick. Not your Rick. It's future Rick. I know I said I wouldn't come back but I need your...

Jess stared at each word in turn. Laughter made her turn away as Erica and Alfie entered the kitchen. Alfie pulled two beers from a cooler Marshall had set by the fridge, handing one to Erica. They clicked the cans and then Erica kissed him, her hand finding his.

Jess glanced back down at the phone and sighed.

She would see it eventually. Jess placed the wrapping paper back over the phone. There was no harm in letting her enjoy the party and Alfie first.

Epilogue

Fingers tapping on the steering wheel, I cleared my throat and looked up at the house. There was nothing extraordinary about it. It was almost identical to the detached executive house next door. One garage, integral, maybe four bedrooms, at a push. Probably a lovely little garden out back with some flower beds. Maybe an artificial lawn. That's what people liked these days, wasn't it. The fake stuff. Couldn't see the point in it myself. If you wanted your garden to look green, you should put in the work. But then, who am I to say that. My garden consists of a window box.

I know I shouldn't judge, but I can't help wondering, when it comes to artificial grass, where do the ants go?

I was procrastinating. Put me in the woods, or in a town or anywhere else for that matter where it's just me and the werewolf, and I'm fine. But talking to people?

Still, it could have been worse. I wasn't going to knock on their door to tell them their son was cursed. No, I was knocking on their door to tell them their son was into some sick and dangerous stuff.

Taking a deep breath, I looked myself in the eye in the rear view mirror.

'You can do this.'

My reflection nodded. As long as one of us is confident, that's usually enough.

I left my old Mini, good car that she is, on the road and walked up the driveway, knocking on the front door. It took a moment before a shape appeared behind the glass, growing larger as the person approached.

The door opened and a pretty middle-aged woman appeared. She looked me up and down.

'Mrs Pryce? Detective Wordsworth. Don't worry, it's nothing bad.' I flashed her the fake warrant badge I carried around with me, the one I'd paid good money for that claimed I was a detective with Avon and Somerset Police. I thought it was quite good. It had almost fooled the locals. If only the police were as stupid as they're made out to be in those television shows.

Mrs Pryce, however, didn't know the difference between a real warrant card and a fake one, so she only glanced at it, saw that the photo matched my face and then accepted it. It probably helped that the police had already been in contact.

'What's going on?' she asked.

'I need to have a chat with your son, Andrew. If that's okay?'

Mrs Pryce nodded and allowed me in.

I walked inside, not offering to take my boots off. No one needed that.

Mrs Pryce led me through to a luxurious but small living room where I sat on a deep, cream sofa. There was a fireplace, complete with log burner, and the carpet beneath my black boots was thick.

'Andy!' Mrs Pryce called to her son up the stairs, wringing her hands as she looked back to me. 'What's this about?'

'I just want to talk to your son about an incident in the local woods, recently. We believe he has some information. I understand my colleagues have already discussed some of it with you.'

Mrs Pryce looked sceptical but didn't object. I wondered what that said about her son.

Andy Pryce walked solemnly down the stairs with dark hair that was fashionably a touch too long so that it just went into his eyes. He scrapped it away. Something he had to do repeatedly. His eyes were just as dark and although he was dressed in jeans and a black T-shirt, one glance told you he was either pining to be a rock star or a Satanist.

'Andy, Detective...'

'Wordsworth.'

'Wordsworth is here to speak to you. Sit down.'

Andy did as he was told, taking a seat on the second sofa in the room. His mother perched on the arm between them.

'Hello, Andy. I'll try and be quick, I don't want to bother you both too much. Do you know anything about these?' I showed Andy the pictures on my phone of the symbols on the trees. His mother leaned to look with him, giving her son a pained glance.

Andy sat back, shaking his head.

'No.'

'We believe some people your age made them. Scratched them into the trees, maybe as a bit of fun. You don't know anything about that?'

'No.'

'Only, my colleagues were shown a couple of your books at school. You scribbled the exact same symbols in them.'

'Andy,' his mother murmured.

284

The boy squirmed and then stared at me hard.

'I don't know what you're talking about.'

He was good, but not good enough. There was a spark of fear in his eyes at being found out, at his mother finding out.

'Right, well, whoever made these symbols needs to know how dangerous this stuff is.'

'What symbols are they?' Mrs Pryce asked. 'Your colleagues didn't say.'

'Satanic symbols,' I told her. 'Actually, these particular ones are summoning symbols.'

That was when I lost her. The woman was pure sceptic so instead of being scared, she looked at me suspiciously. Whoever heard of a police officer going into someone's house and talking about summoning things?

I had to continue, and fast.

'I don't know if you were just having fun, Andy, but these things are real. You, or whoever did this, summoned an actual demon in those woods.'

'Now, hang on, who did you say you were again?' Mrs Pryce stood up.

'The demon killed that girl, Andy.'

That got him. Andy's eyes widened and then it was just me and him, while his mother's voice became shrill in my ear. 'Have you spoken to that girl's boyfriend? Have you heard what he saw? It's real, Andy. And you brought it here. It's gone now. We got rid of it and those woods are now protected. You hear me?'

'I think you need to leave. Before I call the real police.'

'But if you're drawing those symbols in your exercise books, you could summon it again. Into your home. Demons attach to things, Andy. The demon you summoned attached to the trees. But the next one could attach to you.'

'Get out! Now!'

I stood up and made my way to the front door, ushered by Mrs Pryce.

'Get rid of the books, Andy. And stop drawing those damn symbols. And if it's too late.' I paused, pulling out one of my cards. 'Call me!'

The front door slammed behind me and I stood on the doorstep, breathing hard, the card still in my hand.

That hadn't gone quite to plan.

From behind the door came shouting. At least she had taken some of what I'd said seriously. Resisting the urge to put my ear against the door, I began a slow and tedious walk back to my car.

I stopped when I heard the back gate open. Andy poked his head through and for a moment we just stared at each other. Then, silently, I walked over and handed him my card.

'In case you need to get rid of a demon,' I whispered. 'And don't go back into those woods, carving anything on those trees. What protects those woods now won't be as kind as me.'

Andy, pale in the darkness, nodded. He took my card and closed the gate.

There wasn't anything else I could do.

The girl's body had been found, the demon was gone and the boy had been warned.

I fell back into my car and checked over my food supplies. I'd have to stop somewhere. I was dangerously low on cereal and chocolate bars. There certainly wasn't enough to get me into the arse end of Cornwall.

So there had been no werewolf, but there had

been fae and two new ghost-hunting friends. All in all, I call that a success.

Smiling and taking a bite out of my penultimate chocolate bar, I turned on the ignition and gave the house one last glance. Good thing I did too. There, in the window, looking right at me, was Mrs Pryce on her phone. And I could guess who she was talking to.

That was my cue to leave, before the police arrived. My cover well and truly blown, I drove my Mini away, thankful that they didn't live in a cul-de-sac where I could have been trapped, or my registration number taken as I'd been forced to drive back past.

No, all in all, a successful trip.

Now, I just had to get to Cornwall, with a quick stop at Jess's to leave the wrapped gift on my passenger seat where she'd find it.

I drove onto the main road that ran through the town and touched the accelerator, round the roundabout, heading towards the motorway. It was at this point that a blinding flash of light appeared to my right. I touched the brakes as I blinked away the colours.

'What the fuck?' I muttered, looking over to my right. There was no car flashing its headlights, no shops or a gang of youths with arms full of fireworks. There was just a man in a long brown coat looking at his watch.

That was weird. I watched him in my rear view mirror until he was out of sight. It was weird, but it was gone. Anyway, werewolves didn't create bright flashes of light, so that one was probably best left to the ghost-hunters.

෨෬

Author's Note

The woods in this book are real and just down the road from my house. It's now hard to walk through them with the dog without feeling a dark looming shape above me or wondering if Alfie will appear through the trees.

The trees joined at the top by ivy are real.

The dead seagull and mouse were real and found by me and the dog on the same walk, along with a blackbird and a rat, which made me wonder if there was a beast on our nature reserve.

The graffitied trees are real, although thankfully not with Satanic symbols.

The fires were real, as were the repeated calls out to the fire service.

The charred wood and trunks are real.

I maintain that the demon is not real, although since having written this book, trees have been falling for no discernable reason and bark is stripped from branches higher up than any human or deer could reach.

Our local police are in no way stupid and would see through Emily immediately.

But where's the fun in that.

Erica and Jess will
return in
Belonging
Coming soon.

We will also see Emily May
again, in Cornwall hunting a
werewolf...

To get regular updates and be the first to know
about ARCs and pre-orders, put your email address
in at
www.jenice.co.uk/updates

If you enjoyed this book...

Authors love getting reviews.
It's one of the best ways to support
authors you enjoy.
I would really appreciate it if you could leave a
review of this book on Amazon or your favourite
distributor.

Marshall and Ruby's Adventure

J E Nice

Marshall stood out from the rest of the parents near the school gate, by head and shoulders. Not only was he taller than any of the fathers there, he was wider and stockier. He leaned back against his white van that he'd managed to park right outside the school by finishing a job early, his biceps bulging as he crossed his arms against his chest. A few of the mothers looked at him. He didn't acknowledge them, although he appreciated the looks.

He kept his eyes on the school doors as they opened and the small children began running out, searching for whichever adult had come to collect them.

Marshall smiled, dropping his arms and lifting from the side of the van as he caught sight of the child he was waiting for. Her brown hair had escaped the neat ponytail her mother had tied that morning and one of her socks had slipped down, but Ruby actually looked surprisingly neat. For her.

She ran at him, already talking excitedly in bursts as she held out her arms.

'Hey, kid.' Marshall scooped her up easily and gave her a bear hug which made her laugh. 'Got everything?'

Ruby nodded and went to climb into the van. Marshall opened the door for her and helped her up the steps before lifting her into the child's seat. As he strapped her in, Ruby dropped her bag in the footwell.

'Are we going home? Did you bring sweets?'

Marshall blinked.

'No and maybe. I've got one last job to do and you're going to come help me. Okay?'

Ruby loved the smell of Marshall's van. It was thick and tangy and there were often sweets in the glove compartment. She wasn't sure about this job though. It meant going to a strange house when what Ruby wanted was to go home, have beans on toast and play with Bubbles.

Marshall helped Ruby out of the van and held her hand as they walked to the front door. The little house belonged to an old woman who didn't smell anywhere near as nice as Marshall's van. Ruby screwed up her nose and huddled closer to Marshall's legs.

She followed him into the kitchen, not hearing their conversation, just aware that she didn't want to let Marshall out of her sight.

'Rubes?'

Ruby looked up at Marshall who was turning the kitchen sink tap on and off. 'Inside my bag, there's a towel and some big tools. Can you lay the towel out and put the tools on top of it, please?'

Ruby, hands trembling a little, opened Marshall's bag to reveal the glint of silver and a dirty towel. She laid the towel on the floor and carefully and slowly placed each heavy, cold tool onto it.

The smell of the strange kitchen and voice of the old woman vanished as Marshall explained each tool to her and she watched over his shoulder as he used them on the pipes under the sink.

'All done.' Marshall stood and asked Ruby to put the tools away for him.

'My, that was quick. How much do I owe you?' asked his customer.

Marshall hated charging for jobs like these. It had taken nothing. But then, if he didn't charge, he wouldn't have a business, and if he didn't bring in the money, he'd never be able to afford the engagement ring he had his eye on.

'Just a tenner today, Mrs Walker.'

With a smile, Mrs Walker reached into her purse and pushed the note into his hand. He quickly wrote out a receipt and they made their way back to his van.

'That's it?' Ruby asked as he placed her back in the child's seat.

'Bet you think my job is easy now, huh?'

'That was very easy.'

'It was only easy because you were there,' he lied, ruffling her hair. He plonked into the driver's seat and smiled at Ruby, reaching across and opening the glove compartment. 'Thank you for being my plumber's mate today. Here's your share of the payment.'

Ruby's eyes lit up as a bag of chocolate buttons appeared.

He poured some buttons into Ruby's open palms.

'Maybe don't tell your mum about this bit,' Marshall whispered.

හⓈ

Printed in Great Britain
by Amazon

62610450R00177